Secondhand
Charm

ALSO BY JULIE BERRY

The Amaranth Enchantment

Secondhand Charm

Julie Berry

BLOOMSBURY

NEW YORK BERLIN LONDON SYDNEY

First published in the United States of America in October 2010
by Bloomsbury Books for Young Readers
www.bloomsburyteens.com

For information about permission to reproduce selections from this book, write to
Permissions, Bloomsbury BFYR, 175 Fifth Avenue, New York, New York 10010

Library of Congress Cataloging-in-Publication Data
Berry, Julie.
Secondhand charm / by Julie Berry. — 1st U.S. ed.
        p.   cm.
Summary: On her journey to the royal university to become a doctor,
fifteen-year-old Evie, wearing potent gypsy charms, learns of her
monstrous inheritance.
ISBN 978-1-59990-511-2
[1. Fantasy.   2. Leviathan—Fiction.   3. Sea monsters—Fiction.   4. Orphans—
Fiction.] I. Title.
PZ7.B461747Se 2010   [Fic]—dc22   2010008281

Book design by Donna Mark
Typeset by Westchester Book Composition
Printed in the U.S.A. by Worldcolor Fairfield, Pennsylvania
2 4 6 8 10 9 7 5 3 1

For Denny,
and for Phil

"The earth is full of thy riches.
So is this great and wide sea,
wherein are things creeping innumerable,
both small and great beasts.
There go the ships: there is that leviathan,
whom thou hast made to play therein."

PSALM 104:24–26

Chapter 1

"What will you do when school is done, Evie?"

Priscilla peered at me through her thick spectacles. They had the unfortunate effect of making her already watery eyes swim large and fishlike. That didn't bother me. After eight years as academic rivals at Sister Claire's school, Priscilla and I had both decided that it was much easier being friends. And what were fish eyes between friends?

It was mid-August, and the air lay heavy and hot around us as we walked home from classes along Maundley's main street. I lowered my bonnet to shield my face from the sun. My scratchy shift and knickers clung cruelly to my damp, tired skin.

"I don't know, Prissy," I said. "I hate to think of it. The end of school feels like taking a walk, and reaching a cliff, with a man holding a pitchfork behind your back. There's no other choice but to fall off."

"Kersplat," Priscilla agreed. "I know." She hoisted the strap binding her books over her shoulder. "You could always do like Rosie Willis, or Mary Grace, and get married this fall."

I shuddered. "Bite your tongue, Priscilla Hornby," I said. "That's like having an army of pitchforks behind you, and a lake of molten lava at the bottom of the cliff."

"Either way, you're dead." Priscilla could be maddeningly practical.

"Oh, why do good things have to end," I moaned, "while tedious things go on forever?"

"This is our lot in life, Evie. We're now to wash and iron and weed and bake. We'll do it a few years for our folks until some man marries us, then do it for him till we die."

"There's romance for you." I gave her a poke. I happened to know she was hopelessly sweet on Matthew Dunwoody, the butcher's son, and would do his ironing and baking till forevermore with a song on her lips, if he'd only take notice of her. But I heroically didn't tease her about him. Not just then. I would save that fun for another time.

"Sister Claire says learning is the work of a lifetime," I mused. "Do you suppose I could teach myself to be a physician? A bit of reading, a bit of studying, on my own?"

"Not a chance of it."

"Why not?"

"You'll not practice medicine on me if you've never had proper training, I can tell you."

I laughed. "Coward."

But Priscilla was no longer listening. She grabbed my arm and pointed. "Evie, what's going on up there?"

We reached the chapel and noticed a gathering of ten or more people standing outside. For Maundley, this was practically a mob.

A short man in crimson hose and a blue velvet jacket that was rather too tight stood addressing our gigantically fat and eternally sweating mayor, Sam Snow. Beside the stranger an attendant stood, holding two horses by their reins.

"Good people," the man said, in a magnificently crisp, nasal voice, reading from an elaborate scroll. "I come from Chalcedon to announce the joyful news that His Exalted Majesty King Leopold III, Protector and Prince Royal of Pylander, by the grace of God and upheld by his fair and loyal subjects, deigns to favor the village of Maundley with his luminous presence on the occasion of your feast of Saint Bronwyn, next fortnight."

A ripple went through the crowd, starting with Mayor Snow's great girth. A royal visit! Such a thing hadn't happened since Widow Sprottley's uncle's cow birthed a calf with two udders. We'd heard the tale often enough to know. What news!

"Fame of the charm and pleasantness of said country celebration, honoring your village's patron saint, has reached His Majesty's ears, and as it is his good will to visit the towns of all of his Pylandrian subjects, His Majesty now sees fit to time his arrival in Maundley with the eve of your celebration."

Mayor Snow swabbed his cheeks with a dingy handkerchief. Widow Moreau, who lived next door to Grandfather and me, winked in my direction.

"His Majesty begs you to go to no special trouble on account of his arrival," the herald went on, giving us a stern look that clearly spoke otherwise. "He will be pleased to lodge, along with his retinue, at the home of your mayor or chief magistrate. As for dining, His Majesty is sure that the simple fare at the feast will please his tastes. As for entertainment, he is prepared to be exceedingly delighted by the dancing, games, and contests that accompany your feast day."

Priscilla and I stared at each other. Dancing? Games? Contests? And for that matter, lodge at Sam Snow's crumbling house? Lord help us all!

"His Majesty salutes you cordially and with all affection, and joyfully anticipates the day of his arrival among your loyal bosoms."

Mayor Snow wiped his sweating hand upon *his* loyal bosom and offered it, trembling, to the brightly colored herald. "Joyful news indeed," he said in a voice that squeaked like a growing boy's. "And now, er, you must need refreshment from your long journey. May I"—here he cast a terrified look over his shoulder at the ever-growing assembly—"offer you victuals? The Galloping Goose"—here he gestured to our only tavern and public house—"serves an excellent luncheon and has clean rooms for boarders."

This set off a fit of coughing among the villagers present.

"Thank you, no." The herald cast a critical glance at the local tavern, whose wooden goose dangled askew over its door. "I must press onward. I'm due in Fallardston before day's end. I will tell His Majesty how joyfully you received the news of his imminent visit."

The mayor shot us all a panicked look.

"Huzzah! Huzzah!" I cried, before I'd had a chance to think. Others joined in, praise be.

"Huzzah! Huzzah! Long live His Majesty!"

Chapter 2

When the hoofbeats of the herald and his page died out, an outcry broke loose.

"The *feast* of Saint Bronwyn?"

"Were we planning to hold one of those this year?"

"Where will you lodge the king, Sam—in bed with you and the missus?" Butcher Dunwoody slapped his knee. "That's the only spot in your house where the roof don't leak!"

Widow Moreau spoke up. "What you need, Mayor," she said, "is some help repairing your place. Now, if my son Aidan were here, he could mason those stones of yours right up. Carpenter Thomas and his sons could fix the roof snug."

The Thomas men nodded slowly, cautiously. Widow Moreau's sharp eyes saw it.

"Folks'll help you clean and paint. As for the 'feast,'

leave that to us." By "us," we understood her to mean the village women who did whatever Widow Moreau told them to. Life, they found, was just easier that way. "We'll organize it. Food, handicrafts. Father Pius, can you put together games, and music, and contests for the lads?"

The timid village priest nodded.

Widow Moreau turned to my beloved schoolmistress. "Sister Claire, you'll arrange an exhibition from your students. Recitations, and 'rithmetic, and so on, won't you?"

Sister Claire caught my eye. I sighed. Now I knew what I'd be doing at the feast of Saint Bronwyn. Better than baking. Leave that to Mary Grace and Rosie Willis.

"Who'll pay for the repairs?" Harold Flint, the sour-faced treasurer, spoke. "Mayor can't."

"Besides," I said, "Aidan *isn't* here. He's in Chalcedon, and there's no time to fetch him."

Widow Moreau beamed at me and patted my cheek. "Don't you worry, duck," she said. "I've had a letter from Aidan, saying he'll be here for a visit soon. Expecting him any day now. He'll be eager to see you, too, I'm bound."

I felt my face grow hot as the amused glances of the entire village turned my way. There was nothing I wouldn't do for Widow Moreau—she'd been a neighbor and a mother to me all my life—but why she persisted in this foolish notion that either I or Aidan had any regard for each other, beyond neighborly friendship, was more than I could figure.

"The forest's full of wood, and I daresay many of you men have some seasoned lumber set by," Widow Moreau said, addressing the village once more. "Paint can be made. We ought to do ourselves proud when our king comes to visit Maundley, oughtn't we?"

Mayor Snow wisely said nothing. He was on the verge of a free refurbishing of his house. And he also knew that what villagers would never do for him, they'd do for Widow Moreau.

A little slip of a girl, no more than six, came pelting down the road. It was Letty Croft, her ankles long and brown underneath her raggedy dress, her hair and face shockingly dirty. I adored Letty Croft. She reached my side and tugged my skirt, panting.

"Miss Evelyn," she gasped, "Mam says it's time. You're to come, please, if you would."

I handed Prissy my school things, who took them without a word. "Tell Grandfather I don't know when I'll be home, please?" I said to Widow Moreau. "Hannah Croft's having her baby. Sister Claire," I looked at my teacher. "Just in case, the composition for tomorrow, I . . ."

"Go on, Evie," Sister Claire said. "I'll tell Sister Agatha to stop and see if you need help."

Clutching Letty's dirty hand in mine, I ran off to the Croft cottage.

Hannah Croft was a big strapping girl, or woman, I should say, seeing as she already had three of her own, but

I thought of her as a girl. Her face was so smooth and round and young. She was only about half a dozen years older than me, and even in rural Maundley that was young to birth her fourth. I was not yet seventeen. The reason I was playing midwife, and not an older woman, was simple. I'd never known a sick day in my life. Not a fever, not a cold. Naturally, some therefore believed that I had a beneficial influence over sickbeds and birthing tables. "Wholesome vapors," Father Pius once called it. Which, meaning no disrespect to his holy office, was nonsense. It wasn't vapors that helped the ailing and the birthing. It was heat when needed, or cool when needed, soothing care, and lots of washing and salt in wounds. And all that I'd learned from my father's books. Maundley had no doctor, but I'd been bringing babies into the village, or helping a midwife do so, almost since Letty learned to walk.

I found Hannah on her hands and knees in her bed, moaning and panting.

"Oh, thank 'ee for coming, Miss Evelyn. I was so afraid when the time'd come Letty wouldn't be able to find you," she said. She rocked back and forth. "It's coming quick, I think."

"Letty," I said, "take Lester and Mattie down the road to Mrs. Peronell's house, and stay there until I come for you. All right?"

Letty looked like she hated to leave.

"Why?"

"Because I can't tend to you and your mother too," I said.

"Why?"

"Everything will be all right. Mrs. Peronell will give you supper. Ask her, please, to send over any old linens she can spare."

"Why?"

"Letty!" I cried. Then I changed my tone. "She'll have a sweet for you."

Mama was forgotten; Letty and the little ones ran next door. I put logs on the fire and filled every kettle I could fit in the coals to get water heating.

"Oh, Miss Evelyn," Hannah said, "I've been so afraid of this one, I have. It ought to get easier each time, but instead all I get is more afraid. I remember how awful it hurts. It keeps me up nights, remembering."

I rubbed her back with slow, firm strokes. "I know," I said, though of course I didn't. "I know. Do you want me to send for your husband, so he can be here with you?"

"Laws, no," she said. "I'd hate for him to see me bawling and hollering like this. Don't know what he'd think of me."

I knew what I'd think of him if he thought less of her, but I kept my comments to myself and rubbed her back. For hours. Contrary to her prediction, this one wasn't coming quick.

Word reached Abiah Croft anyhow, and he was there in the garden when I opened the door.

"Biggest one yet, Mr. Croft," I said, displaying his infant son. "Isn't he sweet? Hannah says his name is Brom."

Abiah's face parted into the widest grin possible. His leathered peasant's face went soft as warm butter at the sight of the tiny red child. He took Brom in his hands and cradled him under his chin.

In time he remembered I was there. "We don't know how to thank you, Miss Evelyn."

"It was Hannah who did the work."

He handed me back the baby and reached into his pockets. Joy drained from his cheeks. "We haven't any, er, that is, in time we could . . ."

"Oh, no," I said. "Don't think about that."

Abiah shook his head, distressed. "No, Miss Pomeroy," he said. "I'll see to it, and I'll come by just as soon as . . ."

The baby began to fuss in my arms. I wanted to refuse payment, but saw that for his sake I shouldn't. "Tell you what," I said. "I hear you're a fine hand at cheese. How about a slab of it for Grandfather?"

Abiah Croft stood up straighter. "It's Hannah that's got the knack," he said. "I'll bring a whole wheel by tomorrow."

～◦

Mrs. Peronell brought supper and said she'd already tucked the Croft children into bed at her home. I left the

Crofts with Hannah feeding Brom, and Abiah feeding Hannah soup, spoonful by spoonful, and made my way home through the falling twilight. The cool night air smelled sweet, and the lavender sky colored fields full of barley and meadows full of hay. I kept smiling, thinking of that ruddy little baby, thinking what a glad, glad thing it was for everything to go well at a birth. I didn't blame Hannah Croft one iota for being afraid. A little part of me was afraid every time I helped a laboring mother. But that was why I did it. The fear was enough that I had to—*had to*—help in whatever way I could.

That was why I wanted to be a physician, like my father had been and like my mother had studied to be. From the day Grandfather told me how my parents died during the influenza epidemic, after weary nights treating sick patrons at the university infirmary, I'd formed my hope of following in their footsteps. They were martyrs to medicine, heroes in my eyes.

The kingdom of Pylander, since the days of Queen Margaret the Wise, generations before my day, had held school doors open to women and girls, by law at least, if not by widespread practice. There were women at the royal university in Chalcedon. Not many, but enough to prove it was possible. Not many became doctors. Most chose teaching, like Sister Claire.

I walked on, knowing the paths home through the woods by heart, and imagined myself at the university. I'd seen pictures of the robes and caps that the students and professors wore. Even just thinking of those trimmings gave me chills of excitement.

"Ho there! Young lady!"

A deep voice made me jump. A dark shape filled the path before me. Bandits! Could I make it back to town? Not before being caught. Heart thumping, I backed away from the shadowy figure, looking for an escape through the trees.

"Do you know the way to Widow Moreau's house?"

Relief, then aggravation flooded over me in turn. "Well, if you don't know, Aidan Moreau, I'm not about to tell you."

The tall shape stepped out of the shadows and leaned against a tree. I'd recognize those laughing eyes anywhere, but I was startled to see how much older he looked. Hefting rocks all day and working under the hot sunlight had added years to his face and build. He seemed foreign to me now. I'd known Aidan since we were children, though he was a few years older. His mother used to make him walk me to school. Even after he left for a stonemasonry apprenticeship in Chalcedon at fourteen, he had come home once or twice a year to see his mother. But this time I might almost not have known him. For shame, scaring me like that in the woods! He knew his way home as well as he knew his name.

"Aren't you going to say something?" I said. "Or are you waiting for other young ladies to pass by so you can terrify them too?"

"Not a bad idea," he said. "I could easily make a sport of this. But seeing as you're unprotected, I may as well walk you home. I can always come back and lurk more later."

"Your mother'd boil you if you did."

"There is that." He looked sideways at me, and I noted that he'd grown at least an inch taller. "She's probably at your grandfather's, giving him grief. How's the fishing this season?"

I smiled. When we were little, Aidan and I would fish together in the stream beyond our homes. At first it was just me tagging along to pester him when I was a little girl, but soon he began to say the fish came when I called them. He insisted I come along for good luck.

"No time for fishing these days," I said.

"We'll see about that." He pantomimed flicking a fishing rod with one hand.

"What brings you home?"

"Holiday," Aidan said. "My old master's as good as gravy. His family, too. They're very kind to me. Always wanting me to look in on my 'sweet, helpless, widowed mother.'"

I laughed. "He's never met her, then, has he?"

"I suspect she's laid some sort of spell on him," Aidan said.

"Or written him a letter," I said. "Your mother gets what she wants out of people."

"You're telling me?"

"Well, she's got a plan for you, this trip." I told Aidan about the royal visit and the Feast of Saint Bronwyn.

"Oh, no." He laughed and groaned together. "I thought I was getting me some rest for a change. Say, Evie," he said, looking at me with excitement, "I've got some news. You can be the first to know."

News was intriguing. "Let me guess: you're married."

He stopped in his tracks. "No!"

"Soon to be, then."

He shook his head. "No," he said, looking at me closely. "Neither one." He seemed crestfallen, as though now his news wouldn't seem like much. "I'm done being a journeyman. My master, Mr. Rumsen, says when I return, he'll make me a master myself. I may stay on with him, if he can use me. If not, he'll help me find a post somewhere else."

I picked my way over a fallen tree limb. "Is this good news?"

"It's a year earlier than most," he said. "Mr. Rumsen says I'll be the youngest full mason in Chalcedon. Maybe in all of Pylander."

I presented my hand. "Well, congratulations then, laddie," I said. "Let me be the first to shake your hand. Well done."

Aidan smiled, and for a moment he looked more like the boy I remembered.

"Now, isn't this a pretty sight?"

I dropped Aidan's hand. Aidan reached his mother in two strides, picked her up, and swung her around knee-high off the ground. I slipped away, smiling, and headed toward Grandfather's house.

Chapter 3

Widow Moreau made Mrs. Hornby the chairwoman of handicrafts for the feast, and she'd scheduled Prissy's time down to the minute. This left my friend out of sorts, for we both wanted to study for end-of-term examinations. Even though, in truth, they didn't seem to matter much now, we were still both vying for the top school prize. Out of politeness, neither one of us ever mentioned it.

Another school day in the hot, stuffy classroom came to a close, and Priscilla and I had walked so far as the center of town when Matthew Dunwoody appeared, trotting as fast as his father's old horse would oblige him.

"I got it all worked out," he yelled, sliding off his poor horse. "Rode to Fallardston myself this morning, and fixed it all up proper."

Folks came out of homes and shops to hear the news,

like always, whenever the slightest commotion stirred in sleepy Maundley. Some days a breeze was enough.

"What did you fix up, Mr. Dunwoody?" Priscilla asked in a false shy tone that made me want to laugh out loud. She blinked so rapidly I thought perhaps she'd gotten a gnat in one eye.

"A caravan of gypsies camps in Fallardston at harvest," he said. "I got 'em to come here for Saint Bronwyn's. They'll bring wares, music, dancing girls, fortune tellers, all sorts of things."

"Dancing girls," the miller said in a daze. His wife swatted his behind, and woke him up.

"You hadn't ought to have taken it upon yourself to do that, Matt," Mayor Snow said. "I don't know as we want a whole troupe of gypsies mucking up our common and bringing their sicknesses here. We'll have our throats cut in our sleep, likely as not."

"Found some performers too," Matthew said, ignoring the mayor. "Pair of brothers that put on live theatricals, playacting all sorts of stories."

"The stage is an unsavory thing," Father Pius said.

"Now, Father," Widow Moreau said, appearing as if by magic, like she always did when things happened up town. "It's entertainment for the king, not a meat dish. I dare say His Majesty is accustomed to theatricals and acrobatics and suchlike, living in Chalcedon as he does."

Father Pius thrust out his lower lip and said nothing.

"And as for the gypsies, young Matt, you've done well," she said. "I've needed a new skillet for an age. You and your dad need newer knives. Half the women in town need their scissors sharpened. It'll be a boon having the caravan come."

She nodded and put an end to the discussion. Matthew Dunwoody headed back to the butcher shop in triumph. I left Priscilla gazing after him in a humiliating state of reverence.

School had been a flurry of activity, with Sister Claire assigning recitations and poems to memorize to each form, from the young ones on up. I was tasked with memorizing Saint Menelos's fabled discourse on biblical beasts, which was long, but far more lively and scientific than Saint Adelard's treatises on sin, which had fallen to poor Priscilla.

Reaching home, I ambled through Grandfather's orchard before going indoors. On a whim, I dropped my books in the tall grasses, all except for Saint Menelos's, and climbed into my favorite tree. Here was as good a place as any to memorize my biblical beasts.

This particular tree's branches formed a low cradle that I could rest in like a bed. I wondered if the branches could still support my weight, but they'd grown larger too, and I rested and read, snug and secure, rocked by the gentle motion of wind in the boughs.

The golden apples were heavy, warm and fat with

juice. I helped myself to one, testing it. It *was* ripe. My bite broke off with a terrific crunch, showing flesh white as snow. I'd beaten Grandfather to this discovery, which never lost its glory, year by year. The apples were ripe!

I forgot my book as I ate that divine first apple. August light filtered through green leaves, beginning to redden. I thought of Grandfather, his little farm, and these trees where I'd spent so many happy hours. This slow, contented life wasn't so bad, was it? I had Grandfather's love, and Father's books, and all the cider I could drink. Why would I want to leave?

Warm light played over my face. Hay-scented breezes cooled my skin. I closed my eyes.

I didn't notice when my rest turned into sleep. A century might have passed. In my dreams the rocking, swaying motion of the tree branches became rolling, swaying waves on the sea. I swam, effortlessly as a fish, buoyed along by the swelling waves.

A shadow caught my eye. Far out, under the dark water, something was moving toward me, and not by accident. It had singled me out, and somehow it knew my name. Its great, fearsome head drew nearer. I was too terrified to escape. I flung out my hands to protect my head, and the creature opened its mouth, and bit.

I woke with a gasp. My eyes went straight to my hand,

which still felt the stinging bite. Yet there was no bite on my hand.

But coiled around my wrist, like a long bracelet, was a snake.

I wanted to scream and fling it off me, but I couldn't. I was paralyzed. The snake was small and thin, like a delicate, living twine, yellow scales intertwined in a perfect pattern with brown on its textured skin. How I saw all this so clearly, I don't know. Part of me was still underwater, trapped and terrified. The snake lifted its tiny head and looked back at me, then worked its way around my wrist and up my arm.

It's just a small snake, I told myself, like dozens you've dealt with before, in the fields or by the creek. But I'd never seen markings such as these, and how did I know if it was venomous? I couldn't shake my muzzy-headed sense that somehow this little snake meant danger.

The snake worked its way up my arm and onto my bodice, until it lay coiled upon my breastbone. It raised up its head on its thin body and gazed at me, its slip of a tongue flickering. My arms and legs were still frozen, but I managed to lift my head and gaze back. It was so close now that my eyes couldn't focus on it properly. There seemed to be two of them.

Its little head darted forward.

My breath caught in my throat.

The snake's head brushed my mouth.

I felt the faintest prick of a razor-sharp fang on my lower lip.

It stroked its head and neck along my cheek, then slithered away, dropping out of sight among the branches below me.

Chapter 4

I sat up and tasted my lip with my tongue. A tiny drop of blood had formed. Was I poisoned? How quickly would the venom take hold? I flexed my arms and stretched my legs. They worked.

What did it mean, being kissed by a snake?

I ran indoors. If it was venom, at least indoors I could bid Grandfather good-bye. If it was not venom, well, I still wanted to get away from that place.

The cloying, heavy sweet smell of simmering vinegar filled my nostrils as I entered the cottage. Grandfather was pickling today. His pickles were famous in Maundley. He'd spent years adjusting the recipe. The great kettle stood on the stove, full of salted cucumber slices.

"Trouble, Evie?" Grandfather looked up from chopping onions and blinked at me. His red eyes streamed. "You see a ghost?"

"No ghost," I said. "A snake. It bit me, just slightly, on my lip."

Grandfather's knife clanged on the chopping block. He hurried to where I stood, wincing slightly from his stiff knee. "What kind of snake? Where's the bite? Show me."

He took my face in his leathered hands and tilted my head back for better light. I could feel his rapid breathing and smell the onion on his fingers.

"I don't know what kind," I said. "Something small. I'm sure it's nothing."

Grandfather squinted at my lip. "It's a small mark," he said. "Hardly broke the skin at all. Maybe I'd better . . . You'd best lie down, Evelyn."

I wondered whether *he* should. The episode seemed more insignificant each moment. My heart still beat, my lungs filled with air. Perhaps the snake was just addled by the heat.

I stretched out on Grandfather's bed, and he pulled up a chair to watch me. It's an odd feeling, being stared at while you wait to see if you'll die.

"Let me get you a drink of water," Grandfather said. "You feeling dizzy? Nauseous? Your lip's not swollen. That's a good sign."

He forgot the drink and snatched up my wrist to feel my pulse. His lips moved as he counted heartbeats while his eyes followed the clock on the mantelpiece.

I sat up and kissed his whiskery cheek. "I'm fine, Grandfather. Let me get you some more onions from the garden. You need them for your pickles, don't you? Some garlic?"

"Onions can wait. Let me put a compress on your lip."

He folded a clean cloth into a bandage and smeared his all-purpose ointment on it. It cooled where it touched me, and I breathed in drafts of camphor-scented air.

"Camphor's supposed to repel snakes," Grandfather said. "They don't like the smell."

"Bit late for that."

But my grandfather couldn't compose himself. I peeled off the compress and stood up. "I'm perfectly fine, Grandfather."

Grandfather eased himself onto his bed. He wiped his forehead with his sleeve. "I need to rest a bit." He tried to smile. "My old heart can't take the shock of something happening to you."

I put both arms around him and squeezed him close. "Nor I you, Grandfather," I said. "If I could be a physician like my father, I'd doctor you up and keep you with me forever."

Grandfather's smile was sad. "Not even your father knew how to do that."

I gave him another squeeze. "I got a delicious apple off the tree just now."

Grandfather seized upon this lifesaving change in

subject. "Did you, now," he said. "Well, well. Another season's come around."

"They seem to keep on doing that."

"Don't you be telling *me* about time passing, missy," Grandfather said. "You've hardly even started. This old man knows."

"Old man? Bosh. You're barely over sixty."

"Old enough." Grandfather dusted his hands on his shirt, then returned to his chopping block. His slices were so even and precise you could measure a tailor's stitches by them.

He watched me move about the kitchen. I caught him staring at my lower lip, still concerned. He turned back to his onions like a guilty child. "If you're eating apples today, maybe there'll be time to make some fresh cider for the Saint Bronwyn's folderol they're whipping up."

Grandfather was as famous for his cider as he was for his pickles. He was ever experimenting, fiddling with the brew. "You'll win a ribbon, then," I told him.

"Hmph. Not if Widow Moreau has any say in the matter."

Chapter 5

The gyspy caravan arrived midmorning on Saint Bronwyn's eve. Their clothes and their painted wagons seemed
more colorful than all the rest of the world put together.
We gawked at them, I'm ashamed to say, every man Jack
and woman Joan of us, as they tethered their horses and
lit their luncheon fires.

"Do you suppose the king will fall in love with one of
the village girls?" Priscilla asked me as we sat weaving flowers into wreaths. "It happens. Mary Grace is pretty enough."

"Don't be a goose," I said. "Kings only fall in love with
village girls in fairy stories."

"Kings fall in love with whomever they like," Priscilla
said. "He's a bachelor. He needs an heir. He could do worse
than marry a strong, healthy country girl."

I pricked my finger on a thorn. "You sound like a horse
breeder."

"Then what's he coming for, if not to find his one true love?" Priscilla said. "He combs the kingdom, under pretense of royal duty, but secretly he's searching for that face that will leap out from the crowd . . ."

"He's scouring for tax money, likely as not," I said. "What's gotten into you?"

"They say he's handsome," she said.

"Kings are always handsome." I reached for more daisies. "Even when they're half-dead, bald, and toothless. It's a privilege of being king."

"He's not even thirty yet," Prissy protested. "I'm sure he has all his teeth!"

"But is he as handsome as Matthew Dunwoody?"

Priscilla scowled at her lapful of blossoms. "That son of a butcher thinks he hung the moon in the sky, ever since he found those gypsies. You'd think he grew them from seed."

"Matthew has fine, straight teeth," I said. "A mouthful of them."

"He needs them, too, tough as the meat they sell is."

~

We rigged booths from sawhorses and planks and draped bedsheets over the top. The ice man's wife practiced her song for the king until someone threatened to heave a skillet at her. The four Hafton brothers, famous for their hunting prowess, came whooping out of the woods with a massive boar trussed up by his ankles over a long ash pike. Ham and pork roast for tomorrow!

At last all that could possibly be done, and then some, had been done, and still there was no king in sight. No messenger to explain his delay, either.

We waited.

We fussed with our buttons and collars.

Butcher Dunwoody and the Hafton brothers gutted the boar until our stomachs flopped.

We ate bread and butter, saving the dainties the ladies had made all week for His Illustrious Arrival. All save Mayor Snow, who for once had no appetite.

Children fell asleep on the grass. The sun sank in the west. Night birds swooped through the soft twilight air.

I looped my arm through Grandfather's. "Let's go home before it's too dark to see."

"Well said, Evelyn, my duck," Widow Moreau said. "I'll go with you." We headed home.

"Suppose he'll never come?" Grandfather said. "A rude trick that'd be."

"King's privilege, I suspect," Widow Moreau said. "The most trifling thing could make him change his mind, and still we wait upon his pleasure."

"Not I," Grandfather said. "These boots are laced like tourniquets. If I wait any more on his pleasure, soon I'll have no feet."

"For all that, you won't walk any slower than you do

now, Lem Pomeroy," Widow Moreau said cheerfully. "You're so thin Evelyn could carry you. I ought to fatten you up. Don't you eat anything besides pickles?"

Grandfather stamped the butt of his walking stick into the dirt. "There's not many foods more healthful than pickles," he snapped. "They purge the digestion."

"Grandfather!" I said. "Please!"

"Well, they do."

Widow Moreau snickered. Then we stopped. Someone was crashing through the underbrush after us.

"Evie!" Aidan's voice called.

I spun around, searching for him through the gathering gloom. "What's the matter?"

He burst through the trees and stopped, panting. "King Leopold's here," he said. "One of his men grew sick on the journey. The king is calling for a physician."

I felt cold all over. Heal one of the king's fellows? From some malady I couldn't guess? Now, if he was about to have a baby, that'd be one thing . . .

In the dark behind me I heard Grandfather take a step forward. He cleared his throat. "What's wrong with the man, son? Do you know? What are his symptoms?"

Aidan shook his head. "Fever, I think. That's what I heard. He's inside a carriage."

Grandfather and I looked at each other.

I turned to Aidan. "Walk these two home, will you, while I run on ahead?"

Torches and fires from the gypsy caravan illuminated the common, where Maundleyans stood in anxious clusters, well back from the king's coaches, as though they were full of contagion. And well they might be.

I approached the king's carriage and stuck my head in the door. "Did someone inquire about help for a sick man?"

Half a dozen faces turned my way. I felt like a worm surrounded by robins.

"Yes," a voice said slowly, from the darkness. "We did send for a medic or healer. Can you bring us one?"

"I am he," I said boldly. "I mean, I am she."

There were splutters of indignation, but no more. My patience wore thin. I could be home tucking into bed with my medical books. Like me or not, but I could help. At least a little.

"Where is the sick man?" I said. "Time is passing."

The owner of the voice leaned forward in his seat and rose. I had no choice but to retreat from the carriage and onto the ground outside. I backed away before the man trod on my feet, and fell backward, landing hard upon my tailbone. I looked up at the man, now visible by the torch he carried, its light glinting off the medallion he wore at his chest.

"Oh," I said. "You're the king, aren't you?"

Chapter 6

Quick as anything, he reached out a hand and pulled me up. I was more muddied than hurt, and more embarrassed than muddied, but the king made no comment. When I was once more upright I remembered my manners and curtsied to His Majesty.

Priscilla was right. He *was* handsome. His hair was chestnut, his eyes dark and sparkling in the torchlight. I knew he was just a man like any other, but I couldn't help a giddy thrill. *I'm standing next to the king!* The comely, athletic, youthful bachelor king . . .

But those dark eyes were worried. "Please lead me to the patient," I said.

"Do you have tools?" King Leopold asked. "Medicines? What do you propose to do?"

What *did* I propose to do?

"Heal him." Then I panicked. "Or at least do all that I can."

The king's mouth was grim. After a moment's pause, he turned on one heel and led me to the next carriage over.

Chill night air blew through the corners of the carriage. A short, stout man lay stretched across the rear seat. I felt heat radiating off his forehead before I even touched it. From time to time his body was racked with choking coughs. The stuffy air inside the carriage stank of his sickly breath.

I knelt beside him and lay my hands on his forehead and under his neck. He burned terribly. Lumps swelled on either side of his throat. I pressed his head between both hands and palpated his scalp while I tried to think. He needed treatment, but Maundley wouldn't thank me if I brought this illness into our village.

The patient took a long, slow breath. I realized he was sighing with relief at my touch.

"What do you suggest?"

I'd forgotten the king was there.

"Ask Mayor Snow to obtain a room for him at the Galloping Goose," I said. "He'll need to be carried there, stripped, and bathed in lukewarm water. Ask my grandfather to send a bottle of cider, and ask the inn to send up a bowl of broth."

The sick man coughed painfully.

"Also ask Widow Moreau—she's the old woman who runs the town—to find me some catnip and licorice root. And honey."

King Leopold nodded and backed out of the carriage.

"And garlic," I called after him. "Ample garlic."

I rubbed my patient's temples and jawbone. Had I done wrong, giving orders to the king himself? The sober way he received them was some reassurance.

In minutes the king returned with another of his company, and the two men heaved the sick man up off his couch and out of the carriage. I followed after, gulping in the fresh air.

At the Galloping Goose, serving women attended to the bath. By careful eavesdropping at the bar I learned the patient was Chancellor of the Exchequer. A weighty title indeed.

"As I suspected," I told Aidan while we waited at the inn. "A glorified tax collector."

"No wonder the king values him so."

I peeled cloves of garlic, crushed them underneath an empty beer mug, and dropped them into a bowl of water. "Even tax collectors deserve to live," I said.

"That," Aidan said, wrinkling his nose—I assumed at the garlic—"is a matter of opinion."

I set aside my garlic brew, then bathed shredded licorice root and catnip leaves in boiling water, spooned in a great glob of honey, and put a lid on the teapot. My medicines were ready.

The door to the room opened, and a young, pale courtier with a narrow nose appeared.

"The Lord Chancellor will see you now," he told me.

I carried my teapot and garlic water up the stairs. The thin courtier showed me into a room with a lamp lit by the bed, where the Lord Chancellor sat propped against pillows, wearing a clean nightshirt. The king sat in a corner with a cloak draped over himself.

"And this is she?" my patient said. "My ministering angel?"

I couldn't tell if he was sincere or mocking. His face was round and red, with a smooth bald crown on top and a full neck rippling down from his chin.

I set down my brews and placed my hands upon his head and neck one more time. At my touch, he closed his eyes and sighed blissfully.

"You're not cured," I said. "Only cooled and refreshed from your bath. You're still feverish, though less so."

"That's something you do, there, with your hands," the Lord Chancellor said. "Marvelously cool. Like peeled grapes on a summer's day."

"I wouldn't know about peeled grapes," I said. I poured him catnip and licorice tea. "Drain this teapot over the next hour," I said. "Then sleep all you can."

He saluted me. "I must obey the doctor's orders."

"In the morning, you're to drink all the water in this bowl," I said. "You won't be thanking me then. But it will help the aggravation in your throat. The innkeeper can make you more of this tea in the morning. And you should have some thin porridge for breakfast."

He took a swig from his cup, winced, and took another.

"Porridge? Has it really come to that?" He held out his soft, dimpled hand. "Christopher Appleton's my name, my good girl."

"You see, Appleton?" the king said. "Just what I've been telling you. You see what a difference a charming young lady can make, eh?"

"Balderdash," said the Lord Chancellor. "One good apple doesn't mend the whole spoiled barrel. You'd do well to remember that. Meaning no offense to those present." He winked at me.

"Mind your manners," the king said cheerfully. "If I could afford to manage without you, I'd cut out your tongue for that insinuation."

I curtsied and turned to go. "I'll come again in the morning, before the feast begins."

The king startled us both by clapping his hands loudly. "By Jove, that's right," he said. "The feast day. It's what we've come for, isn't it?" Then he reached for my hand. "We are much obliged to you," he said. "I wouldn't know what to do without Appleton. What is your name?"

"Evelyn," I said. "Evelyn Pomeroy."

The king smiled broadly, showing a splendid set of teeth. I would have to report them to Priscilla.

"Evelyn Pomeroy," he said. "That's a name I expect we shall be hearing again."

Chapter 7

The Lord Chancellor's breath was still foul in the morning, but not his temper. He took his porridge and tea, and drank the garlic drink dutifully while I glared at him, so I knew he'd mend. I started another batch of garlic steeping, then headed to Saint Bronwyn's mass much relieved.

The choirboys, under the direction of Father Pius, staged a holy reenactment of Saint Bronwyn's virtuous life. I was fond of Maundley's patron saint, who had been kind to animals and ever carried soup to the suffering poor. But it was hard to remember that this was a *holy* reenactment as I watched a fuming, mortified twelve-year-old boy who had been cast, regrettably, as the good lady herself, stomping through his motions under Father Pius's watchful, bushy eyebrows.

We were all glad to exit the church and make our way to the festivities.

The common had become a wonderland. Bright stalls lined one side, gypsy wagons unfolded like mechanical toys along the next, and cooking fires dotted another. Village women hawked and bartered handicrafts, and gypsy women did the same with their marvelous beads and scarves, knives and pots. Apples stuffed with raisins baked in an outdoor oven, while luscious scents wafted from the fire pit where the boar roasted underground in hickory coals. On the green itself were the games, foot races, sack races, and three-legged races for all ages. Next came contests, wrestling and hammer throwing and archery. Some gypsies joined in the games, and a few Maundleyans got their tempers ruffled when blue ribbons were claimed by gypsies. The king himself watched the games with keen interest, even cheering for the winners.

Grandfather had made me a little present that morning of five guineas, for all my hard work at school. I protested and tried to make him keep it, but he insisted that I take the money. "Treat yourself to something nice at the fair," he said. "Some token to remember this day."

And so I browsed the stalls, taking my time luxuriously, feeling rich as a queen. I fingered fabrics, leather valises and wallets, wood carvings, and hair pins.

"Pretty girl want to buy a pretty charm?"

The woman gazed at me through penetrating dark brown eyes. She was tall and handsome, with broad shoulders and cheekbones, and curls of salt-and-pepper hair poking out from under a red scarf. She seemed to sway slightly, as though she were remembering a dance, and her skirts, spangled with dots, swished around her hips.

She tapped me on the nose. "Come, see my special charms I save, just for you."

Before I could answer she seized my wrist. Hers tinkled with a dozen bracelets as she led me past the trinkets for sale in her stall. She pulled out a wooden box. Inside, on thin woven cords of colored silk, were a gorgeous riot of bangles to be worn as pendants around the neck.

Without thinking, I reached for a charm, a black rock polished to an incredible gloss, with a perfectly smooth hole in the center, through which a red cord threaded.

"How much is this one?"

"Ah, you like that?" she said. She thumped her breast-bone. "Girls like you choose what your heart needs. Centuries ago, that very charm was worn by a duchess in Rovary."

Fiddlesticks, I thought. *These look like she made them last week.* I dropped the shiny stone. "What do you mean, 'girls like me'?"

She watched me sideways, her high eyebrows arching. "Eh? No? *Pani-sap-rakli?*"

I took a step back.

She reached for my hand again. "Nothing, nothing. Don't listen to the old woman muttering! Come, come, I sell you *draba*. Charms. This one, for you? Eight pennies."

She draped the charm over me. It slid into place around my neck like it belonged there.

"Eight pennies," she sang, her hoop earrings swinging. I handed her one of my guineas, not knowing how to do otherwise.

"Tell me what this charm does," I said.

She patted my cheek. "It's *love* charm," she whispered. "Rovarian duchess, she use it to win the heart of daring general in Rovarian army. For you, in order to work, you need to think of one you love, every time you put on."

I laughed. "No fear, then," I said. "Let me buy another of these for my friend."

I found a matching charm with a ring of black stone. Rovarian duchess indeed! What, did she have a sister? Two charms just the same? No matter. I would enjoy presenting this to Prissy.

The woman counted out my change and pressed it into my palm, then folded my own fingers over it. "Tell you what I do for you. You choose another charm, no? Another *draba* for the pretty *rakli*. For only three pennies more I give him to you, you such good customer."

I found a delicate snowflake pattern, made entirely of frail twigs lashed together with what looked like cobweb. The cord was emerald green, and the twigs had their bark stripped off, leaving the pale yellow wood bare. It reminded me of a wild spring blossom.

"You like that? Three pennies."

I handed her the money. "And what does this give me?"

She pursed her lips. "Luck," she said. "Extra special good luck. Used by a princess in Nondavurg, always very clumsy, until she wear this."

I smiled. Preposterous! Yet I could almost believe she meant it.

"Thank you very much." I turned to leave.

"Wait wait! One more, you are needing to have!" she cried. "I feel it in my back teeth. Come, I give last charm, one penny." She thrust the box at me. "Find the charm calling you."

There was something about her that was impossible to refuse. This, I figured, was how she earned a living huckstering worthless trinkets. But the bright silk cords lay tangled in the box like maypole ribbons. At the bottom, on a drab string, was an odd-shaped nugget of waxed bone.

"This is a curious one," I said. "It doesn't seem to fit with the others." I stroked the bone, feeling its tiny nubs, wondering what kind of creature it once belonged to and how long ago it lived. A vertebra, I was inclined to think. As a scientific puzzle, this charm intrigued me.

She watched me through narrowed eyes. "So," she said. "This is what you choose."

"Oh, I didn't say that," I said. "I was just noticing it."

She held out her hand for it, and I found mine gripping it tightly.

I released my grip and laughed a little. "I suppose I

have chosen it," I said. "For a penny. Maybe it has chosen me." I paid my price. "What does this charm give me?"

She put her box of charms away, under the table and out of sight. "Protection," she said. "From snakebite. Good-bye."

Chapter 8

I wandered away from her stall, deep in thought. All that hocus pocus about choosing the charm you needed was nonsense. Wasn't it? Love, luck—every gullible fool wanted love or luck. It was nothing more than coincidence that I'd just had a snakebite, and a tiny one at that.

I found Prissy helping her mother at the handicrafts table, and gave her my present.

"It's a love charm." I slipped it over her head. "Think of Matthew Dunwoody every time you put it on."

"That butcher's son," she fumed. "Thinks he looks so grand for the *dancing girls* in his new leather breeches."

"Well, does he?"

Prissy scowled. "Thanks for the necklace. I see you got yourself one too." She gave me a meaningful look. "Who's the lucky fellow?"

"Hah. I only bought one because it was pretty."

Matthew Dunwoody passed by, deep in conversation with Roger Thomas, the carpenter's son, when both stopped at the sight of us.

"Good morning, Evie," Matthew said. "Don't you look rosy today!"

Priscilla pressed her lips together tightly. "Good morning, Roger," she said, deliberately ignoring Matthew. "A fair day we have for our feast."

"Not as fair as the pretty girls who've joined the celebration," Roger said, bowing. Chiefly in my direction.

Praise be, they left. I tried to compose my face. Poor Priscilla was having a harder time.

She folded her arms across her chest. "What came over *them*?"

It was a reasonable question. I'd never had such attention from village lads before. Neither Priscilla nor I had ever been written in on the list of Bonniest Girls in Town. In matters of spelling and arithmetic we were the undisputed champions, but regarding beauty ...

"Pay no attention," I said. "They probably spent the morning at the Galloping Goose."

The athletic games wound to a close, and everyone headed for the makeshift pavilion erected in honor of Saint Bronwyn's Day. Sister Claire herded us there for the school exhibition, but first I bought a pair of crocheted infant's trousers for baby Brom. It would give me an excuse to stop by Hannah Croft's later and see how he was getting on.

I lined up with the other students and watched the village settle uncomfortably onto the benches under the pavilion. I felt embarrassed, holding the town captive while we students recited our lessons. After the exhilaration of the contests and games, we were bound to be a disappointment. But they sat politely.

Grandfather sat in the very front row, looking smart in his red checkered shirt and brown trousers. King Leopold himself sat and listened to the recitations. I wondered why he was so interested in our small village school. I confess I watched him more than I watched Sister Claire.

The littlest ones sang the well-known geography song. "Fairest Pylander, home and native soil; Rovary, south, where the whalers toil; Merlia, west, on the breast of the sea; Danelind, north, where the hunters be." They followed it with a children's psalm, then bobbed and curtsied to their mothers and received smiles from the king for their charms.

Having the king present for recitation day was such a startling novelty that when my turn came I nearly faltered and called the behemoth a dragon. It was a great relief to finally sit down.

Then Sister Claire rose.

"Good people of Maundley," she said, "permit me now to announce the winner of the top academic prize at my school."

I bit the insides of my cheeks. Let my face show

nothing! *Don't hope for this prize, Evelyn. Be good enough to wish it for Priscilla.* But I couldn't entirely master myself. Oh, how I wanted to end my education with that prize. I was ashamed of how badly I wanted it. I caught myself clutching my good luck charm.

"This year's winner is," Sister Claire said, with maddening delay, "Priscilla Hornby!"

Oh.

I turned and embraced Priscilla and kissed her. Truly, I was glad for her success, but more truly, I needed to do something to mask my disappointment.

Sister Claire clapped along with the rest of Maundley. She watched us both.

What did it matter anyway? Top prize or no top prize. What difference could that possibly make to how the sun rose and set?

Sister Claire held up her hands. She looked like she was about to do something unplanned—which for her was most unusual. "I want to add that this year's decision was especially difficult." An anxious look flickered across Mrs. Hornby's face. "Allow me, please, to designate Evelyn Pomeroy with an honorable mention."

And now Priscilla embraced me, over the fresh wave of applause, and I wondered how to keep my face still. Somehow this was worse, to be singled out as the runner-up. If I couldn't win, I would rather have remained obscure.

The king strode to the platform where we stood with Sister Claire and bowed to her, which made her cheeks flush. The women present gasped at this gallantry. With his elbows cocked at his sides, his embroidered waistcoat, and a green cape flowing over his shoulders, he could even make a nun blush. Why did it irk me that he had seen me take second place?

"We are most impressed with the achievements of your students here in Maundley," he said, resting a hand on Priscilla's shoulder. She looked like she might faint. "Not every village we visit prizes their schools, nor their young scholars, this well."

Sister Claire, that modest soul, lowered her eyes but could not conceal her smile.

"We had occasion to witness last night the quick thinking and resource of one of these young ladies," the king said, and then it was my turn to blush.

"Your families have fostered your studies, have they not?" the king asked us. We nodded.

"Are either of you betrothed, at your young ages?"

Priscilla's mouth opened. She shook her head. My face grew *very* warm. What could this mean? From the corner of my eye I saw Rosie Willis, arm in arm with her beau, and seated behind them, Aidan Moreau, watching me.

"We are convinced that a village lacking schools lacks hope, and a kingdom without learning cannot thrive," the king said. "This blessed sister is to be commended. We are pleased to announce a scholarship for your top prize winner at the Royal University in Chalcedon."

Priscilla's eyes opened wide, and not altogether with delight. I closed mine quickly. University? Priscilla? *Please, do not let me envy my dear friend.*

Mayor Snow leaped to his feet and applauded. "Such an honor for Maundley!" he cried.

King Leopold stroked his chin, then turned to me suddenly. "Maundley's school," he said, "is clearly superior to most like it in the provinces. Therefore, to win an honorable mention here is akin to taking the top prize elsewhere. You are to be congratulated, young lady."

My head filled with buzzing. Somehow I remembered to curtsy, bowing low.

When I rose, the king took my hand. "Would you also like to attend University?"

It took me a moment to hear and understand.

Had my soul and body had come unhinged?

I forgot how to speak. I glanced at Grandfather, whose face was a mask.

"Yes, please. Your Majesty," my voice said, before my brain could intervene. "I would."

Priscilla's eyes were wide. She reached for my hand and squeezed it.

His eyes twinkled. "Then so you shall."

I wanted to scream, I wanted to laugh, I wanted to throw

my arms around the king's neck and kiss his chestnut-bearded cheek. Perhaps the good luck charm restrained me from doing those things.

The good luck charm . . . ?

Oh, my.

Chapter 9

❦

All of Maundley, or so it seemed, turned out to wave good-bye to Aidan, Priscilla, her maiden aunt Charlotte Jessop, and me on Tuesday next, as we waited for the coach for Fallardston. Aidan would accompany us back, but Miss Jessop was our official chaperone.

The coachman reined his horses, and a couple climbed down from the coach and entered the Galloping Goose. Aidan lashed our parcels to the carriage, alongside the daily post.

I wasn't looking forward to long days in a hot coach, but Grandfather insisted I not go by ship up the coastline to Chalcedon from Fallardston. "There are storms at sea, and you can't swim," was his objection. Even Widow Moreau backed him on that one. She hated the sea. I could humor him. It was the least I could do for him, since he was letting me go.

There were tearful adieus from Widow Moreau, Sister Claire, and Letty and Hannah Croft, who came with baby Brom. How could I leave them behind? Others I didn't mind leaving so much. Matthew Dunwoody and Roger Thomas and several of their mates were there. They had dropped by so often, both to congratulate me on my scholarship and urge me not to take it, that Grandfather began hollering if they came more than twice a day. I couldn't go outdoors without tripping over nosegays of flowers, and I couldn't walk to town without them arguing over holding my basket. Even Rosie Willis's beau winked at me once.

And those weren't the only strange doings this last week. My chickens had gone from laying one egg a day, if the mood suited them, to three and even four. Grandfather's final kettle of pickles, which I'd helped him bottle, filled twice as many jars as it ought to have. And the raccoon that had troubled my kitchen garden these last three seasons packed up and moved to greener pastures. I'd taken to blaming all these events, in jest, on my gypsy charms.

The crowd of lads swirled around me until Aidan shouldered his way through with a heavy trunk and they were forced to step back.

And then I had to take my leave of Grandfather.

I felt I hadn't stopped saying good-bye to him since Saint Bronwyn's Day. Now that the time had come to part, I felt spent, with neither words nor emotions left to convey. He planted a whiskery kiss on my cheek, then retreated into the crowd. I wished I'd done better, but it was too late to rush after him now. Good-byes had to end somewhere. I climbed into the dark coach.

Priscilla's maiden aunt was already there. No one seemed desperate to delay her.

Charlotte Jessop was soft of body and hard of jaw. A pewter-colored cap was pinned to her steely hair, which was pulled tightly off her forehead. She sat against a window fanning her face.

I sat and observed the grimy windows and the dank smell of mildew and spilled luncheons. Stiff, cracked leather seats were nothing like the king's plush carriages.

Outside Prissy clung to her mother's and father's necks. At last the coachman bawled that he would leave without her, and her father managed to stuff her into the carriage. Just when we thought we were all comfortable, another body appeared in the door. It was the man we'd seen exiting the coach, followed by his companion. Now we'd be six, wedged like twin calves at an udder. Miss Jessop joined us on our side, while the man and woman sat by Aidan.

The door closed. Release levers squealed. Horses stamped. And then the coach moved forward, tossing me back against my seat. I craned my neck for one last glimpse of Grandfather. He seemed small and pale amid the throng of less abandoned people.

Then the coach turned around a bend in the road, and he was gone.

And the impossible moment I'd thought of ever since Saint Bronwyn's Day was finally here. We were on our way to Chalcedon.

I heard a hiccup beside me. Priscilla fumbled for a handkerchief to wipe her eyes. Poor girl. It was hard for her to leave her parents. Aidan looked away, but Miss Jessop was less tactful.

"What's the matter with you?" she snapped. "It'll be a right miserable journey if you can't so much as ride to the signpost for Maundley without wailing like a sick baby."

Prissy's cheeks flushed with shame. She kept her eyes lowered but glanced toward our fellow passengers. They took no notice of her embarrassment. They seemed intent on sleep.

The man was wiry and lean of build, with a close-shorn scalp. Crawling up from under his ill-fitting collar were a host of dark markings working up his throat and around his jaw. Tattoos! I knew it was only pigment, but their effect was chilling.

His wrists were also decorated with tattoos, but his hands startled me. Instead of healthy brown flesh, his hands were mottled, waxy white and gray, with slick, shiny rope-like scars. Burns. He looked like he'd fallen hands-first into raging coals.

I began thinking of all I'd read about the treatment of burns, until I looked at his face again. His lips had that same scarred gloss to them, and very little beard grew around his mouth.

It was then that I realized, with an awkward start, that his lady companion was not asleep, but watching me as I studied her scarred man. Her dark-lidded eyes smoldered with mockery. She made a flicking gesture in my direction with her finger and thumb, as if I were an insect. Her fingers were long and thin, with sharp nails and tightly bound muscles under pallid skin.

It would be a cruel day, trapped in this close carriage, bouncing wretchedly over every bump, that woman's hateful stare burning me. We wouldn't reach Fallardston until late afternoon, where we'd lodge at an inn, then cross the Ladon River by ferry and continue on to Chalcedon by another coach. I fingered my little pouch of money. It was all I had for food and passage, tied to a rawhide thong around my neck with my gypsy charms. My pendant with the king's seal, which granted me admittance to University, I'd pinned to the inside of my dress.

Charlotte Jessop spent the morning complaining Priscilla was crowding her. Priscilla practically sat in my lap to avoid her. We all felt relieved when Miss Jessop's chin drooped onto her breastbone and she began to snore.

I offered an apple to Priscilla and tossed one to Aidan. Faster than a frog catching bugs, the strange woman snatched the apple in midair and bit into it. Stunned, I handed Aidan another and wondered if people in the jostling city would be as rude as she.

The coach driver opened a hatch to tell us we'd reach Fallardston in an hour.

The sun beat mercilessly upon our carriage. I was becoming intimately aware of certain smells—Miss Jessop's sweat mixed with powder, the tattooed man's scent of ash and lamp oil. His companion smelled like my stolen apple. Sweat ran down my ribs. Oh, to jump in a cool river and swim! Much I knew what that would feel like, but it was heavenly to imagine.

I flexed my feet and wiggled my legs. Circulation in my toes was shutting down for good.

Abruptly, the horses neighed, and stopped. Miss Jessop woke with a snort, and Priscilla, Aidan, and I exchanged glances. Surely we weren't in Fallardston yet?

Voices yelled. The horses shrilled. The coachmen shouted them on. But we didn't move.

"Mercy!" Miss Jessop began to whimper. "I do believe we're—"

"Highwaymen," Aidan hissed. "Everyone down!"

I folded Priscilla's body down on my lap, then lay myself on top of her, my heart racing.

Aidan must be wrong.

Musket shots pierced the stillness, discordant in the autumn sunshine. They echoed in my skull.

This can't be happening.

Miss Jessop whimpered. Oh, let there be some normal explanation!

So this is what terror feels like.

Like hearts pounding. And mad, blind fear.

So much for my gypsy luck.

Another shot, and we felt a thump. It was the coachman, tumbling down onto the road.

The scarred man pushed his side door open and dragged his lady after him.

"Shall we try to go too?" I whispered to Aidan.

"Take Priscilla," he began, then stopped.

A dark shape appeared in the door.

The highwayman.

Chapter 10

Aidan slid down onto the floor, and for a moment I thought him a coward. But with an explosive, double-legged kick, he smashed the door open, clipping the bandit in the face. The bandit staggered back, and Aidan was outside in two ticks, striking him with both fists.

Then he stopped, stepped back, and held his arms up.

Dread came over me. So much for our hope. The man held a pistol to Aidan's belly.

"Stop!" I cried. I pushed Prissy off me and squirmed out the door, which barely opened for Aidan's blocking it. Prissy called after me as I stepped out into the blinding light.

A thin line of blood trickled from the bandit's eyebrow. He dabbed it and stared at the spot as if such a thing had never been dared before. His finger flexed on his trigger.

I pushed myself in front of Aidan and felt the hot metal of the barrel against my chest.

"Leave my friend alone," I told him. "Put your gun away this minute, and let us go."

Aidan tried to move me aside but I resisted. The bandit chuckled. He was thick as an oak, yet he stood with a flamboyant grace, one fist on his hip, the other brandishing a pistol like a rapier. He wore a ruffle of lace at his neck and a black band belting his waist. Robbing poor travelers must be a thriving trade. A wide-brimmed hat obscured much of his face, but his eyes, brown and gold, were as calm as those of a priest saying mass.

Rolling in the dust of the road, moaning, was the coachman. His blood formed a growing black puddle. I made a move toward him, and the highwayman jabbed his pistol at me.

A hissing fury reared inside me. How dare he threaten me and my friends? How *dare* he?

"For shame!" I spat the words. "Does the brave bandit fear a peasant girl? What do you care if I help the poor man? You've picked a coach full of penniless country folk to murder."

He laughed in my face. "Not quite penniless, my fiery little maid," he said, seizing the ornaments around my neck. The rawhide strap holding my money broke, but the gypsy charms, on braided cords of gossamer silk, didn't yield. He decided they weren't worth the bother. Instead, he stroked my cheek with his fingertip.

Aidan growled and lunged toward him. The bandit raised his gun.

"Tie him up," the bandit said, handing me a length of rope. "Bind your sweetheart, missy, and perhaps I won't kill him. Though perhaps I will. Make it tight, now."

I took the rope and cinched Aidan's wrists like a traitor. *My sweetheart.*

He reached into the coach and dragged out Prissy and then Miss Jessop. Miss Jessop kicked him, and I liked her better for it. Prissy's love charm broke off with her money pouch.

"Now," he said. "Tell me why I shouldn't kill you all." The fiend was enjoying this!

"Because God will punish you in hell for it," Priscilla said, and the highwayman laughed.

"Two courageous maidens! But spare me the preaching." He looked again at me. "Well?"

"Because you were born to be more than a ruthless spiller of blood," I said.

He made an extravagant bow. "The lady has spoken. Lie down in the road, all of you, behind the carriage." We had no choice but to obey. Miss Jessop whimpered pitiably.

"Farewell, my tigress," he called, kissing his fingers and winking his cursed hawk's eyes at me. Then, leaping into the coachman's seat, the highwayman threw back the braking lever and cracked the driver's whip. The team of six horses flew forward, eager to flee this frightful spot.

And then he was gone.

I scrambled to my feet, tripping on the hem of my dress, and flew to the driver. He wasn't moving as much now, but lay feebly, bleeding in several places. What could I do? I had no water, no bandages, no medicines, not even any whiskey to relieve his pain.

I placed my hands on his face. "I'm here," I said. "Where does it hurt?"

His eyelids flickered open. "Thorndike," he said. "Jeremy Thorndike."

I was busy unbuttoning his shirt to see where the musket shot had pierced his side. "Who is Jeremy Thorndike?" His wounds made me cringe, but I kept my face calm for his sake.

"Me," he whispered. His face was ashy from loss of blood. The wound on his thigh wasn't bleeding now. He had little left to spare. My delay in reaching him had cost him dearly.

"My wife, son. In Hibbardville."

I began to sob. There was nothing I could do. Except one thing. I moved to his head and lifted it into my lap, stroking his face.

"I'm sorry." I couldn't see his face anymore. "I'm so sorry."

He let out a ragged breath. "S'all right, lass," he said. "God reward you. My wife, my son. You'll tell them."

His head turned to one side, like a child nestling closer to his mother, and then lay still.

"I'll tell them," I said, closing his eyes. "I'll tell them you said good-bye."

Chapter 11

Aidan carried Mr. Thorndike to the shade of a tall maple, its leaves scarlet like the infamy that was wrought upon the poor man. He lay the body down, then moved about restlessly, his face contorted. Finally he picked up a rock the size of a small melon and, with an animal yell, heaved it far down the road where it landed in the dust. At any other time, I would have been impressed.

"Feeling better?"

He sank into the grass and wouldn't look at me.

I removed Mr. Thorndike's jacket and covered his face with it, then sat down and tried to think. Now what?

Priscilla and her aunt sat some ways off, wrung out from shock and fear. Miss Jessop's skin looked pale. Priscilla tended to her the best she could.

"What were you thinking, sailing out of the carriage and ticking off the ruffian, Evie?" Aidan said, with surprising anger in his voice. "You might have been killed!"

I bristled. "Oh? And what about you? Kicking the door in his face? It's a wonder he didn't shoot you for spite."

"What would you have me do, sit and wait for him to murder us all?" Aidan snapped.

I couldn't believe this. "Tit for tat. What gives you license for bravery, and me none?"

"I told your grandfather I would protect you." I'd never seen Aidan's face so red.

"I appreciate that," I said, "but how did you plan to do so, lying dead in the highway?"

He sat up quickly. "I'm not dead, am I?"

"No, and there's at least some small thanks to me that you're not."

"Oh, stop," Priscilla cried. "What's gotten into you two? Aren't things bad enough without making them worse?"

Aidan twisted the seed kernels off a long stalk of grass and said nothing.

"My aunt is unwell," Priscilla said. "She'll need to rest, if we ever reach town. Did anyone manage to keep any money?"

Aidan showed his empty pockets. I shook my head.

"Aunt had a little, tucked away"—she swallowed—"somewhere. What about the driver?"

"You want us to rob a dead man, Prissy?"

She rolled her eyes. "Oh come on, Evie, it isn't robbing.

We can pay his widow back, I daresay. But if he's got any money at all, we need it now far worse than he does."

I did find a few coins in Mr. Thorndike's pocket. I handed them to Prissy. We waited for other vehicles to pass by, but at least an hour passed with no sign of a traveler. Then we heard the clop of hooves from the wrong direction. We shaded the sun from our eyes and peered west. Along came a high-backed wagon, painted all in green and blue, pulled by a single exhausted horse. As it came nearer I could make out large gold letters proclaiming "COMMEDIA DELL'ARTE, TRAGEDIC AND WHIMISCAL THEATRICALS UPON COMMAND. WILL PLAY FOR DINNER."

"Do you think they might take us to Fallardston?" Priscilla whispered.

"It's not the way they're going," Aidan said.

"Let me go speak with them," I said. "Perhaps I can persuade them to help."

I ventured out into the road and waved at the wagon. *Gypsy luck, don't fail me now.*

The driver sat up taller in his seat and pulled on the reins.

"*Mamma mia!*" He stopped the wagon, jumped down, swept off his hat, and bowed.

"Is it so?" he said in a thick accent. "Or do my eyes fail me in the sunlight?" He gazed eagerly into my face. "Is it that you are a maiden in distress?"

"Well, you might say—"

"But no!" he cried, seizing my hand. "To call you a maiden is to call the ocean a puddle!"

"Sir," I said firmly, "I *am* a maiden."

I took a step back and surveyed him. He was tall, with glossy black curls and dark blue eyes. He wore an impossible suit of dark red trousers and a fitted coat, with black trim and gold buttons. His clothes, in fact, seemed quite at odds with the shabby wagon and horse.

I scarcely knew what to think. "Who are you?" I said.

"Those that know me call me Rudolpho," he said, still holding my hand. "Those that know me better call me *Amoroso*."

"Do they." I backed away yet again until we were almost playing tug-o-war with my hand. "That's interesting. As you mentioned, I am in some distress, and—"

"Why do you stop the wagon, Rudy?" came a groggy voice from within.

"Go back to sleep! I speak with an ugly old woman!" Rudolpho cried. "My brother," he whispered to me. "I keep him around for pity's sake. He's half idiot, maybe more than half. But a scandal around young ladies. My little fib, it was to protect you."

A head poked out of the wagon that was identical to Rudolpho's, though rumpled with sleep.

"More than half idiot, am I?" the head said. "Says you, three-quarters ignoramus and two-thirds dunce?"

"Their arithmetic needs work," Priscilla observed from behind me.

Rudolpho's brother stumbled out of the carriage. He wore a suit just like his brother's, except his was black with red trim. He wrenched my hand free from Rudolpho's and stroked it.

"*Signorina bella*," he said, "pardon me for having such a brother as this irksome louse. Alas, I, Alfonso, cannot help it. My lot in life is to follow him around, rescuing him from his own stupidity, for such was our poor dying mother's last wish. But in your face, ah! What an angel! Heaven has rewarded my pains."

"I found her first!" Rudolpho displayed his fists. "Go back to sleep, you great sluggard!"

"Will you both stop at once!" I cried. "If either of you had any sense at all, you'd see that my friends and I are in great need of help."

Then they saw Priscilla, Miss Jessop, Aidan, and Mr. Thorndike. They grimaced.

"The big one, him we cannot carry," Rudolpho said, crossing his arms across his chest. "Our poor horse, she is half-dead already."

"The fat one, she is too sour," Alfonso said. "She will spoil the upholstery."

"The dead one," Rudolpho crossed himself, "may as well stay where he is."

"And the other one," Alfonso said, indicating Priscilla,

"she is . . ." Here Rudolpho elbowed him. "Is she your sister, signorina?"

I was so angry at these two arrogant popinjays I didn't answer.

"Only a friend?" Alfonso said. "Friends come and go, but you, *bella donna*, will go no more, but only come with me in my wagon."

Aidan appeared beside me.

"Is everything all right?" His voice was low and even, but the brothers shrank back a bit.

"I was just explaining to these two gentlemen," I said, "about our unfortunate treatment at the hands of the bandit"—their eyebrows rose—"and about the tragic death of the driver, and how we greatly need a ride to Fallardston, to find lodging for our friends and see to the driver's body."

"Ah, then," Rudolpho said, "our only wish is to be of assistance. However . . ."

"What my brother is meaning to say," Alfonso interrupted, "is that we most regrettably are obliged elsewhere. If it were not for our art, the demands she places upon us, leaping to your aid would be our first and only desire . . ."

"Especially seeing as it is you, signorina," Rudolpho cut in. "But as it happens we are scheduled to perform tonight in the opposite direction from this Fallardston." He wrinkled his nose, as if Fallardston smelled poorly.

"Really? Perform where?" I asked.

"Mundy," Rudolpho said.

"Mandolay," Alfonso said.

"Do you mean Maundley?" I asked.

"The very same!" said Alfonso.

"A thriving city," Alfonso went on, "where anxious crowds await us."

"For the carnival," his brother said, "of Saint Bridget."

"The festival," the first corrected him, "of Saint Bonaventure."

"Do you mean the Feast of Saint Bronwyn?"

"Extraordinary, your grasp, signorina," Alfonso said. "Without you, we would be lost."

"And no wonder," I cut in, "for you've missed Saint Bronwyn's Feast by a week."

Alfonso and Rudolpho glared at each other. Matthew Dunwoody *had* mentioned actors . . .

"I told you the butcher man said it was last Tuesday!"

"No, you didn't. You said it was today."

"No, I said . . ."

"Since the Feast of Saint Bronwyn's has passed," I said, raising my voice, "surely you won't wish to continue your travels to such a remote area as Maundley, a village of no more than a hundred people. You'll wish to return to where the audiences are larger, yes?"

"A hundred people?" Rudolpho burst out. "That butcher, he said . . ."

"Never mind the butcher," I said. "I've saved you two days of travel. Return the favor?"

Rudolpho took my hand once more. "Favors for you, *mi bella, certamente.*" The scoundrel actually kissed my arm! Not to be outdone, Alfonso began kissing my other one.

"*Mi bella,*" Rudolpho said, "have you considered the noble art of the stage? Join us, become an actress, dance and sing for queens and kings! With a face like yours, La Commedia dell'Arte would prosper! The eyes that flash like fire, the hair like spun gold, the lips . . ."

Aidan began to cough, and if ever a cough sounded like a threat of violence, this one did.

"I accept your kind offer to drive the two ladies back to Fallardston," I said, "while my friend Aidan and I walk alongside the wagon."

"But it is unthinkable that you should walk!" Alfonso declared. "You shall ride with me here."

"Ah, but think." I yanked my arms free. "If your horse had a second wind, the young man would fall behind." Second wind, pah. I was certain that's what they'd try.

"You shall not ride with my half-wit brother," Rudolpho said. "You'll ride with me."

"I'll walk," I said. "And when we reach Fallardston, I will repay your kindness."

I confess that here I winked at the two brothers, and without a further word they leaped to assist Priscilla, her aunt, and Mr. Thorndike into the wagon.

Chapter 12

As it happened, Miss Jessop *did* spoil their upholstery. The day's shock upset her so greatly that she deposited her breakfast upon Prissy's lap. Poor Prissy spent a miserable afternoon roasting in the wagon with a pallid corpse, her suffering aunt, and that noxious smell.

I trudged along, thinking of Mr. Thorndike. Oh that I were a man, or better, a dozen men, who could bring that murdering fiend to justice! Why couldn't I have helped the poor man?

More than ever, I wanted to be a physician. But would I reach the university? And if I couldn't enroll this autumn, would I get another chance? The king would soon forget me. Miss Jessop and Priscilla surely wouldn't continue on now. I couldn't travel alone.

There was one other choice.

"Aidan." I watched closely to see if he was still vexed with me.

"Hmm?" His eyes were only tired now.

"Priscilla and her aunt will no doubt stay in Fallardston until they have recovered and received assistance from home," I said. "Supposing I stay with them, what will you do?"

He shrugged. "Go on to Chalcedon," he said. "My master will be wondering after me."

"How will you get there?"

"Walk," he said. "It's not so bad. About three days. Farmers and villagers will often give me a meal and a bunk in return for fixing up fences or porches. A mason's always needed."

I took a deep breath, gathering all my courage. "Aidan," I said, and he turned to look at me. "Will you take me with you?"

He stopped walking. So did I.

"D'you mean, just the two of us, walking?"

I nodded. "I don't see any other way."

He took off his cap and shook dust off the brim, but his eyes never left me. "Well . . . how's that going to look?"

My words poured out. "Aidan, if I don't get to University on time, I'll never get to—"

"What will we say, when people ask us to give account of ourselves as we travel?"

I found myself staring at his boots. "We could . . . we could say that we're . . . married?"

Aidan's eyes opened wide. By now the actors' wagon had left us far behind, and we both ran to catch up before Alfonso or Rudolpho noticed.

"I could say I was your sister," I stammered, "but isn't that, somehow, less safe? For me? If people thought I was your wife, they would be more inclined to leave me alone."

"Men don't seem to leave you alone, do they." It wasn't a question.

I felt my cheeks grow warm. "Honestly, I don't know what's happened all of a sudden. It's never been like that before."

Aidan was watching me with an amused look, and I realized in an instant what a vain, coquettish thing that was to say.

"I don't mean . . ." Oh, be *quiet*, Evie! But I had to go on. "What I mean is that, never in the past . . ." *Oh, help.* "It's probably got something to do with the gypsies."

"The gypsies?"

I forced out a laugh. "Their magic trinkets. I bought a few ornaments at the feast day"—I gestured to my charms —"one of them, she said, was a love charm. Ever since then . . ."

My voice trailed off. Immediately I bit my lip.

"So, you bought a *love* charm from the gypsies, did you?"

"No!"

"No?"

"I mean, yes. But not because it was a love charm. I thought it was pretty!"

Aidan did not look convinced. "May I see?"

I showed him the charm. In the waning light, it was only a dull gray rock and a string.

Aidan gave me an odd look. "I'm no judge, but I've seen prettier trinkets, I think."

"Oh, never mind my trinkets!" I poked it back under the collar of my dress. "The point is, will you take me with you, or no?"

He watched me closely. Never before did Aidan Moreau have the power to make me feel so self-conscious. "And tell folks you're my wife?"

Why must he press this point? "And tell them I'm your *very young* wife."

He sighed and shook his head. "With my luck, if I parade you around as my wife I'll meet a beautiful girl somewhere, one that I would have liked to court. But she'll never have me, no matter how many times I go back and explain, because she'll be convinced I'm a bigamist."

I averted my face to hide my bafflement. Was he teasing me?

"I'll take you, Wife," he said, "as far as Chalcedon, but then I'm seeking an annulment."

Chapter 13

Twilight fell, and my mouth tasted bitter with thirst, when at last we staggered into Fallardston. I could hear the nearby rush of river water racing over stones in the shallows, and the sound only drove my thirst to madness.

As the lights of town began to twinkle in the distance, another sound reached my ears. It was the raucous cry of some sort of bird. My whole body seemed to respond to its call.

"What's that sound, Aidan?" I asked.

He looked up, puzzled, then realized what I meant. "Those? Those are gulls. They live near the seashore and catch fish. Look. There's one."

A flash of white flickered overhead, soaring in a neat arc above our heads, then disappeared again into the gloaming night.

Breezes blew in from the west, sweeping across the sea

toward us, bringing a cold, fishy, salty dampness. I imagined the vast ocean, surging and receding, and was seized with desire to see the blue water and thrust my feet into the wet sand.

The first public house we found was called The Badger, which had a cheerful aspect with its bright red door and orange lamplight in the windows. Aidan went off in search of an undertaker and the coaching line dispatcher. I collected our coins and went into the inn.

The proprietress was a tall, lanky woman of middle age, with a protruding chin and sharp eyes. She took in my bedraggled appearance and pursed her lips critically. My heart sank. But she listened attentively and kneaded a great bowl of bread dough while I told our story. I feared my tongue would trip as I called Aidan my husband.

"Not married long, are you?" the woman said, nodding curtly.

"Only just." I didn't dare look her in the eye. I showed her the money we managed to save, and she nodded again, with a vicious thump at her dough. I wouldn't want to be *her* enemy.

"Young woman," she said, "My name's Prunilla Bell, and I don't do favors. You've got to pay to eat and sleep at The Badger. But there's nothing I hate worse than lawless brigands, murdering and terrorizing the countryside. And I notice the coach didn't pass through today. You look like an honest young woman," she went on. I felt a twinge at that. "I pride myself on my judgment. I'll tell you what. You and your man are bound for Chalcedon?"

I nodded.

"The last ferry's gone," she said, "and you'll not find another coach for two more days. You got anyone that can give you money once you get to Chalcedon?"

Did we? Well, there was the king. If that failed, Aidan had his master. I nodded my head.

"There's a ship," she said, "sailing tonight with the tide, bound for Chalcedon. Should arrive by tomorrow midday if the wind stays favorable. My nephew, Freddie, is second mate."

A ship? And travel by night? Was it safe? I supposed one could drown as well by noon as in moonlight. I remembered Grandfather's strange insistence that I not travel by sea.

"So you take half of this money and put it down for boat passage. Ship's called *The White Dragon*. Not a week ago it brought a princess over, can you imagine? Freddy'll trust you for the rest. He does what I tell him."

I didn't doubt it. She divvied up the coins on the serving counter into two piles.

"The rest of the money, I'll take as a deposit for your friends. They'll share a small room and send letters home. If the mail coach gets through this time, they should hear back from their folks back home within two or three days. I can be patient until then."

Whack, whack went the heels of her hands into the gritty brown dough. Heaven help Prissy and Miss Jessop if this woman's patience should run out! But there was no question of the Hornbys not sending help, provided word reached them.

I stood there debating. I'd never wish to betray Grandfather's trust. But this was so much better, quicker, and safer than walking for three days and posing as married. Wasn't it?

I was on my own now, with only my judgment to rely on. It was time for me to make my own choices and see them through.

"Your new husband treat you good?"

I was so startled by this I dropped a coin on the floor. "Who, him?" I stalled for a reply. "He treats me good enough." Aidan, the kindly husband. Treating me "good." What a farce!

Mrs. Bell nodded, and winked at me. "You got one that treats you good, you hold on tight to him. That's my advice, and I don't charge any for it."

I turned away before this expert judge of honest character could see me laugh.

We eased Miss Jessop into the bed The Badger's proprietress showed us, fetched her soup and wine, and in no time she dropped off into an uneasy, moaning kind of sleep. I brought in a basin of hot bathwater and a nightgown loaned by Mrs. Bell for Prissy, and she crawled into bed next to her aunt, shuddering with exhaustion.

"I want to go home, Evie," she said. "I've done my bit of traveling."

"You don't need to decide anything tonight," I said. "Remember how you've wanted to go on to University. Don't abandon hope. There might yet be a way."

"But I haven't wanted to go, Evie," she said. "Not nearly so much as you."

Surely that wasn't so. All those years of study!

"Before Saint Bronwyn's Day, I asked Sister Claire if she could use me as an assistant teacher," Prissy said. "If she still wants me, that's what I'll do. I always enjoy the little ones."

And I'd thought Priscilla couldn't surprise me.

She was fading fast. "Don't be alarmed," I said. "Come morning, I'll be gone."

Both her eyes flew open wide. "*What?*"

"I'm . . . I'm going to go on. With Aidan. He's going to take me to Chalcedon. Tonight."

She lifted her head off the pillow. "Just the two of you?"

"It's the only way," I said. "He'll keep me safe. I know he will."

"But Evie . . ."

"Prissy, please don't tell your parents what we're doing!"

She sank back down into her pillow. "Don't do anything rash, Evie," she said. "No more than what you're already about, I mean."

I smoothed her hair out of her face. "Dear Prissy, I will

miss you so," I said. "We have a good, solid plan. We'll tell people we're newly married, so they'll leave us both alone."

A tired laugh rose from the bed. "Send a letter and tell us when it actually comes true."

I rocked back on my heels. "Bite your tongue, Priscilla Hornby!"

Chapter 14

Alfonso and Rudolpho waited for me downstairs, like mirror images of each other, black and red, red and black. Too bad, really, that they were such a pair of puppets, for they *were* handsome.

"Well, fair maiden?" Rudolpho said. "We wait."

I halted. "For what?"

"For the token," Alfonso said, with a flourish of his hand, "of your undying gratitude!"

"The what?"

"You said you would repay our kindness," Rudolpho said.

Ah.

"Travel with us," Alfonso said, "and enchant the world with your beauty! On stage, you will be enamored with me, *so*, and when I take you in my arms, *so*,"—he put his arm around my waist and pushed me over to fall backward in his arms—"you will swoon with passionate desire!"

Rudolpho knocked Alfonso aside, nearly sending me to the floor. "But it is for *me* that your flames of love will burn," he said. "And when I give you a lover's true kiss, all the crowd will witness that it is I, Rudolpho, who holds the key to your heart."

"Leave off, swine," Alfonso cried, waving his fists at his brother. "The lady favors me!"

I took advantage of this distraction to address the wide-eyed Mrs. Bell.

"Mrs. Bell," I said to that worthy woman, "these two gentlemen are actors, planning to set up their show here in Fallardston. Would it attract patrons if they performed here?"

Mrs. Bell scrutinized the two brothers. "It could," she conceded. "I don't pay, though."

"But you could offer a room, couldn't you? And supper on the nights they perform?"

She wiped a mug with her rag. "Settled," Mrs. Bell said. She spat on another mug and wiped it. "I want a show tomorrow night."

"There," I said, with a curtsy to La Commedia dell'Arte. "I've repaid your kindness."

I took this as a chance to make my escape, but Rudolpho blocked the exit of the taproom. "*Bella signorina*," he breathed, "it was something different I had in mind, this repayment of kindness that you so temptingly held out like the carrot before the donkey."

I took a step back. "Does that make you the donkey?"

"How about a leetle kiss? U*n bacio piccolo*?"

I looked up, a smart retort on my tongue, and paused. All my words left me. He was leaning closer, closer, his lips parting . . .

"Young woman," Mrs. Bell's welcome voice reached my ears. "Your husband awaits."

Rudolpho tossed his curly head back. "Husband? Who is this husband? The fair maiden has no husband! She is a *maiden* in distress, yes?"

I flew through the door. "Thank you both!" I cried. "Good-bye!"

I ran out into the stableyard and found Aidan speaking to a dour-faced man with a black wagon. The draped form of Mr. Thorndike lay stretched in the wagon's bed.

"Good, you've taken care of him," I cried, seizing his arm. "Come on, let's go. Now!"

"Where are we going?" Aidan said. I tugged him toward the road. "And why the hurry?"

"Halt! Young maiden!" Rudolpho called after me.

"Aidan, run," I ordered. "Rudolpho is making Mrs. Bell doubt you and I are married."

"The deception begins, eh?"

We took off running. The cobbles were brutal against my sore feet.

"I think they've given up," I panted, looking over my shoulder. "Mrs. Bell's got a nephew with a ship. We can take passage and pay the rest when we arrive in Chalcedon."

Aidan stopped. "A ship?"

I paused, remembering. Thoughtless me. Aidan's father, a sailor, had died at sea.

"Never mind, Aidan," I said. "I'm sorry. I wasn't thinking. We'll walk."

He watched me closely, then nodded comprehension. "I don't mind. I'm not afraid of ships, even though I don't often . . . A ship makes the most sense."

We came over a high point on the street. Before us spread the twinkling lights of Fallardston, with more clustered at the very edge. Then, there were no lights, except the frosted reflections of moon and stars on the peaks and valleys of ocean waves.

The sea. I stopped.

"Oh," I said. "Oh, look, Aidan. Isn't it beautiful?"

"It's big, anyway," Aidan said. "Let's get on the boat, and we can admire it from there."

We reached the docks, which smelled of fish, and were lit only by lanterns and the spilled light from the windows of taverns lining the boardwalk. In no time we located *The White Dragon*. An elaborately carved dragon made up the prow, and a dragon was outlined on the largest of its many sails. Aidan explained that this was a galleon, a grand vessel indeed.

I approached a sailor who seemed to have some authority and asked him, "Do you know a second mate by the name of Freddie? Possibly Freddie Bell?"

The sailor cringed. "It's Fred," he said. "Just Fred."

"You mean you're Freddie?" I cried. My charms must be at work again.

Freddie Bell, a beanpole with a huge Adam's apple, goggled at us. "Well? What is it?"

"Your aunt, Prunilla," I said. "She said that with this"—here I showed him our coins—"you would give us passage to Chalcedon, and there wait for us to pay the rest."

He thrust out his lower lip. "She said that, did she? I run a ship, not a charity ward." Luckily, though, he scooped up my coins. "Be ready for the whistle." He moved along.

Aidan reached for my arm. "Let's get off this dock before we fall off."

Steps led down to where foamy water met the rocks. We explored until we found dry sand, then sat, groaning at our stiff limbs. Exhaustion overwhelmed me.

I unlaced my shoes, then, ordering Aidan to look away, I reached under my skirts to unfasten and remove my stockings. I pressed my aching toes into the spongy sand, then, hoisting my skirts, ran into the water.

"Oh!" The cold water shocked me.

Aidan uncovered his eyes. "Evie! What are you doing?"

"Come on in!" I called, trying not to smile. "The water's lovely!"

Aidan looked slowly around, to make sure no one was watching, then he, too, pulled off his shoes and stockings, rolled up his trousers, and jumped into the surf.

He yelped at the cold, and I nearly fell into the water laughing.

"Thanks," he said, kicking a splash of water at me. I splashed him back, but since neither of us really wanted to be soaked, we stopped, and instead amused ourselves by stomping around in the shallows. Wet sand sluicing through my toes and sandy water stroking my feet as the waves lapped back and forth were delicious, intoxicating, marvelous.

"I might never leave this place," I told Aidan. "The king can keep his university. I'll just stay here and play in the sand."

"There's better beaches than this near Chalcedon," Aidan said. "In high summer, it's warm enough to go in swimming. For those that know how."

"Do you?"

"No. I wish I did." I thought of his father once more.

A flash of something pale in the water caught my eye. I grabbed Aidan's arm and pointed. "Did you see something? Out in the water?"

Aidan shook his head. "Did you?"

"Something large and light colored," I said. "So close!"

Just then, the ship's whistle blasted. Aidan and I ran splashing to the shore. We slapped sand off our feet and pulled our stockings on. What felt smooth and luxurious on the beach now felt maddeningly itchy as we wrestled into our shoes.

Farther along the docks we could see the hurly-burly of passengers and cargo boarding the ship. Then my view was blocked by three figures, silhouetted black against *The White Dragon*'s lanterns, who came down another spur of the dock and stood near us, but high above on the board-walk. Two men, and a smaller figure with a girl's size but a woman's poise.

Aidan and I waited, knowing how we'd look coming up from the dark beach alone. One of the men had a creature on its shoulder. A monkey! I'd only seen pictures before. He slid off the man's shoulder and loped along the board-walk to sniff and chatter at us.

"*Chick-eeet! Chick-chick-chick-chick-eeet!*"

The sound jarred me, as did the strange, hairy face. So like a human infant, and yet so different! I held myself very still until the monkey scampered back to his master.

". . . well, so far," the other man was saying. "He's got the costumes, and he swears he's got the payment. He'll meet us there in two days."

"Payment *ought* to be easy," the man with the monkey grumbled.

"It's complicated," the first man said. He handed him a clinking parcel. "Here's a start."

"And do we know we'll be invited onto the ship?" Definitely a woman, from her voice.

"She'll see to that," the first said. "Hurry. Your ship is leaving."

The man with the monkey and the small, trim woman hurried down the dock. The other man watched them, then headed back up the pier toward the shore, the way he'd come.

I caught his profile clearly, and sucked in my breath.

He paused and looked around. I crouched and waited. Finally he turned and went on.

"What's the matter, Evie?" Aidan whispered in my ear.

"The man giving orders," I whispered back. "From the coach. He was the scarred man."

Chapter 15

❧❧

Freddie Bell hollered a last call for any taking passage on *The White Dragon*. Aidan all but carried me up the steps. We skidded down the slip and up the gangplank.

"Oh, it's you," Freddie said without joy. "Listen. For those as don't pay full, there's the poop deck. Fine night like tonight, there's music and revelry. You can make do."

I didn't know a poop deck from a spanker sail, but we followed the direction he pointed, working around swarms of sailors and bales of rope thicker than my leg. There was indeed music. A thin old man perched on a barrel, sawing out a jig on a battered fiddle. Couples had already begun swinging each other around. Swaying lantern light made the whole scene merry. We leaned against the railing to watch.

I'd heard sailors grew starved for female company out on the ocean. Three different ones whistled at me. What passed for manners in country towns didn't seem to apply here.

The ship, when it had left the harbor and spread its full sails to catch the winds, began to roll underfoot. The strange sensation delighted me, and I spread my feet wide to find my balance. Aidan, alas, closed his eyes and clutched at the railing, his great knuckles turning white.

"What's the matter, Aidan?"

He didn't open his eyes. "Nothing," he said. "Some son of a sailor I am."

"Do you need something to drink?"

"Just tell me when we get there."

"If I may be so bold?"

I turned to see a cheerful red-haired young man bowing and beckoning me to dance with him. I hesitated, then held out my elbow and let him lead me to join the dancers.

"Is that your brother with you?" The young man nodded toward Aidan.

Oh, dear. If I said Aidan was my husband, how would it look, dancing with strangers? On the other hand, if he wasn't my husband, I could receive more unwelcome attentions.

"Thank you for the dance." I released his arm. "It warmed me considerably." I went to Aidan and leaned closer into him than I intended. The young man shrugged and moved on.

That was a relief. I ought to have stepped away from

Aidan's side, but the night winds whipping around the sails were bitter cold.

Aidan's eyelid opened a crack. "You slay men by the dozens wherever you go, Evie."

"That's Mrs. Moreau to you, laddie," I said. "And stop talking rot. I do no such thing."

"If you're Mrs. Moreau, then no more dancing with strangers." His smile gave him away.

"Feeling better, I take it?"

"Getting used to it. I'd still rather be on dry land."

"I'm not sure I would. Look."

Water churned in the wake of the ship's stern. It spread two blades of white-capped spray from either corner of the ship. The black water stretched forever, except where the dark shore blotted out the stars to our left. Hanging low over the horizon, painting a shimmering silver ribbon all the way to The White Dragon, was the moon.

Was there ever such a perfect sight in all creation as this?

Did the moon make the sea this lustrous every night, and here I'd only just discovered it?

Peace settled over me, a kind of peace I couldn't explain.

"It's extraordinary, Aidan," I said. "Here, in this moment, I feel I've come home."

"Do you?"

Aidan's face was tilted toward mine, his brown eyes watching me closely. Well, of course his face was tilted down. The lad was a head taller than me, at least. And yet . . .

I forgot about the moon.

The air he breathed, how it filled his chest, and emptied out again, warm, the soft sounds it made rushing past his mouth . . .

Fascinating thing, breath. I could use Aidan as a scientific study.

I felt warm, despite the wind. Or was I still standing too close?

Aidan didn't seem to mind.

"Evie?"

"Hmm?"

"*Chick-chick-chick-eeet!*"

From out of nowhere a furry form leaped onto Aidan's head, snatching his hat and flinging it out into the sea. I shook myself, as if I'd woken from a dream. We reached for the little pest, but it leaped away faster than we could snatch, peeling back its lips and baring ghastly teeth.

Laughter broke out among the other passengers on the poop deck. The music had stopped, and the monkey's owner stepped forward.

"Your creature doesn't like me much," Aidan told the man.

"Meet Deuce," the man said. The monkey did a flip. "He's a wicked imp, but he'll amaze you with his tricks." He laid his hat on the deck. "Deuce needs to pay for his crimes."

People clapped as the monkey did more flips, walked on its hands while carrying a cup of wine with its feet, and guessed which hand held a button. Pennies fell into the hat, but I was more curious about the man than his pet. What was he discussing with the scarred man from the coach? *Hold back, Evie,* I warned myself. *It's no crime to have scars or monkeys.* But something felt wrong. This man, genial though he was, felt false to me. The woman kept her distance.

"You folks want to see some animals?" a tall sailor said. "Oy! Bob! Bobby Natch!"

A reply came from somewhere in the tall riggings.

"Bring your crew," the sailor yelled. "We've got some here 'at wants to see it."

The sailor called Bobby Natch, a much-wizened older man with very few teeth, appeared with a parrot on one shoulder, a three-legged cat at his feet, and a wicker basket. The parrot favored us with language I dare not repeat, and the cat hissed at the monkey, then climbed to the top of a long pole where he sat yowling at us. Many men found this amusing.

Then Bobby Natch opened his basket. "Stand back, stand back, ladies and gents."

At first nothing happened. Then a shape appeared, small, triangular. It tilted, swayed, then slipped over the edge of the basket, drawing a thick, winding, swelling body behind it.

"Snake!"

Women shrieked. My dance partner made no bones of scurrying off the poop deck. All the while the snake kept pouring itself out of the basket, and Bobby Natch cackled with delight.

"That's a sand viper," he said. "Three feet long. Annoy her, and it's the last thing you'll do."

"Why would you keep such a creature?" a woman cried.

For the fun of scaring us, I imagined. "Rats," said Bobby. "This lady kills three times the rats as old Puss. Rats bring disease. So my mates and me call her 'the Doctor.'"

Aidan nudged me. "Stand behind me, Evie," he whispered. "My boots are thick."

"I'm all right," I said, fingering my snakebite charm, and wondering if I believed in it. "Snakes don't bother me."

"Now, now, folks," Bobby said, "you don't have nothing to fear from the Doctor. Leave her alone, she'll leave you alone. Ain't she purty?"

She *was* beautiful. Her amber eyes reflected lantern light like two yellow moons. A symmetrical zigzag of dark scales traced down her muscular back. She coiled herself in a neat pile and surveyed everyone's ankles.

A chill wind blew across the ship, whipping the sails. Bobby Natch and the other sailor studied the sky. The stars in the west had been blotted out by clouds.

"Chick-chick-eeet!"

The monkey, perched on his master's shoulder, chattered

at the sand viper. She raised her head to search for the sound. Bobby Natch, wearing a leather glove, stooped to retrieve his snake, but the monkey leaped down and hissed at her. She swerved her neck back and forth menacingly.

"Get that thing away if you want to keep it," ordered Bobby, and the monkey trainer reached for the little pest.

He saved his monkey, though *he* was a moment too late. The sand viper, striking like a spring-loaded arrow, hurtled across the deck and sank its teeth into the monkey tamer's wrist.

Chapter 16

≈⌢⌣≈

Bobby Natch gripped the viper's head at the jaws, pulled it off the man's arm, and stuffed her back into her basket. He gave the man a mournful shake of his head, then scuttled off the poop deck and disappeared into the bowels of the ship.

The two bites leered like narrow red eyes from the monkey tamer's wrist. The wind whipped the sails, sending spray into our worried faces.

I came forward and took his hand. "Get me strips of cloth," I said to a sailor. "And a blanket for this man to lie down on."

"'Oo's she think she is?" one sailor asked another.

"Get her what she asks for," Aidan said, as I coaxed the man to sit. "She knows things."

If only I did! From what I'd read in my father's books, I knew the procedure would be to slit the bite wound across with a sharp blade, then suck as much blood out as you could.

I might have only moments to spare before the venom took hold, but I couldn't bring myself to cut the man further, nor to suck his blood into my mouth.

It *wouldn't work anyway*, I thought. *How could it?* But who was I to argue with Father's books? Then again, even the books admitted that the method rarely worked.

Luck charm, snakebite charm, both of you, help me now.

The sailor arrived with a blanket and cloths. The deck pitched underneath my knees.

"Sir," I said, "please lie flat on your back." This was what came to my mind, and I seized upon it, grateful for any idea at all. Was half of medicine seeming confident that you knew what to do? If the patients believed you could help, could that save their lives? Pray heaven it was so!

The monkey man was too frightened to protest. His chest rose and fell rapidly, but not, I thought, with actual difficulty breathing. Just with fright.

I placed my hands on his ribs. "Sir," I said, "listen to me. You must remain calm."

Still he panted like a horse just off a run.

"Slow your breathing. Lie very still. It could make all the difference."

His face, now pale, trembled. I pushed back his sleeves, held his wounded arm high, and began cinching his arm just below the elbow with the strips. Not too tightly, but enough to discourage fluids from moving more through the flesh.

There we remained with his hand held high. The worst part was waiting. What would happen to his hand? His eyes? His heart, his breath? I tested him every few minutes to see if he could hear, see, or feel through both sides of his body, and if the injured hand still had sensation.

We waited. The moon was only a dim glow now behind the thick clouds, while the angry wind pushed us closer and closer to Chalcedon.

Oh, let me not see two victims die today. One was far more than enough.

I reached and took off my snakebite charm, draped it over the monkey trainer's head, and settled the strange charm under his collar. The man's watchful eyes never left my face. Minutes crawled, but every minute in which nothing changed gave me new hope.

"You're a healer, you are," a blond sailor said, crouching beside me and watching me with wonder. "I've heard of women like you. From the islands."

Wind was now whistling through the sails. Massing clouds had swallowed all the stars, and the cold was becoming intense.

"Can someone bring this man another blanket?" I said. Then, to the sailor, "I'm not from any island. This is the first I've laid eyes on the ocean. But I hope you're right about the healing."

"Those island women," a shorter sailor said, "they're not healers. And she don't look anything like them. They're *snake charmers*." He produced a wool blanket, which he dropped onto my patient's chest.

"Snake charmers?" I said. "They're from desert countries. Little men with flutes."

"There's them, too," the man conceded, "with the cobras. I seen 'em in Zanzibar. But the island women, they've got snakes following 'em anywheres. Serpents for pets. Pity the poor fool that comes up against one of them."

"Why?"

It was the first thing the monkey trainer had said since his bite, and I was glad of it. If something other than his own plight interested him, he must be calming down. Perhaps he would be all right.

"Put a spell on you, they do," the sailor said, gesturing widely, his eyes dramatic. "Man can't hardly resist the snake women, with their long, black hair. Go chasing the world over if one of 'em asks you to. Yer a slave for life to her wicked charms."

"I hear they're beautiful," the blond sailor said. "Like mermaids." He held his wrists in front of his chest, as if waiting to be shackled. "I don't mind snakes. Sign me up for slavery!"

The short one cuffed him cheerfully. "Yer a fool. Always said so. They'll own yer soul!"

"Better one of them than the devil!"

I checked my patient's wrist again. The skin was soft, not taut with swelling, and the color seemed healthy.

"Can you feel it if I press here?" I touched different points along his hand, fingers, and arm, and his sensation was still strong. "Too soon to be certain, but it looks like you may not suffer any ill effects from this bite."

He nodded, his face expressionless.

"A thank you for the pretty lady wouldn't be amiss." The blond sailor kicked his boot.

"Thank you." A more dispassionate thanks I couldn't imagine.

There was a loud *crack* as the sail nearest us flapped, looking likely to burst its knots. The wind no longer nudged us north, but blasted straight from the west. I pitched to one side as The White Dragon listed sharply toward shore. Spray hit my face and doused some of the lanterns. Bells began ringing, and the captain and Freddie began shouting orders to the crew. The sailors near me didn't wait to be called twice, but sprang into action, taking straight to the riggings.

Aidan crouched beside me and hoisted me up by one arm. "Evie, come this way."

My patient rose and ran off. I staggered after Aidan.

The wind lashed furiously. People fell and objects slid as the ship lolled back and forth in the waves. Rain began pelting the deck, making it impossible to see.

Aidan led me to the rearmost mast of the tall galleon. He wrapped my arms around it tightly. Then, standing directly behind me, he enfolded me in his tight embrace of the stout mast.

"Whatever happens," he shouted over the gale, "don't let go!"

I could barely breathe, trapped between the pine mast and Aidan's ribs. He rested his chin on my head. It almost seemed he wanted to enfold and crush me, like a constrictor snake.

Snake. I wondered how the sand viper felt. Poor, frightened creature.

"Wind's blowing us toward the shore," Aidan shouted. "We'll be dashed against the rocks. But if we're lucky, there's a chance we might make it to the shallow water."

Lucky. No gypsy charm could bend nature that far.

The ship rocked drunkenly, wave after wave soaking us. Neither one of us could swim.

We were going to die.

My ears were full of the groaning ship, the screaming passengers, the shouting sailors, the roaring winds. Yet a strange quiet fell over me. The university, and everything I'd ever planned, faded like a chimera, and the past, my blessed past, filled my view. Sister Claire. Priscilla. Widow Moreau. And one, dearest of all.

"Aidan," I cried, worming my head free enough to be seen and heard. "If you make it safe to shore"—I took a deep breath, for the words were bitter—"and I don't, please, tell Grandfather how much I love him."

Aidan let go of his grip around the mast and turned to face me, lifting my chin. His hair was plastered to his head, his face streaked with rain.

"Evie," he said, "if either of us makes it to shore, or if we don't . . ."

I never heard the end of his sentence.

He bent and kissed me.

Chapter 17

❧❧

If someone had asked me, I would not have believed anything could remove me from the terror of a ship in a storm at night—from screaming passengers and shouting sailors and the roar of angry waves against the ship's hull. I would have been wrong.

It was an awkward thing, our necks twisted, our faces scraping against the mast, the driving rain covering the dark world.

Aidan?

Me?

Aidan, all my life, right there, next door, and now, here, like this?

Of course. Of course, Aidan. And now is all we've got.

He stopped and rested his forehead against mine, his eyes closed, as if he didn't dare look. Then the ship pitched again, and he resumed his grip around me and the mast.

I squirmed around to face him fully, probably driving splinters in my cheeks as I did so, and kissed him back. I felt his sharp intake of breath. He let go of the mast and wrapped his arms around me.

So soft, so sweet, so surprising, as if all the stars in the night sky were bursting out from inside me. How could I have known?

Aidan. And *me*.

What are you *doing*, Evelyn Pomeroy? said a small, bookish schoolgirl voice in my head.

Dying, I told it. *Go away*.

Then inexperience made me nervous. How does one stop doing this? I wondered, and finally concluded, by stopping. I closed my eyes and tucked my head down, suddenly shy. Aidan laughed softly, which I felt more than heard, and he squeezed the mast until I thought I'd pop.

And still the storm raged on.

Then the mast shuddered horribly. Its mainsail ripped, and the wood of the mast screamed as it snapped like a dry twig only a few yards above our heads.

There was a horrible jolt. The whole ship crunched. Its pitching and rolling stopped.

"She's foundered on the rocks!" a voice yelled. "She's takin' on water!"

Whatever jag of rock had snared its hull seemed to want to hold on, despite the seaward waves that lashed its side, soaking us with salt water. No longer did nature's forces seem impersonal. It was a contest between sea and stone, and the sea grew furious at the rock's rebuff. Higher and higher the waves mounted, as each failed wave doubled back and rejoined the rest.

When the last wave came, somehow I sensed its approach. Or perhaps it was the silence that fell over the shouting crew as that last wall of water rose up.

The wave flung *The White Dragon* off its perch and toppled it into the sea like a cat batting a mouse through the air with its paw. I felt myself rise, still holding the mast, still clasped in Aidan's grip, as we all turned a tumbler's somersault in the air, then landed in the sea.

Chapter 18

~⁓~⁓

What happened next was all so fast, yet when told, words will stall the speed, the rush, the fear.

The cold was astonishing, and still more its daggers of sharp, relentless pain. There was no lessening of the cold, nor the fear that my heart would rupture from the shock of it.

My ears filled with a low, vast, steady thrum, chasing away the chaotic din of the wind and the creaking ship.

My mouth and nose filled with water.

Aidan still clung to me.

Salt water stung my eyes, yet I forced them open. There was nothing to see but blackness, but I had to try and see.

My lungs burned. Air! Would there ever again be air?

The stump of mast to which we clung stayed rooted underwater. If we didn't let go, we'd drown. Before I could do anything, though, the mast snapped off the ship and began moving through the water. I felt hope while Aidan still held on.

Then the backswell knocked the mast hard against the bulk of the ship. Aidan's grip around me relaxed, and before I could seize his arm, he was swept away from me in the water.

I bobbed to the surface, still clutching the mast, and gasped in a breath. Then I let go of the mast and plunged toward the direction I thought Aidan might have gone.

Too late I realized how foolish that was. The last fool mistake I would ever make.

But so be it. I would make the same choice again.

I flailed through the water, my mouth and lungs again filling. Thrash as I might, I couldn't bring my head above the surface. Whenever I thought I had, another wave broke over me, plunging me under.

There was no sign of Aidan. In that dark, there wouldn't be.

Still the cold crept through every tissue in my body, claiming my hands, my feet, until I could no longer feel their pain, until they almost felt warm. Let go, I thought. Stop fighting, and slide down into the warmth and quiet at the bottom of the sea.

Aidan is there. Let go.

Down, down the water pulled me, and the less I fought, the quieter all became.

Then another voice spoke in my mind.

I'm coming!

I turned in the dark water, as if I might find the thing, the voice, but all was black.

I'm coming, oh, I'm coming, coming as fast as I can. Oh, it's you, truly you. I'm coming! I've found you!

The voice, though not audible, grew stronger, more near, until something wreathed itself around me, something long and powerful, like a supple tree trunk, and rushed me to the surface, my body succumbing like a cloth doll.

I gulped in a mouthful of sweet rainy air and opened my eyes. I lay like a child in a hammock on the surface of the frothing water, supported by this moving, living cradle. I lifted my head to try to get a glimpse, and saw nothing except a darting glow in the water beneath me.

Coils of this living, glowing rope surrounded me and skimmed me over the water.

It was a serpent. A mighty serpent, half as long as the ship itself. And it had me captive.

I ought to faint, I ought to scream, I ought to panic. These were the words in my head. But something in me was beyond panic, beyond fear, in a quieter state. I wondered if it might possibly be death.

I wished I hadn't parted with my snakebite charm.

Did this creature wish to hurt me? It had seemed pleased to find me. Was that only because I was its favorite meal?

Must get you to shore before you chill, before you choke. It is you, I knew it, I smelled it. Oh, why, why, why have you made me wait so long? The others, they've been laughing at me!

It spoke to me in my mind. I could hear no words, and yet I could feel its words as well as if I did hear them. Better, for I could have heard little in that storm.

"You seem to know me," I said aloud. Now I was speaking to my own delusions! "What are you?"

Later, later. Must get you dry and warm.

I took some small courage at these words and dared to ask what now concerned me most.

"Do you also know the one I came with?" A new thought struck me. "Is . . . one of your kind helping him too?"

There was a slight tremor of distaste, as if Aidan were a dish I'd served to a guest too polite to say it was spoiled.

I know which one he is. I smelled him too.

And suddenly we were on the beach. My fingers closed around fistfuls of sopping sand. The creature backed away, and I flung myself over onto my hands and knees, my whole body shaking with cold and gratitude.

Up from the water rose the creature, glorious and strange. I gazed upward as it ascended, almost hovering over me. Though it had saved me, still, I shrank back in fear.

Its head was flat and angled at the edges like the cut emerald on a priest's ring. Its snout was long and blunt, with whiskers like a catfish, and nostrils that twitched like an anxious horse. Silver blue skin plated with large scales gleamed in the darkness, and jewel green eyes blinked at me.

A sea serpent.

"Please," I said in a voice I barely recognized, "please find my friend and help him."

Now we're together, you and I. There's nothing else we need.

Faster than thought, its answers appeared in my mind. An even more horrible thought struck me. "Did you cause this storm?"

The serpent watched me, blinking, as though this question was not something it knew how to answer.

"Can you stop the storm?"

It will die down soon. Now that we've found each other. If it were possible, the great mouth seemed to smile. *Don't be frightened. I will always protect you from storms.*

I digested these words. "So you *did* cause the storm? People are dying!"

The beast reared its great head back as if confused.

I do not create storms, it said. *But for you and I to be so long apart? It isn't natural. The ocean abhors it.*

This made no sense.

Sixteen years I've waited for you, Mistress. Its eyes blinked with sadness and reproach. *They have called me abandoned. But I always believed I would find you.*

It stretched its long neck down toward me and butted my shoulder, my chin, gently with its head. It caressed me, nuzzling against me with its horned face. Instinctively I recoiled and immediately felt its hurt. So I stopped. I reached a hand toward it.

And halted. This gigantic monster, this behemoth, could devour me in one gulp! And I was having a conversation with it? If I had any strength, I would run. And yet, something in those eyes constrained me, compelled me to stay.

"Please," I said again. "My friend is dying. Already he may be gone. Please, bring my friend to me."

It lowered its head, for all the world like he was bowing. *Mistress*, it said, though its mouth didn't seem to move, *they are only food. What do you want with them?*

"Food!" I cried, aghast. "What do you mean, they're only food?"

Those others. In the water. They're not like you.

"Those others in the water," I cried, crawling closer to dry land, "are every bit like me. You must help them all, if you have any love for me. First, bring me my friend. And if there are others like you that can help, call to them!"

The great serpent hesitated. *You will stay, won't you?*

"I won't leave this beach."

It turned its great head back toward the sea and leaped under the surface, the rest of its length rippling after, flashing before disappearing from view.

The next moments were some of the worst I ever spent. I was wet, with freezing winds buffeting me. I wanted badly to lie down, even if the waves did wash the sand away and take me with it. *Walk,* I told myself. *Walk and warm your body.* But needles of pain shot through every muscle. I was alive, but how many were dead? I fell forward into the sand, striking my knee on a rock, and lay there crying.

A movement caught my eye, and I looked to see a human form crawling up out of the waves. It wasn't Aidan. One of the lucky sailors, it seemed, who knew how to swim, though even an adept swimmer would likely have succumbed to the waves and rocks.

He reached a pebbly place and collapsed, facedown, heaving up water. I went toward him but stopped, seeing another form wash ashore. A more urgent case. It was a passenger. I rolled him onto his front. A spume of water issued from his mouth and he began to breathe.

It was still too dark to see much, but I stumbled about, treading upon ship debris and bodies. Miracle upon miracle, every body I encountered was alive. Barely. But alive.

Something small and dark washed ashore at my feet. I picked it up.

Aidan's hat. I put it on.

Gradually the sea grew calm. The rain changed from a pelting torrent to a gentle shower. Survivors washed ashore like falling leaves blowing against a fence. My body warmed itself as I moved about to help, but my heart was elsewhere. All the while I searched for the serpent. Could I have imagined it? Had I washed ashore like the rest of these?

Yet I clung to the serpent in hopes it would bring Aidan.

There were so many survivors! Could the creature have played a part? And if they lived, could I still hope?

The three-legged cat appeared, wet and miserable, its claws sunk into a piece of decking. The trim woman appeared, and soon after her the monkey tamer, with the cold wet monkey clinging pitiably to his neck. The two of them quickly left the rest of us and headed inland.

The rain ceased, and the winds that had blown the storm in so suddenly blew it away. Stars poked through the thinning clouds, and the moon painted a stripe of light across the water. Survivors from the shipwreck gathered wood and planking that had washed ashore and stacked it into a fire mound, and a crew of them argued about how to light wet tinder. I wished they'd hurry and figure it out. We all needed warmth, and fire would act as a beacon to anyone who might, by enormous luck, still be alive in the water.

Luck. Foolish girl, to believe in luck. I trained all my thoughts on Aidan, alive, smiling, walking the path that led from his house to ours. If thinking of someone could keep him alive, he'd come walking over the water to me.

The faintest hint of a sunrise began to lighten the sky behind me, where now the hills of Pylander came into view. The long night was nearly over. Any hope now must be utterly vain.

Mistress.

I jumped up, trying to understand which way the inner voice was beckoning.

Mistress!

He was all the way down at the end of the beach. Close by, an orange glow illuminated the center of the bonfire. Good. That would divert attention. I picked my way over the rocks toward the serpent, hoping no one would take special notice of me. It was hard not to hurry.

I found the serpent uncoiling himself behind a large rock. It deposited Aidan at my feet, then backed away, its head held low.

One look at him confirmed my fears.

Chapter 19

Salt water could never sting my eyes as much as this sight.

I wanted to scream, to cry, to fall apart.

But that was not my way. Not the physician's way. And it would never help Aidan.

I sank onto the sand next to him and placed my head over his heart. There was nothing. No sound, no movement.

Or was there?

I tipped him onto his belly. It wasn't easy. Water poured out as from a cup, but not enough to make a difference. He was so wet, so cold, so pale and bruised in the predawn light.

I slapped his cheeks. I struggled to elevate his waist as best I could, thinking perhaps the slope would make water gush from his lungs and then he would wake. I applied pressure to his abdomen. It made no difference. Not the faintest flicker of life animated his cold body.

The sky grew gradually brighter, but that made me see Aidan's still form more clearly. The schoolgirl in me wondered what other survivors would think when they looked along the beach and saw a thirty-foot sea serpent. I cared little for the schoolgirl or her thoughts now.

So cold, so cold and still, Aidan, my friend, my neighbor, and now, my heart. If you were warm, would your eyes smile at me?

I lay down beside him, tucking my body close to his. Perhaps there was some warmth in me that I could share with him. My gaze stretched out over the sea, and I thought of his mother, short, fiery Widow Moreau, who ruled Maundley with her tongue. How would I tell her this news, that her only son had met the same watery end as her husband?

Pink lights on the water showed the sun had cleared the hills behind me. The serpent's long body wound back and forth slowly in the shallows. Only its horned head rose above the water, its jade eyes watching me.

Gradually I became aware of something happening to the beast. It stiffened itself straight as a pole, and, in a series of short pulses, it ratcheted itself smaller and smaller before my eyes. At first I doubted what I saw. Its eyes shut tight in concentration as its great body compressed itself down, down, till it was only the size of a great snake, and then a smaller and smaller one. The horns were mere nubs, the eyes, little more than green glass beads, and the silver white scales, so infinitely small his pelt looked as soft as hart's leather.

He sliced through the shallow water until he slipped over the sand, finally sliding up over my arm and shoulder. He was no bigger around than the base of my thumb, and yet he was somehow more fearsome to me now. As he touched my skin, my worries faded. He rubbed his head under my chin, tickling my neck with his horns, then slithered from me to Aidan.

I sat up to watch. It didn't feel right, the beast on Aidan's dead body, yet it was thanks to him that the body was even here.

You are fond of this one, Mistress.

I nodded.

More fond than of me.

He slid down the length of Aidan's body to his feet, which the sea had robbed of his shoes. The serpent opened his mouth wide, and two curved fangs glistened in the morning light.

"No!"

But I was too late to stop it. It sunk its great teeth into the arch of Aidan's foot.

Disgust and loathing overwhelmed me. This foul beast, desecrating my friend's body! I clawed my way to Aidan's feet and yanked the serpent from behind its jaws, my other hand finding a rock with which to smash its head if it tried to bite me.

It turned its dagger-bright head to face me, a drop of Aidan's blood wetting its white lips.

I'd better finish it now, before it resumed its fearsome size and finished me. I raised the rock high overhead. The serpent cringed low in the sand.

A warning, Mistress.

I paused.

What you do to me, you do to yourself.

The rock grew heavy in my hand.

"Explain."

First, let me go.

I hesitated before relinquishing my grip on its neck, and kept my rock at the ready.

It slunk away from me some distance in the sand and coiled itself into a protective cone.

Do you know nothing of what you are? What I am?

I didn't feel I knew anything at all anymore.

Didn't your mother ever teach you? You must have seen her leviathan.

"Her what?"

Like me. Her leviathan.

And suddenly I remembered, from my very own recitation at Saint Bronwyn's feast, a lifetime ago, a scripture verse:

"In that day the LORD with his sore and great and strong sword shall punish leviathan the piercing serpent, even leviathan that crooked serpent; and he shall slay the dragon that is in the sea."

Leviathan.

Oh, love of heaven, what evil thing did I now behold?

Did your mother never tell you? the thing persisted in asking.

"I never knew my mother," I said, "and I don't see what *you* could know about her."

I know what she was, the creature said. *But none of us knows what became of her. She was lost, she and her leviathan. He never returned to the sea to die.*

"She died having me," I said. "She never rose from her birthing bed. My grandfather told me. He is my father's father, and he knows."

The serpent cocked its head to one side, its glance penetrating. For a long time it said nothing, but seemed to be weighing my words, and weighing me, too—as if, finding me after such a long anticipated wait, it now felt disappointed.

"I don't understand anything," I said, my voice rising. "I don't know what you are, or why you're here, or what you want." My breath caught in my throat. "I don't even believe in things like you, and I think it's horrid of you to pretend you know something about my mother, or me. You must be mistaken. And I don't care what you say. I won't let you harm my friend."

The serpent's head slid down along the sand toward me, its sinuous body following. It slithered in circles around where I knelt, round and round, like the marchers around Jericho.

I *hatched the moment you were born*, it said, *with your scent in my nostrils, your feelings etched into my own. I cannot be mistaken about that. For the rest of your days, Mistress, I will be with you, to protect and help you. From now on we can never be far apart for long, and when either of us meets our end, the other will, in moments, follow.*

My stone fell into the sand. If this was true . . . my mouth went dry with the realization of what I'd nearly done. But I was far from ready to make peace with this thing, this reptile that had been thrust upon me. Not after the spiteful thing it had done to Aidan's body.

"If you must be with me forevermore," I said, "then let that be the case. But you must never, ever hurt my friends. You were jealous of him! What you did to Aidan is cruel."

It stopped circling around me and looked up at me.

How can I hurt one who is already dead?

"Then you mustn't molest his body, either." I began to cry. Misery, loss, cold, thirst, and now this. "It's vicious of you!"

I *have waited so long for you*, the leviathan whispered, *yet you don't know me at all.*

Without looking back, it slithered into the waves and disappeared under the water.

Go, then, I thought, *and quickly.* I was glad to be rid of it.

Later there would be decisions to make, messages to send, but now I only wanted to sit and grieve.

Morning sun warmed my back as I watched the little streak of rippling white snake skim over the surf and reassume its monstrous size, then dive deep under the water. I buried my face in my hands and gave in to the tears I'd bottled all through this cold, bitter night.

And in the racking of my sobs, at first I didn't hear it when, behind me, Aidan coughed.

Chapter 20

∽∾

I whirled around, afraid of being wrong, but there he was, hacking and gagging on the seawater that was rapidly leaving him. I scrubbed my face with my skirt to wipe away the crying. Air entered Aidan's lungs, and joy made me laugh out loud.

His coughing ceased, and he ventured to speak. "Jehoshaphat, Evie," he croaked. "I could have died!" He wiped his mouth on his wet sleeve. "What're you smiling at?"

Color flooded back into his face. He sat up, rubbed his eyes, and surveyed the scene.

"How'd I get here?" he said. "How'd it get to be morning?"

His voice was still weak. Trying not to attract his attention, I inched myself nearer to his feet to see where the serpent bit him. I couldn't spot a blemish on either foot.

"Let's get you over to the fire the others built," I said. "You need heat."

I helped hoist him up onto his feet, and we walked slowly across the beach to where the bonfire blazed. The others there made space for him without comment. The ring of people around the fire was deep, filled with sober-faced sailors and ship's passengers. What a sorry-looking, bedraggled lot we were.

"How many missing?" I asked Freddie Bell.

He rubbed his forehead with his wrist. "That's the odd thing, miss," he said. "Everybody's accounted for, besides them two that left."

"Meaning, you've found the bodies?"

He gestured toward the beach. "You see any bodies, miss?"

I followed his pointing hand. No, I didn't see any bodies. Not one.

"Got at least a dozen people here swearing they had died, and came back," he said. "Some say something in the water rescued 'em. A big fish, or nearly."

I gazed into the flames. Around me the ring of bedraggled survivors buzzed with conversation. Even children traveling with their guardians had survived the storm.

"When that ship hit the rock, our prospects were grim," the captain proclaimed. "What we've witnessed is nothing less than a miracle."

"But what about the beast?" asked a woman. "If there really is such an ungodly beast as you say, send the harpoons after it. These shores aren't safe with such a creature in the waters."

"You have an odd notion of safety, madam," the captain said. "If what people say is true, without the beast few of us would be alive now."

Shouts rang out from over the bluffs. A pair of fishermen appeared over the headlands and hollered down to our party. Several survivors ran to learn how far we were from help. They followed the fishermen back to their village to petition for assistance.

I retreated from the ring of survivors and pretended to gather more driftwood. When I was sure no one was watching me, I ran back to the jagged rocks. I'd just begun to feel dry, nevertheless I plunged into the waves until I was thigh deep in the water.

I wanted to call to my leviathan, but I didn't know how, nor what name to use, nor how I could begin to repent of my blindness.

"Leviathan?" I whispered. "Beast?"

Small waves lapped against me, yet I was so worn and weak that they nearly toppled me.

I treaded deeper in until my waist was submerged, my whole body shuddering with cold.

"Le-*vi*-a-than," I sang softly, bending my mouth low over the water. "Please come."

I pressed farther on till only my shoulders cleared the

water, and only then if I stood on tiptoe. Waves crashed over my head, and I held my breath to meet them.

"'Ere! Miss! Don't do that!" a voice bellowed from across the beach. "She's gone mad! Trying to go back and finish her death. Somebody stop her!"

"No, don't!" I cried. But a pack of men broke away from the fire and raced toward me. I panicked, and flung myself forward.

Now I couldn't touch bottom. I had one breath left. I used it to send my thoughts out into the deep. *Please, leviathan, forgive me,* I said. *Please pardon my foolishness. Thank you so much for saving them. For saving Aidan.*

Hands grabbed my shoulders and yanked me from the water. They hefted and handed me ashore like a barrel of molasses and set me down on the sand.

"What in the name of Pete were you thinking, girl?" a harsh voice shouted in my ear.

"Go easy on the child," said another, older voice. "She was one of the first ones, running around helping everyone else. She's worn out."

I heard their bickering as if from miles away. I'd failed to send my message. Then a familiar voice spoke in my ear.

"Why'd you do that, Evie?" Aidan's voice full of concern. "Are you all right? What's happened to you?"

I made no attempt to speak. In a moment I realized no one else was speaking, either. A silence had fallen over the entire beach. Even the water had fallen still.

I looked up.

Morning sunlight glistened pink and green on his silvery scales. He rose from the waves like a tower, arching over where I lay. His great head, horned and whiskered, looked regal in the sunlight as he took in the sight of all those he'd rescued in the night, and saw the terror in their eyes. The men who had grabbed me fell back, cringing.

If you wish to call me, Mistress, he said, *it helps if you give me a name.*

A man pulled a pistol from his belt and aimed it at his beautiful head.

"Are you mad?" I cried. "He saved us all!"

The man pulled the trigger. The wet powder wouldn't spark, and he threw down his pistol. Others ventured forward with knives, but none gathered the courage to come too near.

"I'm so sorry," I whispered to my leviathan, hoping no one would take notice, hoping he could hear. "Please, please forgive me."

He nodded his head toward me.

"She's in some sort of league with it," a lady cried.

"That's nonsense," Aidan said.

I attempted another whisper. "You must go now," I said. "They want to hurt you."

I won't leave you. If I go, they will turn their hatred for me toward you.

"I'll be all right," I said. "Come back to me in your smaller size. I'll wait for you here. Can you hide under my clothes?"

Yes.

"She's talking to the beast! Like a witch to her familiar!"

"Then meet me behind the rock. Now, go."

He reared his head high in the sky before sliding back into the water and out of sight. This gave the men with drawn weapons a jolt of bravery, and they charged into the water, brandishing their blades with battle cries, to no avail. My leviathan was long gone.

They turned to leave, casting dark glances my way.

I went to stand next to Aidan, not wishing to be alone, but as I did he edged away, just slightly, becoming just stiff enough to show a new gulf had sprung up between us. I reached for my neck, to squeeze some drops of comfort from the charms I wore. But the snakebite charm was given away, and now the love charm was gone too. It must have come off in the sea. All that remained, perverse though it seemed, was luck.

Up on the headlands wagons began rolling in, and people hurried to be the first to be rescued. I heard complaints about luggage and cargo lost when the ship went down. People snatched from death, and worried about their Sunday boots!

Aidan went to investigate. I sat on a rock. Something touched my hand. My leviathan, small again, encircled my wrist like a bracelet and wended his way up my arm. He tickled.

Aidan returned to where I sat. "Evie, let's go," he said. "They'll take us to Chalcedon."

I trudged up the slope toward the wagons, watching closely for any sign in his face of his feelings for me. Were there any to see? I despised myself for wanting to know. Had the thought of death alone made him kiss me? Might he have kissed another girl as readily, if he thought it was the last thing he'd do?

Even so, no matter what, I would always remember the holy joy of him waking up from death. Kisses, false or otherwise, couldn't take that from me.

He helped me climb into the wagon, but no sooner did I come into sight of the other passengers than they ceased talking and looked at me as if I were a leper. Some rose to leave.

Before they could exit I backed down the ladder.

"Never mind, this wagon's full," I said loudly. "I'll wait for another one."

Aidan, missing nothing, nodded and waited on the ground.

He opened his mouth, closed it, then tried again. "Were you . . . speaking to that serpent?"

I thought of ways to deny it, ways to lie, ways to shield him from the truth. But then, I didn't want to. Not for his sake, not for mine, and not for loyalty to the lifegiving snake around my arm.

"I was, Aidan," I said. "I was talking to it."

He closed his eyes. He reopened them.

"And could the serpent talk to you?"

I saw the fear, the revulsion in his eyes. I owed him no further explanation.

"You can go ahead, Aidan," I said, feeling my face burn. "I'll wait for the next wagon to come. I'll walk if there isn't one."

Aidan shot me a look of vexed disbelief. "Really, Evie?" he said. "I told your grandfather I'd see you safely to Chalcedon. You think I'd leave you alone now?"

There was no mistaking his meaning. Duty, a promise, his sense of honor. They were all that kept him here.

"Grandfather will thank you." I fought to keep my face neutral, to prevent it from betraying my hurt. "When we reach Chalcedon, your task will be finished."

Chapter 21

The sun was high in the sky by the time we climbed into our rescue cart, driven by a freckled boy of about thirteen and pulled by an ancient mule. I crawled into the straw in the bed of the wagon and lay there, wondering if I'd ever have the strength to rise again.

We rode past fields and pastures, watching cows chew cud faster than the mule could lift his hooves. Under my dress, my leviathan slept. Odd though it would seem to have a sleeping serpent wrapped around me, there was something sweet and soothing about it. Had it been only me and Aidan in the cart, my loneliness would be unendurable.

Was it really yesterday that I woke up in my own bed, in Grandfather's house, feeling all the world lay before me, a shiny oyster to be opened?

And now I had a leviathan. Or it had me. Why me? Of

all the people in the world who might inherit such a prize, how did I come to be the one?

And what did my mother have to do with it?

More than once I looked up from my stupor to see Aidan looking at me, but when our eyes met, he turned his elsewhere. Once he opened his mouth to speak, then changed his mind.

After an hour, the driver clapped his hand over his forehead and swore. "Ma'd have my hide!" He reached underneath his seat and pulled out a box. "I forgot. She sent some food for the poor shipwrecked folks. Too bad there's only two of you to eat it."

Bodies will not rise faster on Resurrection Morning than Aidan and I rose from the straw, practically fighting over the lunchbox. We caught ourselves and almost laughed, then wrestled the box open. Inside, shining like manna from heaven, were a dozen cooked eggs, four thick slabs of greasy cooked bacon, two sliced loaves of bread all spread with butter, and a jug of milk.

We attacked that food like starving hounds. Aidan shucked and stuffed two eggs into his mouth at once, and I gnawed at my bacon. We had to rest between bites and gather strength. When I'd finally sated my initial, overwhelming hunger, and gotten down to the business of slowly eating some good solid bread, I felt a stirring underneath my sleeve that made me squirm. My leviathan was rousing and sniffing the air.

Food? it said. *Nice fish?*

I took morsels of egg and bacon and, when Aidan wasn't looking, slipped them under the collar of my dress. It was a ghastly thing to do, and I began to think longingly of a hot bath.

My serpent moved over my skin, up and around my shoulder, and I felt the tiny movements it made as it worked its mouth over the bits of food and swallowed them.

I felt its sensation of shock and surprise. *Ffaugh,* it said. *What kind of fish is that?*

"Not fish," I whispered as softly as I could. "Not fish at all."

Strange.

"People like that food." I held my hand over my mouth as though I might cough.

People are strange. Is there more?

"We're nearly to Chalcedon," Aidan said, watching the road pass by. "When we get there, I'll take you to my master's house. When I explain what's happened to us, they'll put you up for the night. And in the morning I can take you to the Royal University."

And lose no time about it, I thought.

What would I do with my leviathan at the university? If what it had said about my mother was true, she'd had one there too. Perhaps I could conceal him under my dress.

Under my dress!

While Aidan's eyes were elsewhere, I reached down

under my collar, probing for the king's pendant, my ticket to school.

It was gone.

I patted myself all over, as discreetly as I could, searching for it. It wasn't there.

It must have fallen loose in the sea.

What's the matter, Mistress?

Aidan saw me searching. I decided to tell him. Even if he regretted his ill-considered kiss, he was a Maundleyan, and Maundleyans looked out for one another.

"I've lost something," I said in a low voice. "The pendant the king gave me, which will admit me to University. It was pinned under my dress, but now it's gone."

"Are you sure?" Aidan said.

"Quite."

You should have told me.

"That's a bad business." Aidan shook his head.

"I've lost everything," I said, giving way to misery. "My money, my clothes, my books. Without the king's seal, what have I got?"

"We all lost everything, Evie," Aidan said. "We're lucky to be alive."

I sulked at his rebuke. He was right. That didn't mean I had to like it.

The wagon stopped. Chalcedon's towers rose against the darkening sky. The sun was just beginning to sink into the ocean, and lamplight began appearing in windows along the city wall.

I stepped down from the wagon, brushing dirt and debris off me, and gazed upon the vast city. So many buildings, so ancient and strong, built of massive blocks of hewn stone—hewn by masons like Aidan for centuries. Which ones belonged to the university? I saw churches, towering cathedrals with spires reaching to heaven, and there, on high ground, that must be the king's castle. In all that great metropolis, would I find any comfort, any help?

Bells began to ring, tolling the evening hour. I'd never heard such music before. Deep, sonorous tones and high tinkling chimes floated across the wall to where we stood.

My gaze rested on the castle, its banners shining in the last sun's rays.

"If your master will shelter me tonight, Aidan," I said, "I'll seek an audience with King Leopold himself tomorrow. I'll tell him of the bandits on the king's highways, and ask him for a letter to present at the university." I gave my luck charm, the last of the three, a squeeze. "If my luck holds, he ought to remember me."

Chapter 22

Morning found me waking slowly from a deep, soft bed into a cheerful room decorated with a green bedspread and yellow curtains. It took a minute to remember where I was, and why.

I sat up and felt the leviathan slide over my skin. He'd slept on my collarbone. Would I ever grow accustomed to this?

A small mirror hung over the washbasin. I was horrified to see how dirty and disheveled I looked. But a dress lay draped over the chair for me to borrow, and my stockings had been washed and left for me. The basin was full of warm water, and a mound of soap and a cloth had been silently provided as well. Countless blessings upon Mrs. Rumsen, Aidan's master's wife, who had taken me in, fed me, and led me straight to her daughter's bed.

I came downstairs to find them all at the breakfast

table—bald Mr. Rumsen, plump and cheerful Mrs. Rumsen, their daughter Dolores, Aidan, and a skinny apprentice of thirteen. I felt shy as they greeted me. Dolores Rumsen was a pretty girl, with bright red hair, charming freckles, and striking green eyes. Her mother, I could tell, had looked very much like her in her day. Dolores might be a year older than me. She sat by Aidan and sliced him a piece of bread.

"Good morning, Miss Pomeroy!" Mrs. Rumsen rose to greet me, which made the curls poking out from under her cap bob. "Our Aidan here's been telling us more about your misfortunes along the way. What a frightful journey you've had, my dear!"

I took the chair she offered me and sat down. *Our Aidan*. Aidan practically belonged to them now, after six years' apprenticeship. Once he looked like that pimply apprentice.

"Say good morning to Miss Pomeroy, Henry." Mrs. Rumsen prodded the young apprentice, who obliged with an unintelligible sound. He was too busy stuffing what looked like half a dozen eggs into his mouth to bother with visitors.

The homey smell of hot eggs and toasted bread overcame any awkwardness I felt about accepting help from strangers. We'd made it to Chalcedon, to friendly, smiling faces. The king would assist me, and I'd be tucked away in a cozy cubicle at the medical college by tonight.

"As I was saying, Moreau," Mr. Rumsen said, waving

his toast at Aidan, "you're ready to go it on your own now. I've been thinking it over, and I don't see any point in you staying here."

The Rumsen women made little peeps of displeasure, but said nothing. I watched Aidan to see his reaction, but whatever he felt, he mastered it well.

"Your work's excellent," Rumsen went on. "But we don't need two masters here. I don't aim to retire anytime soon. You'd best find a post and make your fortune." He swallowed a drink of coffee. "Time you did, if you plan to set up housekeeping of your own."

Here his gaze moved to his daughter, and hers to me. I looked away. Not to be ignored, she passed me the platter of eggs. "Aidan tells me you and he are neighbors back home?" I couldn't miss the thousand meanings tucked into her inflection on "Aidan *tells me.*" Tells me all his secrets, tells me anything I ask him, tells me my bright red curls are the prettiest in all Chalcedon. Oh, stop, Evie, stop!

"Yes," I said, spooning myself some eggs. "We've known each other forever."

Food? said a little voice inside my head. *Strange fish?*

"Not now!" I whispered into my hand, resolving to save my leviathan some scraps when I cleared away my plate.

"Well, we think our Aidan is as fine a young man as they make nowadays," Mrs. Rumsen said, patting her husband's huge hand. "Don't we, Everard?"

Mr. Rumsen gave a grunt as he chewed his bacon.

"Nowadays," I repeated, unwilling to concede this point entirely. Undoubtedly there had been better young men, once upon a time.

This left an awkward silence. Dolores was the first to fill it.

"Such a commotion since you've been away!" she said brightly. "You probably haven't heard, Miss Pomeroy. It's just been announced, two days since, that King Leopold is getting married, and soon. To Princess Annalise of Merlia. They say she's *desperately* beautiful."

"They're strange folk, those Merlians," Mrs. Rumsen said, cutting her ham with deep disapproval. "But I suppose it doesn't matter if you're strange, if you're beautiful."

Food, Mistress. Food.

I stroked my collarbone as though I had a slow itch and thought of King Leopold and his sparkling teeth. Married? It should come as no surprise. Too bad for all girls like Prissy who could no longer dream of the bachelor king.

"Sounds like a rushed business," Mr. Rumsen said. "I don't hold with rushed marriages."

"I met the king," I said, to my horror, "when he came to Maundley last week. He presented me with a school prize."

Dolores giggled slightly, and Aidan looked away. I wanted to crawl under the table. I never said such boastful things! It was that infernal redhead that flustered me so.

"Isn't that nice?" Mrs. Rumsen served Aidan a second slice of fried ham. "It must be a treat for the provinces to get a peek at His Majesty. Of course, for us in the city, it's not so rare."

Of course not. The eggs in my mouth turned to rubber.

"I heard some interesting talk in the marketplace myself this morning," Mrs. Rumsen continued, and I blessed her for it. "It concerns your ship. What was it? *The White Flagon?*"

"*White Dragon.*" It was the first peep I'd heard out of Aidan all morning.

"Just so," said the lady of the house. "I heard that when the ship capsized, several passengers claimed they were rescued by a hideous sea creature!"

Henry's mouth gaped open, revealing a good portion of half-chewed breakfast.

Dolores smiled. "You can't believe that, Mother." She gave me a wink, as if humoring credulous mothers was a hobby we shared.

Aidan's eyes met mine for a moment. Was he worried that I might speak?

Under my dress, my leviathan scuttled his head back and forth. *I'm not hideous. Other males envy my size and color, and my . . .*

I nearly choked on my glass of water.

"Are you all right, Miss Pomeroy?" Mrs. Rumsen threw down her napkin and rose to help me, but before she could, Mr. Rumsen thumped me vigorously on the back.

"I'm fine," I said, before the elder stonemason could whack me into kingdom come.

"They said it was like a giant snake in the water." Mrs. Rumsen took her seat. "Laws, but I despise snakes! Stomp on their tails whenever I find one underfoot in the back garden."

"Now, Betsy, I've told you before . . ."

I didn't listen to Mr. Rumsen's defense of snakes. "It's all right," I whispered under my napkin, for now my leviathan was nearly frantic. "Stay calm. Please. I won't let them hurt you."

"But surely, Miss Pomeroy, you can lay the matter to rest, can't you? Aidan tells me"—there was that little smirk again—"that he was unconscious on the beach after his ordeal in the water. Did you see the monster everyone's talking about?"

I kept my eyes on my plate. "Everyone?"

Skinny Henry broke the silence. "Did you, miss? Did you see a foul beastie in the sea?"

Food, Mistress. I must have food soon.

"I saw no foul beast," I said firmly.

Dolores looked surprised by my tone of voice.

Aidan seized on a sudden idea. "It was dark anyway," he said.

Now I was the one surprised.

"Well, thank heavens you didn't see it," Mrs. Rumsen said.

"I think you're disappointed, Mother," Dolores teased. "You were fascinated by it."

I slowly raised a fork of ham to my mouth. Would this torturous conversation never end?

"I most certainly was not." Her mother blinked indignantly. "If I thought there were such horrid creatures in the ocean, I'd never sail again."

"Fortunately, there are none," said Dolores.

Strange fish!

And, poking his head out from my collar, my leviathan snatched the ham from my fork.

Chapter 23

Spoons clattered. Mrs. Rumsen and her daughter screamed. Mr. Rumsen sprayed breakfast as he swore, and the apprentice jumped up and snatched at my neck. I threw up my arms to block him.

"Snake!" Mrs. Rumsen cried. "In your dress!"

Down under my collar, my leviathan was working hard on his slimy ham prize.

"It's not . . . ," I began.

"You mean . . . you *knew* it was there?" Mrs. Rumsen squealed. "Everard!"

"Did that thing sleep *in my bed* last night?" Dolores was now standing behind her chair, clutching it as if ready to wield it at the creature. "A*aaagh!*"

"That was no ordinary snake," Henry said, hopping back and forth. "It had a funny head. Like a little dragon. Oh, lemme see it!"

"Aidan Moreau," Mrs. Rumsen said through clenched teeth, though her eyes were on me, "what is the *meaning* of this? What unnatural thing have you brought into our Christian house?"

Aidan's face flushed crimson. "I didn't . . . I mean, I never knew . . ." His halting apologies couldn't get far. Mortification was written on his face.

"Where'd you get that, miss, offa some sailor?" Only Henry wasn't horrified.

"No," I said, rising from my chair. "Aidan did not know I had this, Mrs. Rumsen. I'll go now, and send the dress back when I've found another."

"Keep it," Dolores said, her freckled face full of loathing. "I wouldn't wear that dress for a kingdom, even if it was washed ever so many times."

"Thank you for the food and shelter," I told Mrs. Rumsen, who wouldn't look at me, and I pulled the door shut behind me.

I hurried up the street. I didn't want to be found, or caught, or helped. Not anymore. Aidan could stay there in his second home. I didn't need his kisses, or his aid. Not now or ever.

I ran until my sides hurt, and regretted eating breakfast. I found a little church with open doors and strains from a wheezy organ reaching outside. I went in and sat in one of the rearmost pews, half hidden by a thick pillar, and waited to see if my lungs would cave in on the spot.

And then, without warning, I began to cry. I ducked my head down so no one would see.

What had I done?

I wiped my eyes on Dolores Rumsen's sleeve.

No matter what my leviathan could do—rescue the drowning, raise the dead—serpents inspired loathing. Mankind had hated them since time began. Women didn't think, they just squashed them underfoot. Now my welcome would be the same.

And I'd have him with me until I died. Which meant, if the Rumsens were any indication, I'd be spending my days alone. Who would have me now as a friend, a granddaughter, a neighbor? When granny grew ill, would loved ones call the snake doctor to come and help?

I felt the leviathan creep over my shoulders, around the back of my neck, and then curl himself lovingly under my chin.

Why are you sad?

"Because I am alone and penniless in this great city," I said. "Isn't that reason enough?"

You are not alone.

There was nothing I could say to that without revealing too much bitterness.

Why did you leave the one you were fond of?

My leviathan must consider it a wasted effort now to have brought Aidan back to life.

"Because he is no longer fond of me."

Why?

I thought of little barefoot Letty Croft, ceaseless in her questions. Why, why, why. Because of *you*, I thought, but wounded as I felt, I had no heart to wound anyone else.

"Because people change their minds," I whispered.

"Was someone chasing you, my child?"

An aged priest appeared at the end of my pew. I froze, realizing my leviathan was in plain sight around my neck.

But the ancient priest, with his back stooped under his robe, took no notice. His eyes must be fading. Seeing his obvious pain at every step, I felt ashamed he should be offering to help me. "I saw you run in. You looked distressed."

"No, thank you, Father," I said. "I am well. I just needed a place to rest and think."

"You've come to the right place," he said. "Enjoy the music, and stay as long as you like." And he shuffled slowly down the left-hand aisle toward the nave.

I held up a hand for my leviathan to crawl onto.

Mistress?

"Hmm?"

I *did badly, didn't* I?

I didn't know how to answer this.

I'm sorry about the trouble.

I stroked his soft, supple back. "I'm sorry I was slow to feed you."

He sniffed the air. Is *there any more?*

Hah. "No."

He paused. *Too bad.*

I chuckled in spite of myself. "How bad, you scarcely realize," I said. "I don't know where or when either of us will eat again."

He flexed his long back so it made a wavelike motion. *We're near the ocean. I smell it. I will need a swim soon. Throw me in, and I can catch you a nice fish.*

I rose from my seat. "We may soon reach that depth of despair," I told my leviathan, "but we're not there yet. There is one last hope we can try. We're off to see His Majesty, the king."

What is a king?

I made my way out of the chapel. How did one explain a king? "It's . . . he's a man who rules other men and women. The most important person there is." A poor definition, to be sure.

The little serpent actually laughed. *There's no one more important than you, Mistress. Especially, no man. I told you. They're just food.*

What kind of bloodthirsty brute was I stuck with? "You are not to eat people, no matter how they behave. Or taste. Kings are kings, and queens are queens—those are like lady kings—and I'm just a common girl from a tiny town in the provinces. I'm nobody important."

I elbowed my way through the crowded marketplace, keeping my sights on the castle.

Would Mistress like to be a queen?

I laughed, then thought of the king's dark eyes.

"Who wouldn't?" I said. "But I don't waste time thinking of things like that."

What would Mistress like?

I stopped in my tracks. No one had ever asked me that before, not with such earnest sincerity. As if whatever I might like would be possible, as if whatever it was, they'd try to get it.

"I used to think I wanted to be a physician," I said. "I thought I was the sort of person who could heal and save others. I've had a bit of luck with babies and fevers in the past."

You are that sort of person.

"Was that just some noble fantasy I created?" I said. "The great hero, the ministering angel? Was it an excuse to travel to University and have an adventure away from Maundley?"

Why would you doubt you could heal sick people?

"I've seen enough death to last me a long time," I said. "I don't have the courage to face it often. All my grand talk, and now, I want to go back to Maundley, like Priscilla."

My leviathan said nothing.

"Perhaps that's what I'll do," I said. "Instead of asking the king for funds to go to University, I'll explain all that's befallen me and ask for help to get home."

Still my creature brooded on my arm.

"Excuse me, madam," I asked a woman passing by who seemed friendly, "but can you tell me which of all these great buildings houses the Royal University?"

"Not one building, but a dozen at least." She pointed due east. "See those towers? They're the corner points of the university. All the other buildings lie in between."

The four towers were vast and imposing. Though miles from where I stood, they dominated the eastern landscape, just as the castle dominated the western one, toward the sea.

I let my eyes linger over the university a moment longer.

At long last I reached the king's castle. A paved courtyard, lined with trees, spread before it. It seemed a man-made mountain, with arching roofs and towers reaching to the clouds above. Guards in lion-emblazoned tunics crisscrossed the courtyard in measured treads, passing each other en route, their bayonets resting upon their shoulders.

I do not think you are as sure as you say.

I was perfecting the art of muttering to my leviathan without others noticing. If all else failed, I could take up ventriloquy next.

"As sure of what?"

Changing your mind. About helping sick people. And about going home.

"Oh, you think not, do you?"

And Mistress?

"Yes?"

There is no ocean near your Maundley. If there was, I would have found you.

That full reality had not struck me before. We could not be far apart, he'd said, and whatever happened to me happened to him. I was now an exile even from my child-hood home.

Stranded in Chalcedon, with no path forward or back.

And Mistress?

Oh, would he never stop? "What is it?"

I will never change my mind about you.

Chapter 24

"State your purpose," snapped a stout porter at the doors.

"I wish to see King Leopold." My voice squeaked like a child's.

The porter snorted into his moustache and sneered. "Have you been invited for tea?"

"No," I said. "But I met the king. He gave me a school prize to attend University."

The porter rolled his eyes. "One of *those*, are you? His Majesty thinks every schoolgirl in pigtails and every schoolboy wet behind the ears is a scholar."

Shall I bite him, Mistress?

"Not yet," I muttered into my hand, feigning a cough.

"Well, I made the trip," I said. "And I need to speak with King Leopold. It's an urgent matter. Bandits on the king's highway. Shipwreck at sea."

"That's a fine tale. Run along now, you hear?"

"I wish," I said slowly, firmly, "to see the king. I have traveled for days to see him, and I have no intention of turning back now."

"Well-o-well." The doorman opened a bag and pulled out a pheasant drumstick. "Little Miss Bossy, eh?" He took a large, moist bite, greasing his whiskers. I could feel my leviathan sniffing. "Maybe you've been sleeping under a mushroom lately, but King Leopold's just announced his nuptials. He ain't sitting around waiting upon callers. There's party after party. He'll be celebrating right up until the wedding Saturday."

Curiosity overcame me. "He just announced it, and he's getting married *this Saturday*?"

The porter shrugged and took another chaw at the pheasant leg. "Love don't keep, I guess. Sure enough won't keep long after the wedding!" He slapped his knee with a greasy paw.

It was hard to think with that walrus glaring down on me. Parties, a wedding, then a honeymoon . . . how could I wait? I'd freeze to death, or starve, long before his return.

"Is there a place I could sit and wait, out of the cold?" I said.

"Be off with you," he brandished the thighbone, "or I'll throw you into vagrant's prison."

A sudden inspiration saved me.

"In that case, I wish to speak with Christopher Appleton," I said.

The guard opened his mouth to blast me with another rebuke, then paused. "Who?"

"Christopher Appleton. The Lord Chancellor of the Exchequer."

He took a sidelong look at me. My request had flummoxed him. He shrugged and opened the door. Before I crossed the threshold, I knelt, pretending to lace my boot, and retrieved a morsel of dropped pheasant meat for my leviathan. A regular beggar I was becoming.

I entered the castle blinking at the change from outdoor to indoor light. The room in which I stood seemed even bigger than the castle had seemed from the outside. Grand staircases on either side of the chamber swept up to higher promenades. Banners hung underneath deeply recessed windows, admitting shafts of light onto the patterned stone floors. It must have taken an army of masons to build this place, I thought. An army of Aidans.

Never mind him.

People passed to and fro along a vast corridor. Where in all this cavernous space might I find Christopher Appleton?

My leviathan wriggled and poked his tiny head out from under my collar. I fed him the gristly bit of meat. "Please," I whispered, "swallow it quickly, before I gag."

He ducked back under my clothes.

I set off along the right hallway. A serving girl in a black dress and white apron passed by, loaded down with covered platters on a tray. They smelled delicious.

"Excuse me," I said. "Where might I find Lord Appleton?"

She looked annoyed. "Keep on going," she said. "The Exchequer's down this hall, then up a set of stairs." She took a critical look at my appearance. Did I smell like the ocean?

At the Exchequer, stern sentries shared the servant girl's surprise at finding a young woman coming to see Lord Appleton. After making an inquiry inside, they let me in.

I waited in a plush antechamber for His Lordship, growing more uneasy by the minute. When the idea appeared in my head, it had seemed inspired. Lord Appleton had been so appreciative back in Maundley, calling my hands cool peeled grapes. But here in the velvet chairs outside his chambers, things took on a different hue. Through a windowed door into the inner office, I saw black-clad clerks pass slowly back and forth carrying leather-bound ledgers, for all the world like priests officiating in the temple of money. And the high priest of all this pomp was Christopher Appleton.

At last the door opened, and a wizened older clerk frowned at me through his pince-nez. "Miss Pomeroy?" he said, as if the name were a regrettable one, then gestured for me to follow.

I crossed the long chamber filled with clerks bent over their counting tables. They paused and watched me pass, ignoring their tidy piles of dully glinting coins.

Only a few of those coins would solve all my immediate

problems. I kept my eyes riveted on my escort's shoulder blades, poking out through his too-small jacket, and marched on.

We reached a door, and the elderly clerk rapped on it with his knobby knuckles.

"The young lady is here, Your Lordship."

I had seen Christopher Appleton clad in a nightshirt and wet from his bath. I scarcely recognized him now. Gold buttons shone on his blue coat, and an odd velvet hat, like a maroon muffin on his head, hid his baldness.

"Well, well," he said. "If it isn't the little healer girl, come to see me." He leaned back in his chair and rested his heels on his desk. His boots were blue, too, with pointy toes. "You've come at just the right time. Staring at numbers all day gives me a splitting headache. Why don't you come over here and rub my temples like you did back in . . . what was it? Marysvale?"

Suddenly the room felt very large.

"Maundley," I said.

"That makes you pretty far away from home, doesn't it?"

It was a question that needed no answer.

Lord Appleton removed his hat and tossed it on his desk. A few of the long hairs that grew around his neck and ears stood up straight.

"Right here," he said, rubbing the side of his head. "That's where I need it."

"If it pleases Your Lordship," I said, "I'm glad to find you in good health now, and recovered from your illness. I've come to beg for assistance. I journeyed to Chalcedon with the funds you provided, for the purpose of enrolling at University."

He put his ankles down and rose from his chair. "What would you say," he said, "to discussing your need for assistance while we take a little carriage ride?"

I took a step backward. He was right. I was a long, long way from home.

"No, thank you," I said firmly. "The money the king gave me was stolen by a bandit on the king's highway, one who brutally killed the coach driver."

His eyes narrowed at this. "Where?"

"Between Maundley and Fallardston." I was glad we were sticking to facts and not carriage rides. "And my pendant that the king gave me was lost when the ship I took from Fallardston capsized during a storm."

He closed his eyes and began to chuckle. He pulled a snow white handkerchief from his pocket and dabbed his eyes with it. I noticed again those soft, plump hands.

"For a moment, you had me worried," he said. "Bandits on the highway are a serious threat to provincial commerce. But this is obviously a delightful yarn you've spun to amuse me."

"It's no yarn," I said, my voice rising. "Anyone in the city can tell you about the wreck of *The White Dragon* yesterday, miles south of here."

He shrugged and tossed down his kerchief. "What do you want from me?"

I paused. What did I want? To go home. That was what I came to request. I wanted to go home to Grandfather.

But I still wanted to learn. And my leviathan was right. There was no ocean in Maundley.

Would my own villagers gaze at me in horror, as the Rumsens had done? The university, once my impossible dream, now seemed like a last refuge, like the one place I might successfully hide myself as a quiet stranger with a serpent under my cowl.

"I want what the king first gave me," I said. "Enrollment to the university."

He cocked his head to one side. "This is what I tell King Leopold about women. Got their hands in your pockets, every single one of them."

That smug look on his face made me forget my place. "How can you say such a thing?" I cried. "I came in good faith, and was twice waylaid by misfortune. I haven't cost the king anything other than what he freely offered me. All I want is what he promised."

"You'll want to watch your tone with me," he said. "Why should I give you anything?"

He took a step toward me.

Don't worry, Mistress, my leviathan said. *I won't let him hurt you.*

A felt surge of relief. That's right. I had a leviathan with me now. I held my head higher.

"You should give me what I've asked for, if you honor the king's promises," I said. "Give me an introduction to the registrar at the college, and payment for room and board."

He took a step closer. Close to my skin, my leviathan shifted, poised and ready.

"Kings make all sorts of promises," he said, "but it is I who hold the purse strings."

A door opened. It wasn't the door through which I'd come, but one behind His Lordship's desk, one that seemed more private. A woman poked her head through.

She was young and beautiful, with dark hair piled high in loops and braids, and glittering necklaces at her throat. She wore a yellow and gold gown that swept against the doorway, and she clutched a soft velvet purse. I'd never been so relieved to see another soul, for at the sight of her, Christopher Appleton scowled, resumed his seat, and dipped his quill into his inkwell.

"Oh, you're busy," the woman said, noticing me. "I'll just wait outside—"

"No, don't," I cut in quickly. The woman looked at me curiously.

"We were just finishing," I said. "Lord Appleton has kindly agreed to assist me."

The Chancellor of the Exchequer's cheek muscle twitched. He plied his pen to his paper.

The young woman seated herself on Lord Appleton's desk as casually as if she were his own daughter, and aimed her smile in my direction. "Marvelous! It seems I've caught him in a generous frame of mind, then. I have a small request for him myself."

I could not understand why this woman, obviously a grand lady of some means, and perhaps even some title, would regard me as closely as she did, and speak with me so freely.

"'Course you do," Lord Appleton said. "You may have the king hoodwinked, but I see just what you are."

The young lady winked at me, smiling broadly.

"And what am I?"

"A woman," said the Chancellor of the Exchequer. "A conniving, stealing, slit-your-throat-open-to-see-if-there's-a-penny-in-your-gut woman." He nodded in my direction—as if he and I were now, somehow, comrades. "Here she comes with her purse, expecting me to fill it."

"He's just sour about the honeymoon ship," the young lady said in a friendly whisper that was easily heard. She thrust out her hand prettily at me. "I'm Annalise. Has this old weasel been giving you trouble? You look distressed."

Before I could stammer a reply, she turned to see what Appleton was writing. "Hurry up, Lord Appleton," she said. "I want to discuss roasted peacocks, and truffles, and the dress. And entertainers! We'll need amusement on our voyage. What are you giving this girl, anyway?"

"She wants to go to University," the chancellor growled. "Get off my desk."

"The desk belongs to Leopold, so in a few days it will belong to me too," she teased.

Annalise! Of course. Why didn't I realize? This was the princess the king was to marry.

"University sounds thrilling," she went on, giving me a closer look. "If I had the patience for studying, heaven knows it'd be good for me."

"Patience is hardly your strong suit," Lord Appleton said.

"But I still haven't learned your name," Princess Annalise said, ignoring him.

I felt small and filthy, introducing myself to the princess. "I'm Evelyn Pomeroy."

"Evelyn Pomeroy," she repeated, rolling the words around on her tongue. "Pomeroy. An interesting name. That's a pretty frock you have on. Simple, yet sweet. I can just picture you picking flowers in it. I want to hear all about you. Where you're from, your people, your story."

"What for?" Lord Appleton said, replacing his quill in its holder. "She's a schoolgirl from the provinces who recited her lessons nicely for the king. Why should she matter to you?"

"Where'd you learn your manners, Lord Chancellor, in the stables?" She turned her scornful look toward the chancellor into a beaming smile for me, and reached out her hand with an inviting little twist to her wrist. "Come, child. You look like you need rest and refreshment. As it happens, this afternoon is leisurely for me. Let's get acquainted."

"But . . ." I was so bewildered, I didn't know how to respond.

"Have you finished giving Miss Pomeroy what she needs, Lord Chancellor?"

The chancellor's lips pressed tightly together. He would comply, but not with goodwill. He handed me documents bearing his seal, with blue wax still soft. "This letter will suffice for the registrar at the university. They will outfit you with tuition, a residence cloister, and board at the common table for female students. And this," he presented me with a slip of paper, "is a ticket for the cashier. He will issue you a sum to meet your needs until you enroll."

I took the papers from Lord Appleton's soft, unwilling hands, and Princess Annalise tugged me away with hers. "Lovely, lovely," she said. "Don't forget, Chancellor, I need a trusty crew, and ship's cooks. Silks this year are more dear . . . but we can discuss all this later."

"The later the better."

Laughing, she pulled me out the rear door through which she'd entered, and led me along a tapestried corridor.

"Such pretty hair you have, my dear," she said, loud enough that Lord Appleton, should he care to listen, might hear. "What a striking golden color."

"Is it?" I said, feeling numb. "It's common where I come from."

But Princess Annalise was no longer thinking about my hair. "Evelyn," she whispered in my ear, "I'm so thrilled to find you here, you have no idea. I'm starved for a friend in all this glut of Pylandrians. But, child, you should be more cautious in front of strangers. It's a wonder that old weasel didn't notice. The whole time you were talking, I could see your leviathan squirming under your dress."

Chapter 25

❧

Before I could respond, she poked me through a doorway. A canopied bed lay buried under mounds of scarlet cushions, a fire burned brightly on the grate, and a table of luncheon was just being cleared away by a young serving girl clad in black. Other servants pressed and brushed gowns bulging from an armoire near the bed. They looked like they'd rather be elsewhere. A door led out onto a balcony, from which I could see the castle grounds unroll themselves down to the sea. Autumn trees burned in glorious red and orange, while the ocean was the purest china blue.

The fragrance of the leftover lunch hung in the air, and I gazed longingly at the little table. My leviathan sniffed hungrily.

"Dorothy," Princess Annalise said, "this is my friend, Evelyn, visiting me from Merlia for the wedding. She's weary after her long journey. Run and bring a tray for her."

The girl with the heavy tray nodded mutely and disappeared.

"Rhoda, Erma," she said to the servants tending to her dresses. "Fill a bath right here for my guest, and pick out a frock and slippers, everything." The girls rose and left the room.

"Stupid girls," Annalise fumed when they were gone. "So cold to me, *a foreigner.*" She pressed her lips together tightly. "Soon I'll be queen and make them mind me differently. But listen to me fretting!" She smiled apologetically and pushed a chair my way. "Sit! Sit!"

She sat and crossed her legs, one slippered foot dangling in midair. My head felt foggy.

"Why would you . . . ," I began, then stopped. "I'm just . . . How did you know?"

She tilted her head. "Know what?"

I patted my shoulder. "About . . . him?"

She laughed. Even her laugh was pretty. The little bits of jewelry around her neck, in her hair, at her ears, all danced with her movement, catching sparkles of light like snowflakes. Silly Priscilla, to think a village girl's charms could hold up to those of a lady like this.

"Evelyn, dear," she said, "do you think I can't spot another serpentina when I see one?"

I looked down at my lap. I tried to keep my face very still. Embarrassment and confusion overwhelmed me.

Serpentina.

So *that* was what I was?

There was a name for people—for women, and girls—like me?

Princess Annalise opened the velvet purse that laid in her lap and made a soft clucking sound with her tongue. "Come on, Bijou," she said in a coaxing voice, wiggling her fingers. "Come out and meet your new friend."

Her little leviathan poked his head out from under the top of the purse. Whereas mine was pearly white with a tinge of silver blue in his soft scales, Annalise's—Bijou—was amber colored with a caramel belly. He, too, was beautiful, his tiny horns curving regally from his brow, his delicate whiskers trailing, and his green eyes dark, like an evergreen.

My leviathan had grown anxious to the point of agitation. I pulled back my collar and allowed him to crawl out onto my hand, then placed him on my knees.

Annalise made a soft sound of delight. "What a handsome fellow you are," she crooned. "Would you two like to play?" In no time they slithered off our laps, landing with soft thuds on the floor, where they sniffed each other curiously. Soon they tangled and wrestled on the carpet.

Annalise watched them with an indulgent smile. "Bijou told me you were here. I was passing near Appleton's offices, and he grew so excited, I had to poke my nose in to see who I'd find. Marvelous thing, their sense of smell. What do you call your leviathan?"

"Call him?" More jitters. I felt like a drugged patient waking up from a heavy sleep as I tried to comprehend all she was telling me.

She turned an amused face my way. "Yes, call him. His name."

What would happen, I wondered, if I just ran out of this room?

"I don't really call him anything." I felt very small. "I only discovered him yesterday." Was it really only yesterday?

Her eyes grew wide. She reached forward and clutched both my hands in hers.

"You *what*? How is this possible?" She fingered a strand of my hair that had come loose. "Where did you say you were from?"

"I didn't say," I said. "Why did you tell the servants I was from Merlia?"

She spluttered. "But *aren't* you?"

"No," I said. "I grew up in a small village called Maundley, far inland from here. Two days ago was the first time I'd ever laid eyes on the ocean."

Princess Annalise rose from her chair and began walking around me, looking me over as if searching for clues. "Fascinating," she breathed. What was fascinating? "Raised in Pylander? Who ever heard of such a thing?"

There was a knock at the door. Princess Annalise's eyes darted to where our leviathans lay warming themselves by the fire. She made a clicking sound full of warning with her tongue, and her leviathan scurried behind the wood box. In moments, mine followed.

"Come in." Dorothy returned with a tray loaded with luncheon. She set it down, then held out a chair and flicked open a napkin. I sat and let her cover my lap. There was enough food for a family of six. Pheasant must be the fowl du jour, accompanied by potatoes, beans, squash, and roasted onions, a dish of cold fruit, a salad of greens with oil, and a loaf of piping-hot bread.

"Thank you, Dorothy." Annalise waved her hand, and Dorothy left.

I forgot conversation and plied my fork and knife for several minutes. It was all I could do not to groan, the food was so delicious. Annalise took a piece of fruit, just to be sociable. Then she cut up little morsels of meat on a saucer and set it down for the serpents. Her eyes never left me. As I ate, Rhoda and Erma returned, whichever one was which, tugging a beautiful tall-sided copper bathtub, followed by a procession of young boys with yokes on their shoulders and buckets of hot water dangling from either end. The boys poured my bath and left, staring at me as they went. Erma and Rhoda unfolded a standing partition before the tub.

When they were gone, Annalise spoke again. "Into the tub with you," she said, "and tell me, what did your mother teach you about your leviathan? What did you learn about hers?"

"First, do you have a place where I may keep these papers from Lord Appleton?" I asked. Annalise pointed toward a drawer in a small writing table. I slipped my letters inside. They were now the most precious things I owned.

Then I went behind the partition and removed Dolores Rumsen's dress—for the last time, I hoped—and my underthings, realizing as I did so just how much I smelled of the road and the sea, then stepped one foot into the tub. A warm, drowsy bliss came over me as I lowered myself down into the water. I'd never had such a deep, hot bath in all my life.

"Well?"

"It's very nice, thank you."

"No, I mean, what did you learn from your mother?"

Oh. "I never knew my mother," I said. "She died of influenza not long after I was born."

"But that can't be true."

I pinched my nose and dunked my whole head under the water. I'd always wanted to do that back home, but our little tub was nothing like big enough. When I came up and opened my eyes, I gasped to see two little serpentine heads peeking over the edge of the tub, Bijou and my leviathan. They slid into the tub, and I screeched to feel them sliding around my wet skin.

"Oh, don't mind them, they love a warm bath," Annalise's voice said from beyond the partition. "Your mother can't have died of influenza. You must be mistaken."

"Well, I'm not," I said. "My grandfather told me. Both my parents died treating sick people at the university infirmary."

"*Both* your parents?" she said. "At this university, here, in Chalcedon?"

"Um-hmm." I kicked at the wrestling little serpents frolicking around my ankles.

"I wonder," she said. "I heard of a serpentina cousin, years ago, who left Merlia to study. Quite a scandal she was at the time. They said she married a commoner."

I stopped washing. "Married a what?"

Annalise took a guilty little breath. "Oh. Tactless me. I'm sorry. It's just that, usually, if serpentinas marry at all, they . . ."

"They marry kings, like you."

"Oh no, not everyone marries a *king*, certainly, but . . ." She opened the drawer in her desk. "I must write to Grandmother and ask her about it." She peered around my partition, and I ducked lower underneath the suds. "Serpentina women live to a frightful old age, you know. Don't you know? Unless something happens to them, which is well-nigh impossible." She rubbed her hands together. "My land, but what a treasure you are. What a find! A maiden child from . . . what was it? Maundley? A born serpentina, and she doesn't know it. Why, that means you've never had your initiation . . . My heavens, can you even swim?"

I shook my head.

"Well, you'll learn in no time. I didn't think there were any of us here on the continent. I was sure I was going to be so lonely here."

She turned and looked out the window toward the sea. For a moment all her vitality left her. She took a deep breath.

"You're getting married, aren't you?" I said. "You shouldn't be lonely then."

She closed her eyes and laughed once, then again, a little too hard, too high, pressing her hand into her belly. "You sweet girl," she said. "You are just the kind of company I've needed." She wiped her eyes with a finger. "What's that you're wearing?"

Again I sunk lower in the bath, and this time I covered my upper half with a washcloth.

"I'm not wearing anything," I said.

"No, around your neck."

"Oh, that. It's a good luck charm."

She smiled. "And does it bring you luck?"

I shrugged. "Who knows where luck comes from?"

"Well said. Now, where are those wretched girls with your clothes?" She disappeared again. "I'll have the tailors up, to take measurements and make you some gowns. We will need one in time for the wedding—you shall be my maid of honor! And we'll go riding, and sailing, and perhaps you can even teach me needlework for the long dull winter evenings."

The leviathans' slapping tails flung soapy water into my

eyes. They needed no long introductions in order to become immediate fast friends. Was that how it was supposed to work with serpentinas too? Using that title for myself made me cringe. But how else could I account for it, this reckless way in which Annalise had scooped me up and adopted me? Half an hour ago I'd never laid eyes upon her, and now I was to be her maid of honor? Priscilla and I had taken years to learn to get along.

There was a knock on the door. "Ah, that will be your clothes now. Come in!"

The door opened. Too late I realized the serpents were still in the tub with me, their eyes poking out of the water like frogs' eyes in a pond. I should have thought soap would bother them, but perhaps it was nothing compared to ocean brine. The water wasn't quite so warm as at first, and my skin had begun to wrinkle. I looked forward to climbing out and getting dressed.

"Oh, it's *you*," Annalise said, in a voice clearly not intended for Rhoda or Erma. There were soft rustling sounds for a moment.

"Only three more days, darling," said King Leopold.

Chapter 26

I froze. The king was in the room! And I was *naked in the tub*!

I wanted to take a deep breath and plunge underwater, but that would make noise. All I could do was sit stock-still, growing colder and pricklier by the minute, hoping and praying that the leviathans wouldn't splash and give me away. But as if by some signal, Bijou ceased his playing and glided silently through the bathwater. My leviathan did the same. How did Bijou know? Did Annalise have some way of telling him? Or did he simply understand that he must hide when other people came around?

"You'll be ready tonight, won't you?" the king whispered. I'd recognize his voice anywhere, but now it was husky and low. I felt positively vile eavesdropping on this exchange, but what else could I do?

"Seven o'clock." She was playing a game of sounding like an obedient child.

"Don't keep me waiting a single moment," he said, and there was another sound suspiciously like kissing. Not something I wanted to be reminded of. "We can't keep our subjects waiting, deprived as they are of your beauty."

"*Our* subjects?" she purred. "How have they managed all these years?"

"Like me," he said. "It's been agony."

Lord love me, but if they didn't stop this soon, I was going to be ill right in the bath. My skin was wrinkling, but my ears were burning. Tender moments that are not your own . . . *ffaugh!* And the strangest part was the tiny feeling of resentment in the pit of my stomach that the king favored Annalise so. For having met him only once, I felt absurdly possessive.

"Darling," Annalise said, "a friend has just come to visit me. A young cousin, who's come for the wedding. May I bring her along tonight?"

"Of course you may," her fiancé replied. "Where is she? I'd love to meet your family."

Oh, no!

"She's resting now, after her journey," the princess replied. "And sadly, all her luggage was stolen. I'll just have some frocks put together for her, shall I?"

Another kiss. "Whatever my darling needs," the king said.

"What I need now," she said, "is a bit more private time, to get myself pretty for tonight."

"You couldn't possibly be prettier than you are now." And another kiss.

"I'll take that as a challenge."

I stuck my fingers in my ears. That didn't stop me from hearing the closing door, though, so I pulled my fingers out cautiously. Annalise soon reappeared, looking proud of herself.

"Well, Cousin Evelyn," she said, "we got that all straightened out."

I shuddered. Those last moments were horrible from every angle.

"What's the matter?" Annalise asked.

"There's a problem," I said.

"Oh?"

"I'm not your cousin."

"Of course you are."

She crossed the room in search of something, and I rose, dripping, from the water and wrapped myself in a towel.

"What do you mean, of course I'm your cousin?"

"Oh, we have so much to discuss, and so little time." She handed me a robe warmed by the fire. "You'd have to be a relative of mine to be a serpentina. It's all in the family."

I crouched by the fire and raked my fingers through

my wet hair. Nothing could surprise me anymore after today. "You mean, I'm related to the royal house of Merlia?"

"Distantly, at least," Annalise said. "It only passes from mother to daughter. Unfortunately, serpentinas have a bad habit of bearing sons, so there have never been very many of us, really. We will have to explore to find out your ancestry."

"Does it matter?"

"Why, don't you want to know?"

Water dripped from my hair onto the hot hearthstones, where it sizzled, then vanished. "Yes," I said, "I do. I've always wanted to know more about my mother. Grandfather couldn't tell me much. My parents were married only long enough to have me. They died soon after."

Annalise crouched and put her arm around me. "You poor dear," she said. "Without a mother to love you or teach you about your leviathan. There's so much you need to know."

I looked back into her face, shining with kindness and concern for me.

"Stay here with me, Evelyn," she said, "and I'll make a princess out of you."

What?

Such an invitation! But why? Why would she want me to?

Firelight moved across her face. She could be a painting.

A portrait of female perfection. Lips dark and full, cheeks flushed with color, features delicate, lashes long, eyes dark and mysterious.

Yet even as I searched her face, she watched me with such hope I could almost believe she was nervous, anxious to know my response. Why? Why would the opinion of a poor girl of no consequence from the provinces matter to a soon-to-be queen?

"Will you stay, Evelyn?"

"My friends call me Evie."

She squeezed my arm. "But Evelyn," she said, "is a name for a princess."

The knock finally came, and Rhoda-or-Erma appeared with an armful of clothes. Annalise took them. "Stay to help Miss Pomeroy get dressed," she said, but I shook my head.

"I can do it," I said, giving her a pleading look. "Please."

She hesitated, then nodded. "You may go, Erma."

Erma. Must remember. I took the clothes behind the partition and began dressing myself.

"Becoming a princess has never been my intention," I said. "I always wanted to be a doctor. Like my parents."

Annalise appeared and helped me lace the corset they'd brought. I began to see why dressing help might be needed.

"Becoming a princess," Annalise corrected me, cinching my laces tight, "is your right and privilege."

But why?

I took a deep breath. I'd never worn a corset like this one before. I wasn't sure I ever wanted to again.

"Princess Annalise?" I said.

"Please, Evelyn, no titles with me."

"All right. Annalise?"

"Yes?"

She pulled a purple frock over my head and began fastening buttons along the back.

"There is another problem. You can't present me to the king as your long-lost cousin from Merlia, come to see your wedding."

"Oh, tush," Annalise said. "Men are simple creatures, Evelyn. They can't handle complex information. They're all charge and attack, no nuance whatsoever. A little concealment is ultimately for their own good. What difference does it make?"

"He met me a week ago, when he came to Maundley," I said, gathering up my stockings. "He gave me a school prize. And I helped Lord Appleton recover from a feverish illness."

Annalise stopped buttoning and pursed her lips.

"A week ago?" she said. "He *met* you? You should have told me."

"You never asked."

She waved her hands in the air, near her face. "Let me

think. Let me think." She studied me like I imagined a mason would study a block of stone to see if it was solid and worthy. "We can do this. Of course we can. A disguise will be fine. After the wedding, it won't matter at all."

"What won't matter?"

"Why, that we had to disguise you." She experimented with my hair, lifting wet strands. "Then again, he's never seen you dressed in gowns and jewels," she mused. "That's disguise enough for any man alive. When he saw you, you were dressed like you were an hour ago, yes?"

"Near enough," I said.

"That's all I need to hear," she said. "Did he learn your name?"

"He did."

"Ah. Then ... for these next few days, why don't you be ... Marie. Marie ... um ... Bellinger."

"For the next few days?"

She played with my damp hair, experimenting this way and that to decide how we might set it for the evening. "Well, after the wedding we can explain that it's all a jolly joke, can't we?"

I took a step back. "But I don't belong here anyway. I was headed for the university. I'll go there, and your cousin can vanish. The king will forget her."

A hurt look passed over her face. "But Evie," she said, her voice musical. "Don't you want to stay and learn about your leviathan? And your mother? And all that you can do?"

I hesitated.

"I can teach you so much," she said. "Without a proper initiation, you can't begin to understand your abilities." She took my face gently between her two hands. "Evie," she said. "You are not like other girls. You are not like ordinary people. You were born for better things. You can make things happen in this world. And I can show you how."

I pulled away. I wished I knew better how to choose. In the last two days I'd seen my hopes and plans roll and tumble like cart wheels. I'd gone from homeless and hungry to apprentice princess in one afternoon, and while most girls, I knew, would not think twice about such a proposal, I felt only tired, muddled, empty. I wished I could lie down.

Something soft brushed over my feet. It was my leviathan. He rubbed himself against my foot and twined around my ankle. I bent to pick him up and cradled him against my cheek.

It's all right, Mistress, he said. *She doesn't want to hurt you.*

"How do you know?" I whispered to him.

"Talk to him in your mind, just as he does to you," Annalise said. "It will go better once you've named him."

I stroked my leviathan and tried hard to send thoughts to him the way he sent them to me.

How do you know? I asked.

She is lonely and anxious, my leviathan told me, *but truly happy to have found you.*

It worked! He understood me without my speaking.

Do you know her? I asked. *Is she someone I should trust?*

My leviathan pulled back his head as if he was surprised. *Not trust a serpentina?*

Chapter 27

❦

I accompanied Princess Annalise arm-in-arm, at her insistence, down the long corridors of the castle from lamp to lamp. This didn't endear me to the other ladies following behind us, all of whom seemed so much more accustomed to their gowns and jewels than I felt.

I had endured an agonizing hour of having my hair set in place by Dorothy, who took out her frustrations with life upon my scalp. Then she buried my tall hair arrangement under a canister of talcum powder. This, Annalise assured me, was a necessary part of my disguise. Dorothy informed me coldly that it was the height of fashion, and didn't they powder their hair in Merlia? There was pink powder for my cheeks and red tint for my lips, all of which made me long for a good scrub. If I couldn't bear the beauty treatments, how would I mimic the manners to pass myself off as a young Merlian lady at a duchess's soiree?

My corsets clamped me like a vise. I carried a velvet purse just like Annalise's, with my leviathan snoozing inside, and tried to step gracefully down the winding stairs in my satin slippers, though the steps were uneven and I couldn't see my feet. The women generated a roving cloud of powder and perfume, which made it hard to fill my corseted lungs with air.

Dorothy had looked askance upon my gypsy luck charm, but I refused to part with it. It would take all the luck I could muster to make it through this night without exposing myself as an impostor, a girl from Maundley playing dress up.

I kept my wrap close around me, and my face pointed down, as we exited the castle. The heavy door guard with the thick mustache and the belt full of keys was there, but he took no notice of me. Would to goodness the king might be as unobservant as he.

It was a cold, crisp night with a sky full of stars. We proceeded down the steps to the courtyard where the ceremonial guards still marched, their breath forming frosty puffs. Just beyond them, a pair of carriages stood waiting, their horses stamping their feet. At the sight of Princess Annalise, the guards ceased marching and stood at attention, bayonets up. Annalise pulled me closer to her, and we hurried on through that tunnel of men and weapons.

"Evie?"

I nearly tripped and fell. Annalise paused to locate the voice. But I had already found it. Not that I needed to look.

Aidan stood near the gate, close to where the carriages awaited us.

"Evie!"

My heart leaped into my throat. I tried to stuff it back down behind my ribs where it belonged. Him, here, now? Seeing me in these ridiculous clothes?

Or would he perhaps not find them ridiculous?

You don't care, Evelyn Pomeroy, I told myself. *You don't care a whit, and stop thinking you do. Don't look at his lips.*

Aidan waved his hat in the air and ran toward us. A chorus of shocked noises emerged from the ladies who were gathered behind us.

So much for gowns and jewels fooling any man alive. What was he doing here?

It's your friend, Mistress, my leviathan said from the depths of my purse. *The one you are fond of.*

Stop calling him that, I told him. *I'm perfectly well aware who he is.*

Aidan stopped a few yards away from us. He stared at me, his face full of bewilderment. His gaze took in my powdered mound of hair, my altered figure, my clothes, everything. He looked down at himself, at his canvas workman's trousers, his worn boots and faded shirt.

Princess Annalise's eyes missed nothing.

"Ladies," she said to her retinue without looking at

them, "into the carriages with you, tout de suite! Mademoiselle Marie craves privacy to speak with her acquaintance."

"But . . . he called her 'Evie,'" one of the young ladies protested.

"Her middle name, naturally," Annalise said. "We'll be along momentarily."

She watched the others leave. My need for privacy did not, it seems, extend itself to her.

"So, Evelyn," she said aloud, when the other ladies had been tucked into equipages by the attending footmen, "aren't you going to introduce me to your handsome friend?"

A stab of possessiveness startled me. I didn't like her calling him that, nor looking at him that way. *For the love of heaven, Evie,* I scolded. *She's only toying with him. And why should you care? One kiss doesn't mean you own him.*

Aidan cared. His jaw dropped. Remembering himself, he whipped off his hat and bowed.

"My lady," he began, his face flushed. Then he turned. "Mademoiselle . . . *Marie?*"

"What brings you here, Mr. Moreau?" I said, finding my voice for the first time. "I had not expected to see you after this morning."

A silence hung in the air between us. Then the Man of Duty reasserted himself.

"I've been looking for you," he said. "I thought you might come here. The man at the door, he seemed to think a girl of your description might have passed this way. But how . . ."

"So charming!" Princess Annalise said, before I could think of an answer. "Your kind, gallant Mr. Moreau has spent the day searching for you, dear. Do you have a Christian name, Monsieur Moreau?"

He looked at her feet. "Aidan, my lady."

"Aidan Moreau," she repeated. "A handsome name. Tell me, Aidan Moreau, what it is you do. What is your occupation?"

"He's a stonemason," I said.

"Of course you are," Annalise said, nodding. "I can see it in your build. The keen eye, the careful hands, the broad shoulders. But so young! Are you apprenticed?"

"No, my lady," Aidan said, holding himself a bit taller. "That is, I was, but I've completed my journeyman status, and now I'm searching for a post."

"Then you shall have one," Annalise said, relinquishing my elbow and taking Aidan's instead, which instantly annoyed me. Realizing it annoyed me annoyed me even more. She drew us close together. "Did you know, Evie dear, that King Leopold has promised me a wedding gift of a menagerie, to be built on the castle park?"

I shook my head. No, I didn't know. How on earth would I?

"I adore animals," she said, giving me a wink, "as you well know. And my husband-to-be has granted me that a building be built where I can take a stroll every day and visit with my beloved creatures. It will be the wonder of

Chalcedon. Scientists and foreign visitors will come and marvel. An elegant building, large enough to house spacious pens for bears, and apes, and even tigers. And there will be whole indoor pools for sea creatures, tortoises, and fish . . ."

"Why were you looking for me?" I asked Aidan.

Oh, I could read volumes of science books half written in Latin, but what I would give for the wisdom to read his face.

"To make sure you were all right," he said slowly. "Chalcedon is no place for a young lady to be alone. Especially at night."

Annalise patted Aidan's arm. "Why didn't you tell me you had such loyal friends, Evelyn?" she asked. "He *must* come help the workers with my royal menagerie. Mustn't he?" She elbowed me but addressed Aidan. "I insist upon it. The work has already begun, and you will live in the lodges where the other workers reside." She flashed her smile at both of us. "Then you can see more of Evelyn, when she is free."

Over in the carriages, I could see the faces of two of the princess's young ladies flattened against the glass to watch us.

"You will come, won't you?" Annalise said. "Tomorrow morning, report for duty. I will send a message for the architects to expect you."

Aidan looked to me for a moment. I got the impression he was looking for my advice. I had none to offer him. I shrugged slightly.

Aidan bowed his head. "And who, my lady, shall I say has sent me?"

"Tell the foreman that Princess Annalise herself has sent you."

Aidan's eyes grew wide. He bowed again. "You're really all right then, Evie?"

Princess Annalise laughed. "You can see that she is, Master Aidan."

Still he watched me. "You don't need anything?"

"Only just look at her! She lacks for nothing now." Annalise gave my arm a squeeze.

And still he waited for my reply. "It's kind of you to ask, Aidan," I said. I meant it. "Thank you for everything you've done for me."

He nodded, once.

"Congratulations on the post." I tried to smile in a neighborly, friendly way. A prekissing, back-in-Maundley kind of way. "You'll build a beautiful menagerie."

Trumpet fanfare broke out from the entryway to the castle, and a herald announced the coming of King Leopold, who appeared in the doorway.

Aidan took another step back.

"I guess I'll be moving along, then," he said. "Got to get home."

Home. "Are you staying with the Rumsens?" I asked him.

"For tonight," he said.

"Please give my regards to Mrs. Rumsen," I said. "And Dolores."

Aidan gave me a odd look. "If you say so," he said. "Good-bye, Evie."

"Good-bye."

Chapter 28

❧

"Curried duck egg, mademoiselle?"

Out of nowhere a silver tray of quivering half-eggs, art-fully drizzled with a fragrant orange sauce, appeared almost under my nose. Not that I had much experience being waited upon, but this struck me as obtrusive.

"Thank you," I said to the server at the soiree in the meekest, weakest, most genteel voice I could produce. "I would love one." He spooned one onto my plate. Its surface, I saw, was sprinkled with little dark, moist spheres. What could those little round things be? Capers?

I *smell fish eggs!* said an eager little voice in my head, coming from the purse in my lap.

Oog. I pushed away the curried duck egg sprinkled with caviar.

"You sang like a nightingale, darling," King Leopold

told Princess Annalise. "Did she not, my friends? Does not my future queen have the voice of an angel?"

"Of a Siren, even," said a young lord, who struck me as rather too pleased with his russet-colored beard. A lady slapped him playfully with her napkin.

"Right you are," the king replied, raising his glass. "To Annalise, the enchanting lady from the sea whose beauty and singing have ensnared my heart completely."

"To Annalise," they all replied, some more eagerly. Annalise favored them with a smile.

Annalise's radiant beauty drew all eyes in the room to her like fruit flies to a cut apple. She so far outshone all other ladies present that neither those ladies nor their husbands could take their eyes off her, ignoring the server and his platter of hors d'oeuvres. The ladies, in particular, could only soothe their bruised feelings by criticizing everyone else in the room—their clothes, their weight, their complexions, their gambling tendencies.

I amused myself by diagnosing and cataloging the illnesses I imagined I saw in those at my immediate table. Lord Franklin, jaundice, by the look of his yellow, flaccid face. He could use a less rich diet and some sunshine. Count Andrin, from the burst vessels in his nose and cheeks, was visiting the wine tray far more than he should. Both the duchess and Lady Louise Sauvage, I was sure, could benefit from daily doses of prunes.

Not everyone at my table was cold and haughty. I almost

wished they were. To my immediate right sat a pale young courtier who'd been introduced as Anthony Boudreau. He sat there, I might add, at Princess Annalise's insistence, and he'd spent the entire evening trying to draw me into conversation. He chewed with his mouth open.

"Eggs, Princess?"

Annalise glanced up at the server. Her fork clattered onto her plate. "Oh! I . . . I detest eggs." She waved the platter away. "Their smell nauseates me. Away with them, quickly, please, if you would, my man." She shot him an annoyed look. I'd hate to be him.

The server, a tall, oily, spectacled man fairly bursting out of the seams of his starched shirt and stiff suit, bowed and disappeared on silent feet. Princess Annalise whipped out her fan and fluttered it before her face.

"My dear," King Leopold said with concern, "I never knew you were so affected by eggs. Are you quite well?"

"Oh, it is nothing. Nothing at all," she said, still fanning madly. She took a sip of wine from her glass, then placed it back down on the table, but missed, knocking it against her plate and spilling its contents all over the table linens.

"Clumsy me!" She rose quickly.

Servers appeared like rabbits popping out of holes and sponged away the spill. Annalise sat back down, fanning herself, fidgeting, and watching the room. At last she rose once more.

"Pardon me, ladies, gentlemen," she said, "but I believe

a moment of fresh air would do me good. Please excuse me for a few moments."

The king and several ladies rose to accompany her. Ought I to have done the same?

"Pray, stay where you are and enjoy your supper," she begged. "I'll only be a moment, composing myself." And, gathering up her purse and clutching her skirts very charmingly, she hurried off toward the draped glass doors that led to the balconies.

Her departure left me only one empty chair away from King Leopold. I stared at my plate to avoid any danger of him recognizing me. This left me face-to-face with the offending egg.

"It was an odd song the princess sang, I daresay," said a weedy-looking woman clad in an orange gown. "Those Merlians do express themselves strangely."

"Come! Our manners!" cried the king, looking my way with great concern. "Gentle ladies, do not forget that this lovely young woman, Lady Marie Bellinger, is Princess Annalise's own Merlian cousin. I dare say Merlians are as apt to find our Pylandrian music odd, as we are to marvel at theirs. Isn't that so, Cousin Bellinger?"

All eyes at the table fixed upon me. What could I say to sound like a gentlewoman at all, never mind a Merlian?

"But that's scarcely a fair question," the king said, reproving himself. "Tell me, cousin, does music run throughout your family? Won't you favor us with a song as well?"

Oh, *no*!

"It lacks a few days yet before this young lady will *be* your cousin, sire," observed the duchess, seated at supper with us.

"Mere formalities," said the king. He raised his hands and clapped for our hostess's butler, who appeared instantly. "Tell the conductor of the orchestra, please, to prepare his men to play a piece for Lady Marie Bellinger to sing."

"Oh yes, Lady Bellinger," said Anthony Boudreau, working his way through a roasted quail. "I should be most eager to hear you sing."

"My lord king," I said, affecting a stuffy, congested voice. "Pray do not inconvenience the orchestra master. I do not, I confess, claim anything like unto my cousin's gift. I lack both the native talent and the will to polish my art that she has shown."

The king, who looked resplendent tonight in a crimson coat with his coat of arms emblazoned upon the front, looked unwilling to surrender. An admirable quality for a king, in general, but at present I found it extremely vexing.

"An instrument, then," he said. "Or perhaps an exhibition of dance?"

"My lord," the butler intoned with a voice of velvet. "At present, the orchestra is preparing to vacate the stage. Lady Fitzmaurice has engaged a circus of extraordinary performers to amuse us next."

"A circus!" cried the king. "I haven't seen a circus since

I was a child, visiting the Rovarian court with my father."
He raised his glass to Lady Fitzmaurice, the duchess. "Bravo,
my dear duchess. You do know how to treat your guests."

The duchess beamed. I brushed the caviar off my curried egg with my fork and blessed the advent of the circus. It had saved me from a ghastly fate, and I planned to
cheer their performance. The caviar rolled around my
plate, and I contemplated trying to flick some into my
purse for my nameless little leviathan, but decided the
risk was too great.

No fish eggs?

I'm sorry, I told my friend. *I can't give them to you here.*

I must go swimming soon, Mistress, he said.

I know.

I'll take him as soon as possible, I promised myself. I
remembered clearly this morning's disaster at the Rumsens' and I imagined my leviathan leaping into a bowl of
punch . . .

The king's gaze kept drifting toward the door where
Annalise had slipped outside. He seemed on the verge of
going after her. I thought of Aidan coming after me. My
thoughts had traveled this well-worn track all evening.
Why had Aidan come? What did he feel for me?

And why had I treated him so coldly?

And still, why, oh why had he kissed me in the first
place? And how soon could I abolish the thought of it? All

this aggravation, just because some brute of a neighbor boy, with two full lips but only half a brain, had used me for kissing practice. Oh, I made myself sick!

The party showed no signs of stopping. Servants cleared away the orchestra's chairs. Conversation buzzed at each table. Perfume drifted from imposing centerpieces of fresh-cut hothouse flowers. Repulsive though he was, it was tempting to lay my powdered head upon Anthony Boudreau's shoulder and fall asleep.

I raised my glass to my lips and paused. I had the uneasy feeling someone was watching me.

Someone was. King Leopold.

I met his gaze for an instant, then lowered mine. My heart thumped in my chest. Please don't recognize me.

"Cousin Bellinger," the king said, "did we meet when I visited Merlia last summer?"

I kept my face low. "No, my lord," I said to my roll and butter.

He stroked his close-cropped beard. "Are you sure?"

"Quite sure, my lord."

He frowned. "I could swear I've met you before."

Once again I felt all eyes at the table upon me. Wherever the king's interest lay, their curiosity followed.

"I am sure that my lord's far-reaching acquaintances include many young women who resemble me." I took a sip from my glass.

"The odd thing," the russet-bearded courtier said, "is how little you resemble a Merlian."

How I wished Annalise would return! "Oh, is that the circus about to begin?" I said. "I've never seen one."

Lord Redbeard favored me with another welcome piece of his intellect. "Small wonder, that," he said. "Those wild islanders of Merlia aren't civilized enough for a circus of their own."

"That'll do, Ralph," the king said.

"More civilized in Pylander, are you?" I retorted, before I could quite stop myself. "As it happens, I spent some time touring the countryside of Pylander before arriving here in Chalcedon, and while I was traveling along the king's highway just a few days ago, my coach was robbed by a highwayman!"

"How romantic!" cried the wispy woman in the orange dress.

"Not at all," I snapped. "It was brutal and horrid. He could have killed us all. As it is, he killed the driver in cold blood and made off with the coach, horses, luggage, and all the mail."

"Salmon fillet?" said the oily servant, who'd returned with a new tray.

Annalise returned to her seat, which King Leopold held out for her. His attention, however, was all on my story.

"Where was this, cousin?" the king demanded. "Which stretch of road? What province?"

"I was en route to Fallardston, heading north," I said. "I am lucky to have my life. The bandit was a lone desperado, but he was threat enough to subdue and rob an entire coach of passengers. Is this how the civilized peace of Pylander is upheld on the king's roads?"

"Lord love me, Cousin Marie," Annalise said, placing a fluttering hand over her heart. "You never told me you faced such perils on your journey. I should have died of fright!"

"Salmon *fillet*?" the server repeated, waving his platter before me.

"Yes, please," I told him, for he was rather imposing, but even at awkward times I was fond of fish. I wondered if I should regret my outburst, wondering if I'd said too much or said it too poorly to maintain my disguise.

The server dropped the fillet onto my plate with his tongs, and its juices splashed all over my bodice.

"For shame, man," the duchess cried, giving the server a scathing look. "Be more careful!"

Princess Annalise giggled slightly. The server's spectacled eyes closed in mortification. He made a silent retreat. I dabbed myself with my napkin.

"I apologize, Lady Bellinger," the duchess said. "These extras one hires in for parties . . ."

"It's all right," I said. Heaven knew, the purple gown was not my own.

"Lady Bellinger is a brave young woman!" Anthony Boudreau declared, without pausing on his artichoke.

"Nothing of the sort," I said. "It takes no bravery to be robbed."

"We're missing this marvelous circus," Princess Annalise said, with rather a forced smile. "How droll of you to find them and bring them here for us, Lady Fitzmaurice."

"Well, I only just heard of them two days ago," the duchess replied. "They came and did a demonstration for me, and I couldn't resist. They're Rovarians. They call themselves 'The Circus Phantasmagoria.'"

I abandoned my salmon and turned toward the dais where the orchestra had been. There stood the circus, two men and two women clad in tight-fitting, garish-colored, tasseled clothes with hoods that covered their hair. The women, especially, were shocking in that their skirts barely reached their knees, while their legs were clad in bright hose like the men. One man wore face paint and juggled colorful balls while the other, who was shirtless and wore no paint, juggled flaming batons. One young woman astonished us all by leaping and tumbling across the stage in front of them while the other woman twirled a spinning baton, then pulled a series of daggers from her belt. With them she impaled the four corners and then the center of a square target, with deadly precision.

The duchess's guests all gasped, then clapped. On cue, one by one, the ball juggler ceased, the flame juggler quenched his torches in his own mouth, the acrobat landed in an impossible split-legged pose, and they all bowed together. Then the ball juggler whistled, and the guests exclaimed in wonder.

For, prancing out onto the stage, in a tiny jacket and cap, came his monkey.

"*Chick-chick-chick-eeet!*"

Chapter 29

~⁓~

"Weren't they captivating?"

Princess Annalise hadn't ceased exclaiming over the circus the entire carriage ride back to the palace.

"Captivating," King Leopold concurred for the third time, drawing his arm tighter around her shoulders. He looked as though he'd rather be discussing other subjects with Annalise than the circus. He also looked as though he wished I weren't present in the coach at just that particular moment. But he kept up his manners bravely.

"Wouldn't it be delightful, darling, if they accompanied us on our honeymoon voyage?"

I was busy with my own thoughts about the circus. The man who juggled and swallowed flames was the scarred man from the coach. His lady companion was the dagger mistress. The monkey man sailed on *The White Dragon*, and I treated his snakebite. His lithe companion was the lady acrobat. All four seemed like completely different people when they performed.

But the strangest part of all, the thing that would haunt my dreams, I was sure, was what happened when the Circus Phantasmagoria was taking its bows. The little monkey loped all around the room, holding out his cap for coins. Whenever someone paid, he shook his or her hand, which delighted most guests, if not all. I had no coin for him, and I shrank back. But the little monkey shook my hand anyway. When he finished, there in my hand rested my gypsy charm. A vertebra on a dirty brown string. The snakebite charm I'd given to his master.

How had he recognized me? And why did he give it back?

And what if . . . but that was impossible.

What if it was not the man, but the monkey who recognized me and returned my charm? What if the charm had a mind of its own?

What nonsense. I slipped the charm over my head and felt oddly relieved to have it back.

"I had rather hoped," King Leopold was saying, "that our honeymoon would be a secluded affair."

Princess Annalise planted a kiss on the king's nose. "Darling," she said, "your vessel could accommodate the royal orchestra and half of Parliament, and we'd still have all the privacy in the world. But we *should* bring musicians, dancers, actors aboard. It's a month at sea. Won't you want some amusement in the evenings?"

He kissed Annalise's forehead. "You're all the amusement I plan to need."

"Darling!" Annalise cried in a shocked voice. "Consider Marie, if you please."

"Oh, don't mind me," I said.

A carriage is far too small a space in which to be confined with two lovebirds. I didn't know how they even had the energy to carry on. The clock had read two o'clock in the morning as we left the duchess's home. I doubted I'd ever been up so late before. I could settle down to sleep for the night right in the carriage . . .

The next thing I remembered was Annalise waking me up and dragging me across the courtyard and into the castle. I stumbled up the flight of steps and followed her to her room. I was dimly aware of the king lingering to kiss Annalise goodnight, but my main intent was to crawl into the bed she'd laid out for me on a couch near her fire. Dorothy, the serving girl, was already asleep in the other couch, playing chaperone to the unmarried princess. I kicked off my shoes and lay down, dress, jewels, corset, powder, and all. I let my leviathan loose from his pouch, and he curled himself up in a nest of hair right next to my ear, but out of sight if Dorothy should wake. Together, we went to sleep.

It was still dark when Annalise woke me. The fire had burned out, and the air in her chambers was cold.

"Evelyn!" She shook my shoulder. "Evelyn, it's time to get up."

At first I didn't know where I was, or why. I turned onto my side and moaned. "Why? It's still dark. And it's cold. What do we need to get up for?"

"Shh." She pointed across the room. "Don't wake Dorothy. Put this on."

She handed me some sort of clothing.

"Let me help you out of your things," she said, and I turned so she could unbutton my gown and untie my corset.

"What are we doing?" I asked.

"We're going for a swim," she said. "It's time for your initiation."

When I was finally released from my oppressive clothing, Annalise disappeared behind her partition, leaving me too astonished to do anything but comply and put on the new things. There were two pieces of clothing. One was silky and thin, made of a smooth knit fabric, pale in color, though what color, I couldn't quite tell. It had straps for my shoulders, and it ended in two leg openings instead of a skirt. It was so loose and slippery-smooth that it slid over my skin, which felt delicious. After the hellish corset, my flesh was now in heaven. The second piece was a rough coat or cloak with sleeves and a hood, and a deep pocket in front for warming one's hands. It reminded me of the humble clothing worn by friars and novitiate priests, who sometimes visited Maundley's parish church.

There was a pair of clogs for me at the foot of the sofa, and I slipped them on. "No stockings," she whispered from across the room, so I obliged and removed my garters and hose. I tucked my sleepy leviathan into my pocket.

When I was ready, she snuffed her candle and tiptoed to the door. She opened it slowly and peered down the hall, first left, then right, then, tugging at my sleeve, she beckoned for me to follow. She was dressed like I was. Her raven hair hung loose down her back.

"I can't swim, you know," I whispered.

"Yes, you can."

There was no use arguing. I followed on, holding a corner of her sleeve to stay in step with her. Our leather-clad feet made scarcely any sound on the stone floors. A single lamp lit the stairwell, thank goodness, but the light couldn't even reach the far walls, making the grand entryway feel like an endless cave. Instead of leading me to the doors, Annalise turned to the right and made her way down the long hall leading to the kitchens. Here it was less quiet, fragrant with woodsmoke and the scent of baking bread. Annalise pulled me aside into a root cellar that smelled of earth and potatoes. A narrow door led outside. It creaked as she opened it.

Moonlight made the castle's kitchen gardens feel magical. Annalise hurried toward the park, where perfect rows of tall, majestic trees still clung to their autumn leaves. We kept close to the trees instead of cutting across the open expanse of lawn, lest someone see us.

Breezes off the water blew right through my cloak and made my skin prickle.

Ocean, Mistress, my leviathan sang. *I smell the ocean!*

At least he was glad for this excursion.

We reached the headlands. Annalise's head disappeared from view as she clambered down the rugged slope that led to the water. I ventured much more cautiously. It was a long stretch of rocky, scrubby bracken between the slope and the stretch of smooth sand.

And there it was. The ocean, once again. All my resistance faded as I watched the waves, crested with moonlight, reach toward the sand, then pull away again.

Annalise pulled Bijou from her pocket and kissed his horned head, then flung him far out over the water. I feared he'd be injured. But he twisted in midair, growing larger, finally entering the waves in a graceful dive, and resurfacing a huge, shining, amber gold leviathan.

My leviathan wriggled inside my pocket. I pulled him out and made ready to toss him in.

"Kiss him first," Annalise instructed.

I hesitated, then kissed his head behind his horns. He nuzzled me in reply. The tip of his tail quivered. I flung him out over the sea. I meant to toss him gently, but he flew from my hand like a cannonball, writhing and expanding as he sailed. He dove into the water, reared up, leaped out and in again, growing each time, and began cavorting with Bijou.

Annalise kicked off her shoes and unbuttoned her cloak, letting it slip and fall off her body. The wind tossed her hair over her shoulders where it fluttered like a living thing. Her eyes shone in the moonlight as she reached for both my hands.

"Welcome to your home, Evelyn Pomeroy," she said. "The ocean belongs to you. You are a queen here. Come and see."

Chapter 30

~⁓~

There was nothing else in the world then but the roar of the ocean, the limitless stretch of dark beach, and Annalise standing before me, no longer a society princess but a wild creature, her hair afloat, her skin washed silver in the moonlight. The wind ruffled her garment, and it seemed to swim over her body. The wind swept over me, too, but I was no longer cold.

"Come with me, Evelyn," she repeated. "You are a serpentina, the daughter of a proud and ancient family, and heir to powers unknown among men. It is time to claim what is yours."

"But what kind of powers?" I asked, feeling once again like the schoolgirl, face-to-face with a goddess.

"You will see." Annalise took a step toward the water.

I wasn't ready to let go of solid earth yet.

"What is that around your neck, Annalise?"

She smiled and showed me the ornament she wore. "It's an unopened oyster," she said. "Inside is an exquisite pearl of unequaled size and beauty."

"How do you know, if it was never opened?"

"I know," she said. "The ocean keeps no secrets from me. Nor will it from you."

"Why do you wear it?"

She bent and scooped up a handful of sand, which she let filter through her fingers. "Each serpentina, as she approaches the age of womanhood, fashions herself a talisman. It symbolizes the gift she has inherited, and what she hopes it will make of her."

"Is that when she becomes a serpentina?" I asked.

"That is when she becomes a woman," Annalise said. "She is a serpentina born."

"Does the talisman . . . do anything?"

Annalise shrugged. "Perhaps. People do tell their strange stories. But I would rather think of it as the serpentina who does something."

"Do I need to make one?"

"I think, instead," she said, "you bought yours from gypsies." She parted the collar of my cloak with one hand. "There's another one, now," she said, looking puzzled. "What is this?"

I placed my hand over the bone charm. "It wards against snakebite."

Annalise threw back her head and laughed. "Snake-bite? You bought that?"

I didn't see why this was so amusing. "Yes." I was glad she hadn't seen my love charm.

"You sweet child," she said, "don't you know that no snake alive can harm you? Serpentinas are completely protected from snake venom. Snakes on land or sea will adore you."

I thought of the little snake in Grandfather's apple tree. And then, I thought of Grandfather. Who was I? Lem Pomeroy's granddaughter from Maundley, or the lost daughter of an alien clan of snake women from over the sea? How could I be both?

"We waste time talking," Annalise said. "Come into the water, sister serpentina, and swim as you were born to do." And without a further word she turned and ran toward the water, neither hesitating as she neared the waves nor pausing to shiver as she entered them. As soon as the water reached her waist she dove under its surface.

I watched and waited. Far out in the deep sea, flashes of silver and gold showed me the leviathans at play. But where was Annalise?

I hurried toward the edge to watch for her, dreading to see her drowned body drift to the surface. I was back on the beach by the sunken *White Dragon* all over again, and drowning in my own fear.

"Evelyn!"

I scanned the whole wide beach, looking for the source of her voice. A hundred yards or more away her wet head appeared, and her long white arm waved to me.

She swam that entire distance without coming up for a breath!

She dove under again, aiming back toward shore, and soon rose dripping from the water. Even soaking wet, her poise and grace were undiminished. She stood knee deep, holding out her hand to me.

"Join me in the water, cousin," she cried. "This is your initiation."

"A bath in the sea is my initiation?" I called back to her over the waves.

"Knowledge is your initiation," she cried. "Knowledge of what you can do, and showing the courage and faith to do it. Throw yourself into the water."

"But I can't swim!"

"Yes, you can."

My leviathan raised his whiskered head from the waves.

It's true, Mistress, he said. *You can swim as well as I can.*

But I nearly drowned before, I told him.

You didn't know before. I will be here to help you, but you won't need my help.

I don't want to be a serpentina, I thought, looking at the inky black water and at Annalise's outstretched hand.

I don't want to swim, and I don't want to spend my life alone, cast out from society. Nor do I want to spend life trying to hide my secret. I don't want to be a strange woman with strange powers. Once upon a time, a thousand years ago, all I wanted was to be a doctor and healer.

You are a healer. Because you're a serpentina.

I looked up, surprised. My leviathan, it seemed, could hear more of my thoughts than I realized. His emerald-cut head tilted to one side, and his jewel green eyes watched me without blinking. Wise eyes. Loving eyes.

You are magnificent, I told him, *even if this was not what I wanted.*

You are magnificent, Mistress, he said. *Swim with me. And, please. Give me a name.*

I took a deep breath, and placed one foot in the surf. It was cold, but soon I didn't feel it. I placed another foot farther in.

A name. What kind of name did one give a mighty sea serpent? Names like John and Harold didn't seem to fit.

I took another step in. Water reached the legs of my garment.

I reached Annalise and took her hand.

"If we were on Merlia, your initiation would include a swim at sunrise with the entire sisterhood of living serpentinas," she said. "What a thrill that would be for you. But for serpentina girls on Merlia, the initiation is mostly ceremonial. They swim before they can walk. They name their leviathan as soon as they can speak. They know their powers from an early age by watching their mothers. But for you, today, this is a true initiation. You face your fears, you claim your identity, you leap into the sea. It's an honor to share this moment with you."

Well, Evie, I told myself, you can either stand here with wet ankles or you can take the plunge. My leviathan, watching me, did a sudden sideways roll, coming up dripping. I envied him his freedom in the water, his complete power and confidence. And suddenly I was sick of standing on the shore.

I let go of Annalise's hand, counted to three, and then to four for good measure, and finally launched myself out into the water. My dive wasn't graceful like Annalise's. I more or less fell forward. But the water received me softly. I rose up with my hair plastered over my face, and sputtered out water.

"Take a deep breath, love," Annalise said, "and go under."

"I need to breathe, do I?" I said. "I thought perhaps I'd sprout gills."

Annalise laughed. "Your leviathan needs to come to the surface to breathe too," she said. "But watch and see what you and he can do."

My leviathan slid over the surface of the water to me and rubbed against my legs.

Ride my back, Mistress, he said. *Let me show you the ocean.*

"But what happens when I need to breathe?" I insisted.

When you do, I'll bring you up.

I threw one leg over his back and leaned forward, wrapping my arms around him.

I'm trusting you, leviathan.

I know.

Chapter 31

He shivered with delight, reared up his head, and dove under the water. I rode the curve his body made, rising high over the water, then plunging in.

It was a shallow descent at first, then I felt him turn sharply downward. His muscles rippled under my body, and I held on for dear life, my eyes clamped shut, my ears ringing with the pressure. Water rushed past my face, pressing my cheeks into my teeth. With each powerful beat of my leviathan's long body we went lower and lower into the black underworld of the sea, farther from the surface, and from air.

Then his pace slowed.

Open your eyes, Mistress.

What good would that do? It's night at the bottom of the ocean. But I obliged him.

At first I saw only darkness. My leviathan's body

gleamed, and from that faint source of light I gradually made out more. My vision changed, and things became clearer, sharper. A small gray fish fluttered before me like a blowing leaf, and then another, chasing the first. Craggy rocks covered with moss descended below me, a mountain range beneath my feet. I felt a moment's vertigo. Was this how eagles felt?

A school of fish swam past in perfect coordination, each one longer than my arm. They took no notice of us—except for the one that my leviathan snapped between his jaws and gulped down his great maw. Part of me—the schoolgirl—wanted to be revolted by the sight, but down here, in my watery home, I was glad he found a proper meal.

We descended until my toes skimmed the surface of the rocks, and I bent over to study their surface. They teemed with life and movement, with swaying fronds of undersea plants and small creatures I couldn't name, crabs scuttling and tiny fishes darting through plants and crevices. I reached down my hand to touch a clamshell and saw tiny things retreat, close, and fold in on themselves. What a world! I would have to find a book about sea creatures, if there was one, perhaps at the university.

Annalise, riding on Bijou, swam into my view and waved to me. A pocket of air escaped from her lips and rose through the water.

That's when I realized I hadn't taken a breath in a while.

Air, please, I told my leviathan. *Quickly!*

213

It's all right, Mistress, he said. *I'll take you up. Stay calm.*

Slowly, leisurely, we drifted up in lazy circles, watching bubbles rise faster than we did. I fought back fear until I realized, I'm all right. I'm still all right.

The sea grew darker and more cloudy the higher we went. Pent-up air burst from my mouth, leaving me empty, utterly empty, and now truly afraid.

And then we were on top of the waves, filling our lungs with sweet air.

Annalise and Bijou surfaced too, and Annalise slipped off her serpentine mount. "Swim to me, Evie," she said. "Kick and stroke, and be calm in the water. You'll be fine."

"No, wait, I . . ."

But my leviathan wriggled out from under me, and I had no choice but kick and stroke or sink. I tried to mimic Annalise's smooth strokes, but my arms were unused to this. At least I was able to keep my lungs filling with air now and then.

"Well done."

I had reached Annalise, to my astonishment. She grabbed my hand and squeezed it.

"Oh, Evelyn, Evelyn, what a day this is for you!" she said. "And for me. I feel I've gained the sister I've wished for. I thought, when I left my native land, I would always be alone. But now you're here, and there's nothing we can't do."

I pumped my arms and legs, trying to keep my head up.

"You're learning quickly. We'll swim again soon. Let's go to shore now, and talk."

We swam to the shallows and walked up onto the sand. Annalise helped me into my robe, then put on her own. She gathered bits of dried driftwood and in no time had a small fire blazing. We sat in the sand, toasting our ankles, and watched the shifting light of the fire, while beyond, out over the dark waves, our leviathans frisked and fought mock battles in the shallows. I couldn't stop thinking about the ocean world beneath the surface. Could I really go there and explore whenever I wished?

Annalise interrupted my thoughts. "Can you keep a secret, Evie?"

I nodded.

"Once I'm queen, things will change here in Pylander," she said. "And wherever I go, you'll be beside me." She lifted a lock of my wet hair and twined it over her fingers. "You'll have dukes and princes clamoring for your favor."

"I'm not sure what I would do with that," I said, pulling back. My hair slipped out of her fingers. "I came here to pursue my studies."

"Of course," she said. "All in good time. We're young, Evelyn. There's time for everything we want to do. If learning amuses you, by all means, you shall."

I flexed my toes in the firelight. Out of the water, being wet made me cold.

"It doesn't *amuse* me," I said. "It inspires me. There's so much I want to know. Especially about the body. I want to understand how it works. Like my father tried to do."

Annalise tossed a bit of bark onto the fire.

"There's so much I want to know about *you*, Evelyn," she said. "Your background, your hopes. If it's knowledge you want, then knowledge you shall have, more knowledge than mankind has ever comprehended. You don't yet know all that a serpentina is, my love."

I felt a flash of annoyance. I *knew* that I didn't know, and I wished she'd stop reminding me. "What are they, then?"

"What are *we*, you mean," she said. "Legend has it that our first ancestor was a Merlian princess who fell in love with a sea god. She sneaked out of her room each night to meet him in a cave near the sea, and they would swim together."

I was glad that in the dark, Annalise couldn't see my reaction. Who could believe such a preposterous tale?

Then again, who could believe in serpentinas?

"Her father forced her to marry a prince. From Pylander, as it happens. So she wed the prince, but refused to leave Merlia and her true love."

A scandalous beginning. I leaned forward to hear more.

"The sea god was jealous of the prince, and the prince knew he did not own his wife's affections. He followed her to the cave one night and challenged the sea god to a duel. Naturally, he was a fool."

"Naturally?"

She laughed. "Men can be such fools, love. Especially jealous ones. The princess tried to stop the duel, for she felt no malice toward her husband, but neither the prince nor the sea god would listen. She threatened to leave them both if they didn't desist.

"The prince stood no chance against his opponent. His body was found dashed in pieces against the rocks in the cave. But his sword was missing, and the legend has it that before he died he managed to get a disfiguring stroke in, destroying one of the sea god's eyes."

"How would that be possible?" I asked. "If any of this were possible. How could you hurt a sea god? If there were sea gods, which I don't believe, wouldn't they be beyond injury?"

"So you would suppose," Annalise said. "Perhaps it had something to do with justice being on the prince's side. I wasn't there. This is only how the story is told."

"Well, go on, then."

"The princess returned and mourned her dead husband, even though she'd never loved him. She called to her sea god, but, ashamed of his disfigurement, he refused to appear before her.

"Soon it became known that the princess was carrying

a child. Naturally everyone assumed the child's father was the dead prince."

Ocean breezes from the west—from Merlia—blew across my cold skin. Whether this myth had any truth to it or not, I took no pride in descending from such a dark, gruesome legacy.

"But of course, the prince wasn't the child's father."

"The princess gave birth to a girl with hair as black as ink," Annalise said. "When the child could barely walk, her mother took her to the beach to play in the waves. A leviathan appeared and wrapped itself around the girl. The princess ran to rescue her daughter, but the leviathan pulled the child out to sea. Instead of drowning, the little girl swam easily, and played with her serpent all afternoon while the helpless mother watched. The child returned to shore and asked for her dinner, and the leviathan swam back to its home in the depths. It was then that the princess realized that the creature was a gift from the sea god to his daughter. A protector. An eye, so to speak, symbolizing the one that was lost, to keep watch over his child."

"So she was the first serpentina?"

Annalise nodded. "Wise as a serpent, cunning as a god, radiant as the moon. She grew to be queen of Merlia *and* queen of the sea. And so her daughters have been ever since."

Driftwood on the fire hissed and sputtered.

"Surely you don't believe that," I said. "Does everyone in Merlia believe it?"

Annalise watched me from far away, as if she could see past me, and far out to sea.

"This is the legend of how we began, Evelyn," she said. "And here we are now. It matters little whether the facts are facts."

I turned away. If this was supposed to be my initiation, why did I feel more confused than before? I was a scientist. At least, that was how I tried to think.

I picked up a handful of sand and flung it out onto the sea. The grains sprinkled into the surf, sounding like rain on a rooftop.

"You can dispute the legend all you like, Evelyn. But how can you dispute your leviathan? Present knowledge forces you to think twice about strange old stories, doesn't it?"

I felt sulky and cross then. "What present knowledge?" I said. "I still know nothing about serpentinas. Nothing!"

"Ah," Annalise said. "And so, to business. For starters, serpentinas do not grow sick."

"I'd pieced that one together."

"You can speed healing where sickness is present, and your touch can help send the mortally ill or wounded to a swifter, sweeter death."

I thought of Jeremy Thorndike, the coach driver, and felt again that bitter sadness. Send him to a swifter death? Had I killed him?

No. I remembered his wounds. It wasn't I who killed

him. It was that ruthless highwayman, may his gold canker and may rust corrode his soul.

"You possess, as your companion and protector, a wise and loyal and mighty creature, the king of the deep, a master of concealment, a creature whose bite can kill or revive, even from the brink of death, as he wishes and as you command."

I'd seen that firsthand. Remembering that morning Aidan died gave me chills.

"You will have influence over things. Influence over others. In a room full of people, eyes will turn to you. Where decisions must be made, your advice will be sought."

"That sounds like all sorts of people," I said. "In Maundley, there's a little widow woman who runs the entire town. Wives would scarcely change their stew recipes without consulting her first. And I'm quite sure she has no serpent."

Annalise smiled. "You will remain young and beautiful for years past when most girls' beauty fades. And your power over men will be legendary. Other women's husbands will go to bed at night dreaming of you."

I kicked at a falling stick, sending showers of sparks in the air. "No thank you! I don't want a bit of that."

"You can't help it, Evie," she said, "unless you hide in a cave."

"Then perhaps I shall. I don't believe you, anyway." I

220

didn't, did I? "I've never been beautiful, anyhow." Not that I cared. I felt petty for having spoken this out loud.

"The kind of beauty that truly captivates isn't always apparent when you're young," she said. "It sneaks up on you, and on those who've known you for years, then suddenly they see you for the first time. This has already begun to happen for you, has it not?"

I moved closer to the fire. Behind us, behind the city, a pale glow crept into the sky, illuminating the tallest spires and buildings. Annalise noticed the change too.

"What does a serpentina do with all this power?" I asked.

"Whatever she wants," Annalise replied. "A serpentina is free to direct her life. And she gains a long life in which to do so."

"So, let me be sure I understand," I said. "We have sea serpents. We swim naturally. Snakes like us. We're good with sick people. And we stay beautiful and . . . influential. That's what a serpentina is? That's it?"

Annalise hugged her cloak around her. "What more did you want?"

I stared into the fire. "Oh, I don't know. I didn't want any of this. But you mentioned powers, and I thought of some sort of . . . magic, I suppose."

Annalise rose and shook sand from her cloak. "Bijou! Bijou!" Her call was high and piercing. "You're young, Evelyn. The young often think power must be measured like weapons and cannon fire. Ostentatious miracles, impossible displays. Someday you will learn that subtle power is the most potent. Influence is enough to turn the world from its course and align it to yours." She winked at me. "And with beauty, you can own it."

I rose and helped Annalise sprinkle seawater over her fire while our leviathans wound their way up the beach, shrinking themselves down in size, looking like disappointed puppies cheated out of a longer romp.

"Do all serpentinas think this way?" I said. "Do they all try to change the world?"

She shrugged. "Serpentinas do whatever they want. Every now and then you find one who wants nothing to do with the others, who goes off and disappears into society and devotes herself to alms and whatnot. Feeding the poor, tending the sick."

Like my mother. My vision blurred. I watched as a last bright ember refused to be snuffed by my sprinkled seawater.

"It's fine for them, I suppose, if it makes them happy," Annalise went on. "But I want more from life than that. And I suspect a bright, ambitious girl like you does too."

The last ember surrendered with a hiss and turned to muddy black ash like the rest.

"I don't know what I want from life," I said. "Not anymore."

She looped her elbow through mine. "You don't have to want anything now, dear. All I want now is a bit of rest and some breakfast. Let's hurry inside before they find us missing."

Chapter 32

I was exhausted by the time I reached my couch. I peeled off my things and gave them to Annalise, who hid them in the back of her armoire, and pulled on the underthings I'd worn the night before. In minutes I was fast asleep on the couch.

When I woke hours later, the sun was already in view over the ocean, westward. Late afternoon. Annalise prodded me out of bed and into a bath. Again I smelled like the sea.

"Hurry! You've slept the morning away, and tailors are coming to measure you. They're spitting needles at me, but I've insisted on a heavenly gown for you. You're my maid of honor."

I climbed into the tub. All I could think of was the sea. Could I really explore the water anytime I chose? Could I go for another swim tomorrow morning?

I resolved to wake early tomorrow for a solitary dip. I had a name to choose. I helped my leviathan into the bathtub with me and stroked his soft textured hide with my fingertip.

What kind of name shall I give you, friend? I asked him.

Any kind you like.

He blinked his emerald eyes at me and purred as I stroked him.

I *do love you, little one.*

He made a playful snap at my finger. *Who do you call little?*

I wanted to rest and soak in the tub, but Annalise was a cruel taskmistress. She threatened to drag me out by my hair, so at last I washed myself and climbed out and put on the frock she gave me. This one, at least, was not so restrictive and fussy as the one I wore last night.

"Tonight, for the masquerade ball, what would you say to this costume?" She held up a feathered mask designed to look like a peacock, and a shocking purple and green dress to match.

"Masquerade ball?"

"It's part of the prewedding celebration," she said. "Pylandrian custom."

"Must I go?" I said. "I don't want Anthony Boudreau chasing me around. I think tonight I'd rather sleep."

Annalise's lower lip pouted out, but then changed her mind and smiled prettily. "Of course you're tired. Young men's hearts may break, but I'll make your excuses. It's just as well."

"Don't be a goose, Annalise," I said. "They only have eyes for you. And you may have them, as far as I'm concerned."

Annalise made a comical face. "A goose am I, Miss Evelyn?" She honked like a goose, then socked me with a cushion.

I lobbed one back at her, and the battle ensued for a moment or two, our leviathans getting into the spirit of the thing and nipping at our ankles until we collapsed, laughing and thoroughly mussed up, on the couch.

"Just look at us," Annalise said, shaking her head. "Do we look like a queenly bride-to-be and her cousin bridesmaid?"

"I hope not," I said. "*You* signed up to be a bride. I don't know where this bridesmaid nonsense entered the picture. Gowns and whatnot hold no interest for me."

"That's bound to change." She pulled a gown from her armoire. "While we're on the subject of young men, we should give some thought to your future. Of course there's no need for you to think of marriage just yet—"

"*Marriage?*" I squawked. "What are you *talking* about?"

"That's what I say, dear, there's no need for you to worry about that yet. But you should still allow some of the more eligible young men to court you. Too bad tonight is a masquerade. If I could see faces I could keep watch for the handsomest young lord for dear cousin Marie."

I shuddered. "Please don't. Why don't you just focus on getting *yourself* married for now, and leave my future for later. Much later."

Annalise chuckled. "I think there's something underneath all this protest of yours."

"Hah."

I finished donning my stockings and slippers, then shook my wet hair out before the fire.

"Annalise?"

"Hmm?"

"Does King Leopold know about your leviathan?"

She picked him up from the floor. "Bijou? Little Bijou? No. He knows I'm fond of animals. Which reminds me, I'll have to inquire whether or not your stonemason is settling in well at his new post. What was his name again? Andrew?"

"Aidan," I said, feeling my face grow hot, for like it or not, I was suddenly and instantly reminded of that kiss. That infernal, unasked-for kiss. I clung resolutely to my original subject. "How can you not tell your future husband about a creature that follows you everywhere?"

"Oh, he'll learn soon enough," she said. "Romance requires a steady supply of little surprises. Men want to feel they possess you entirely, Evie. They're really incredibly jealous creatures. But he'll settle into the idea once the wedding is behind us." She stroked her amber serpent. "How could anyone not love Bijou?"

I watched Annalise fuss with her dress, and marveled at how different her thinking was from my own. Here we were, both serpentinas, yet so very unlike each other. I couldn't fathom deceiving someone I loved about my leviathan or my nature—if, that is, I loved somebody.

"Are you in love with King Leopold?"

She left off buttoning her waist. "Now there's an odd question."

"I was just curious," I said. "You are, after all, marrying him."

She smoothed the bodice of her dress. "Are you in love with someone, Evie?"

"Me?" I wasn't prepared for the question. "No."

She gave me a wink, then looked out her window. The sinking afternoon sun hung low over the water, painting the sky violet pink, like Annalise's cheeks.

"Have you been in love for a long time?" I asked.

She kept her gaze on the sea. "I've only known King Leopold for a short time, really." She went back to her buttons. "But it feels like I've been in love for a long time. Perhaps that's one of the signs."

"What does it feel like?"

"There!" The last button was done, and she twirled around. Her skirts kept on swirling after she'd stopped twisting. "What does it feel like to be in love?" she repeated. "Well, it's . . ." She gazed out the windows and down at the beach. "You can't bear to be apart, for one thing."

"Like the king said," I said. "He didn't want you to make him wait an extra minute."

She clipped an earring on and adjusted her hair in the mirror.

"You feel like you'd do anything within your power to see your love happy. Remove any obstacle, any nuisance, if it would please him. That's what it feels like."

"And how do you know when he is happy?"

Annalise forgot about dressing for a moment.

"Are you *sure* you're not in love with someone, Evie?" She watched me closely.

I shook my head. "Certainly not!"

"If you are, I can teach you how to win him," she teased.

I shook my head. "If I was," I said, "which I'm not, I wouldn't want to use any art for that. Whoever wants to love me had better do it with no special help from me. He'd better love me, leviathan and all."

~⌀~

I endured hours of being measured and stuck with pins by a team of tailors, all of them thin men with nimble fingers and squinty eyes. They looked like they must be related to one another—the Royal Ancestral Guild of Dressmakers, I imagined. Annalise described the dress she had in mind by drawing it, or nearly, right upon my person. The tailors responded in kind until I asked them to please stop touching me, at which they disintegrated into piles of apologetic dust. Finally surly Dorothy appeared with a tray of tea and toast and sausages, and I nearly attacked it.

A swarm of castle ladies appeared in our rooms to update us on three dozen trifling wedding matters. Acting as maid of honor required a whole elaborate ritual, involving numbers of steps this way and that, and bows, and promenades, and meeting the bride at the eleventh pew, and so on. The ladies made little attempt to conceal their dismay that I, a stranger, had upstaged them all for this coveted position. They could have it, as far as I was concerned.

The ladies made a great to-do of presenting Annalise with lacy garters they had sewn for her wedding. By tradition, she would wear the garters during the ceremony. During the party to follow, just before she and the king left for their honeymoon, the king would remove the flimsy, ornamental garters and toss them to the male guests. It amused me to see that this bawdy tradition, even practiced at Maundley weddings in the parish church, made it all the way to the royal wedding party.

The ladies left, and Annalise dressed for the masquerade. She deliberated between a swan costume and a mermaid suit—an obvious choice—but finally settled upon a snow fairy, dressed in powder blue and silver, with a snowflake-studded mask and snow-tipped wand to match.

"Will people recognize me?" she asked, turning so I could examine her from all angles.

"Well, they'll know you're not Lady Fitzmaurice," I said. "Anyone deeply inquisitive will be able to figure you out. But this might be one night where the other ladies of Leopold's court don't want to claw your eyes out."

Annalise laughed. "They're just a bunch of cats. Cats hate newcomers. They'll get used to me in time." She examined her reflection once more in the mirror. "Wish me luck."

"What do you need luck for?"

"Hmm? Oh, nothing. To not trip and break my ankle before the wedding, I expect." And off she went.

I loaded the fire with more logs from the hob and curled up on a cushion by the hearth. My leviathan climbed onto my lap for a snooze, belly-up. I traced the paler scales of his underbelly with my finger, and he wriggled happily. I let my eyes drift out of focus, watching the fire. I was glad I'd opted out of the masquerade. I looked forward to a quiet evening.

Eventually I felt too warm, so I rose, much to my leviathan's annoyance. I went out onto the balcony to feel the night air. Light spilled from the ballroom windows. Music from the party floated upstairs, and I leaned over the railing, enjoying the orchestra. Couples snuck outside onto the terrace and stole kisses behind large cement plantings of flowers and trees. I looked more closely. There was Annalise herself, as the snow fairy, whispering with the king!

We'd already seen his costume. He was a gladiator, which

let him display his well-upholstered chest to Pylander's noble ladies. I wanted to hide behind the couch when he appeared in Annalise's doorway, showing off his leather sandals, wide-belted loincloth, horsehair helmet, spear, and shield. After he was gone, Annalise nearly asphyxiated laughing.

But there they were now, far from the rest of the party, whispering to one another. The king pulled Annalise close and kissed her. I retreated back into our chamber.

I lay on the couch to see if sleep would follow, but now I was wide awake. Finally I decided to search for something to read. I'd heard of a library on the lower level. With everyone at the masquerade, I ought to go unnoticed. I pulled my shoes on and took a candle with me.

Once down the grand stairs, I headed toward where I thought the library might be. I peered around each doorway cautiously, not wanting to stumble into a billiard room or salon full of party guests. Finally I found a door with neither light nor noise spilling from underneath. I turned the handle. This produced no protest from within, so I pushed the door open.

This was the library, all right. My candle revealed dark leather chairs, a writing table, and glass cabinets displaying curios from around the world. Most of one wall was devoted to books. I let the door close behind me and examined the shelves by candlelight.

Then a movement from the shadows behind the door made me jump in terror.

"Oh, Your Majesty!" I cried. "Forgive me, but you startled me . . ."

He stepped forward into my circle of candlelight, looking like a true gladiator from ancient Roman days, not a king playing dress up. Here in the shadows he seemed larger than his true height.

Then I realized something was wrong.

Fear made me speak before thinking. "It's you."

Staring down at me, under the visor of a horsehair helmet, was a pair of brown eyes with gold centers. Hawk's eyes.

The highwayman. Here, at the king's masquerade.

"It's who?" he said, in a deep voice I could never forget. "Who do you think I am?"

I closed my eyes and tried to force myself not to shake.

"It's who you're not, I mean to say," I said, making my voice sound very young and silly, like one of the castle girls, like anyone else but myself. "I thought you were the king."

"I am not the king."

"It was the costume, you see." I kept my eyes riveted to the door. Trapped in a dark library with a murderer, and no one to realize I was missing!

"Four different guests are wearing this type of costume tonight," he said.

"I'm sure the ladies are thrilled." I reached up and pulled the first book my fingers touched from the book-shelf. "Let me wish you good night."

I approached the door, and for a horrible second he didn't move to let me pass. Light from my candle played over the bronze of his shield and the sweat on his skin.

He stepped aside.

As soon as I cleared the library door, I ran.

Chapter 33

I passed a dreadful night waiting for the ball to end.

Should I tell King Leopold the bandit was here? Would he believe me?

If he investigated more fully, he might uncover my ruse about being Merlian. I shouldn't let that stop me, though.

I resolved instead to wait up until Annalise returned, to tell her what I'd seen, but still the orchestra played on and guests' laughter spilled into the night. The book I'd snatched from the library was, alas, an inventory of tactical maneuvers and military casualties in the ground war conflicts between Pylander and Danelind, our neighbor to the north, some 175 years prior. Try as I might, I could not make diverting reading out of it.

I sank into sleep and dreamed of the coach disaster over and over again. Each time I was powerless to save Mr. Thorndike. The dreams changed, and Aidan, too, was shot by the bandit, and I had to choose between helping him and Mr. Thorndike.

I woke abruptly in the predawn hours. The fire on the grate had burned out cold, and from the breathing sounds coming from the bed I knew that Annalise was back, but asleep. I felt startlingly awake. My leviathan sensed me rousing.

Swim, Mistress?

A swim might clear my head of unwelcome thoughts. *All right.*

I tiptoed to the armoire and felt around inside for the hidden cloaks and swimming shifts. Hanging from a hook on the door were the lacy wedding garters. So that was where she'd put them. She'd made a little show of hiding them.

I changed clothes, put my leviathan into my pocket, and left the castle. When I reached the beach, I didn't hesitate. As soon as I could get out of my cloak and shoes, I ran into the waves. Once again the initial frigid shock faded into pleasant warmth. I practiced the smooth strokes Annalise had demonstrated while my leviathan frisked around, butting my side playfully. My body felt strong, awake, alive. There was nothing to fear here. Nothing to fear anywhere in the world.

I swam far out, took a deep breath, and dove under, letting my eyes adjust to the underwater landscape. A large, savage-looking fish with fierce teeth and a pointed snout and fins approached me fast, and I looked around for some means of help. Then my leviathan appeared and shook himself menacingly. The fish turned and darted off, and I climbed onto my leviathan's back. We rose to the surface and sailed for a time over the low waves.

Where are you taking me? I asked.

Down the coastline, he said. *I can travel fast.*

In the dark it was hard to gauge how quickly we traveled, except by the breeze on our faces. The lights of Chalcedon were far behind us now.

I want to give you a name, I said, *but I don't know how to name someone like you. Everything I think of feels so inadequate.*

Don't worry about that.

What are some other leviathan names? I asked.

He seemed puzzled for a moment. *We don't think of each other by the names the serpentinas give us,* he said. *We know each other by scent.*

Then why is a name so important?

It is for you, he said. *You can't fully love a nameless thing.*

I felt rebuked and ashamed.

Take a breath, Mistress, he said, *and hold on tight.*

With only that brief warning, he plunged down, straight down and deep into the water, and my ears were not happy about it until they cleared. My eyes tried to adjust, but he hurtled through the depths at an alarming pace. The rocky bottom rushed up at us.

What are you playing at? I said. *Stop!*

He halted, nosed around the bottom, snatched at something, then began his gradual, circling ascent. My head was still rushing with the changing pressure, and my eyeballs felt like they'd pop. I hugged him around his body and clung tightly until gradually we broke the surface again. He shook his whiskered head.

Then he took off again, skimming over the surface of the water at a breakneck pace. The shore was now on our right-hand side. We were going back the way we came.

Did you come all this way for some special fish you wanted to eat?

No fish, he said. *I'll show you when we get back.*

And on we rode. The predawn glow in the east began to peek over the edges of the mountains, and the morning sky began its majestic birth. What would it be like to greet each new day this way, swimming in the ocean and watching the entire, slow, miraculous dawn?

I closed my eyes and felt the rhythmic pulse of my leviathan's muscles propelling us.

When you love me more, Mistress, he said, *you will trust me more.*

But I do trust you!

My leviathan didn't answer that.

Didn't I? I was here on his back in the middle of the ocean, wasn't I?

When you trust me, you'll understand that I will never hurt you and I will always protect you. And when you know that, you won't need to be afraid, and you will love me more.

You hurt my feelings, leviathan, I said. *I have told you already that I love you.*

Then name me, he said.

Don't I keep you with me always? Didn't I bring you here this morning to swim?

He said nothing. How could I defend against the charge of loving weakly?

I'm doing all I can.

He took an unannounced dip underwater. I only barely caught my breath before the plunge. I choked back the impulse to complain.

We were back near the beach adjoining the castle park. A pink sky hovered over Chalcedon's towers. My leviathan slowed to a standstill in the water and curved around his great head to look at me with sad eyes.

One day, he said, *either I will die for you, or you will die for me, or both of us will die peacefully together.*

The pain in his words smote my heart. I couldn't bring myself to look at him.

I slid off his back and pumped the water with my own limbs. I didn't feel worthy to ride on his strength anymore. I wanted to run away from him, from the remorse I felt because of him. But where could I go that he would not follow?

I *am sorry*, I said, *for my ignorance. And my foolish, selfish ways.*

He lowered his great head down into the water beside me. The touch of his great scaly horn was as gentle as a baby's.

I am sorry, Mistress, for grieving you. Forgive me.

No, I said, *it is you that must forgive me.*

No need.

I *promise you*, I said, *that before this day is through, I will choose a name for you.* I set out stroking toward shore, determined to begin the day and the business at hand.

Don't promise, Mistress, he said. *Let it come on its own time.*

I reached the beach and climbed ashore, wishing I could start a fire as easily as Annalise had yesterday. I sat in the sand and dripped.

Would you like to see what I got from the sea floor? he asked.

All right.

He slid toward me through the shallows and onto the beach, and dropped a small, heavy object into my lap.

My love charm.

Chapter 34

~ ✤ ~

"Evie?"

I stiffened. My leviathan's head snapped up, his nostrils sniffing the air.

It is the one you are fond of, Mistress.

Stop calling him that, I said. I know his voice.

I turned to see Aidan standing on the headland, a shovel in one hand. The rising sun lit his back, and light streamed around him from every side. I slipped my love charm over my head and hid it underneath my clothes.

He has seen me. Do you want me to leave?

You don't have to, I said. But if you want to swim a bit more, you may. The sun is up, so you should probably think of hiding yourself.

Aidan began walking toward me. It was then I realized I was still dressed only in my loose, shimmery swimming garment, which now clung to my wet skin. Love of heaven!

How long had he stood there? I dove for my cloak, which lay nearby, and wrestled it over me.

When my head popped out, there he was, standing before me, looking like . . . well, like Aidan. Tall and brown and . . . familiar. That was all. Familiar.

That *was* all. Wasn't it?

The leviathan blinked as he studied Aidan from every angle, his head darting this way and that, sniffing like a suspicious bloodhound.

Then a rogue thought appeared. Did that love charm bring him around? Was he just like those other boys back home, who wouldn't leave me alone once I put the gypsy charm on?

"Good morning," I said.

"Good morning." He took an uneasy look at the leviathan and added, "Good morning to you too."

My leviathan nodded his great head once, then turned and slipped back into the sea, leaving me very much alone with Aidan.

I didn't want him asking me questions, so I thought the best defense might be offense.

"What brings you here this morning, Aidan?"

Aidan was still staring out over the water, where my leviathan leaped and chased fish.

"Sand," he said. "For mortar." He gestured toward a cart and a mule, up on the highlands. "I saw someone down here by the water, and when I took a closer look, it was you."

I rubbed my goose-pimply arms.

Aidan turned to look at me. "Why didn't you ever tell me about the creature, Evie?" he said. "All the years I've known you. All the times we played and fished together when we were little. How could you keep a thing like that a secret?"

So that was what he thought. Evie the deceiver.

"Does your grandfather know?"

All the things I could say rose up in my throat—defenses, explanations. My innocence, my ignorance. But what, really, did that amount to? I was a serpentina born. If I asked Aidan not to blame me for it, I was agreeing it was something wrong.

And that, I was no longer willing to do.

"I figure that must be why the fish always came when you called them," Aidan said.

I couldn't help it. I let out a laugh. Aidan tried not to smile, and then we were both laughing, absurdly, stupidly, contagiously.

We both stopped, and in the ensuing silence I felt even more awkward than before. And suddenly I wasn't afraid of what Aidan thought.

"My mother was like me," I said. "But I never knew any of this until the shipwreck. I guess there's a lot I never knew about myself until the shipwreck."

Aidan watched me closely. "What do you mean?"

What *did* I mean?

"I mean . . . about being a serpentina."

"A what?"

I dug my toes in the sand. "Serpentina is the name for women like me," I said, "who have a sea creature—a leviathan—bonded to us for life."

Aidan pursed his lips. "For life?"

I wished I could read what was going through his mind then.

He turned to look at me from head to toe. He laughed a little. "You're a far sight from how I saw you last."

I became conscious of my rough cloak and my wet hair clinging to my scalp and neck. I raked my fingers through my hair.

"Were you swimming? I thought you didn't know how."

"I do now."

Aidan bit his lip. "Teach me how?"

I took a step back. "What, now?"

He grinned as he pulled off his suspenders and unbuttoned his shirt. "Why not?"

I tried not to watch him. "I've only just barely learned myself, I—"

"Come on, Evie. Let's. Your snake will save me if I drown again."

I shuddered. Easy for him to be casual about his drowning. "Don't say that!"

Aidan dropped his shirt in the sand and wrenched off

his shoes. He appeared to hesitate in the matter of his trousers for a moment, and I nearly turned and bolted for the castle, but he pulled his suspenders back up over his bare shoulders and headed for the water.

"He's not a snake. He's a leviathan."

Aidan hollered when the water hit his thighs, and I couldn't help smiling. His back was toward me, so I pulled off my robe and ran into the water, diving under the surface, and surfacing some yards out, where I could watch Aidan from a safe distance.

My leviathan was by my side in an instant.

What's this, Mistress?

My friend wants to learn to swim.

We both watched Aidan, hugging his chest against the cold, taking tentative steps forward and yowling at the frigid water.

"Maybe this wasn't such a good idea," he called. "I'll just—"

"Oh no you don't," I cried. "You got me back into the water. You're going to swim."

"Well, aren't you going to help me?"

"You come to me, and then I'll help," I replied.

My leviathan butted his head playfully against my ribs. *Shall I teach him, Mistress?*

I couldn't wait to see this. *Feel free.*

The creature shot forward like a racehorse, closing the gap between him and Aidan in seconds. Aidan saw him coming and stumbled backward, tripping and landing on his tail in the surf. The leviathan caught him up in his coils and tossed him into the air. Aidan didn't know whether to fight or play. It didn't matter; my leviathan was in control. He dragged Aidan out to the deeper water near me and left him there.

Aidan immediately began to sink.

"Kick with your legs, like this," I called to him, "and sweep front to back with your arms. You'll stay up that way."

Aidan tried, but panic made his movements ineffective.

"Be calm," I said, swimming closer. "I won't let anything happen to you."

He churned his limbs through the water, but his face barely cleared its surface. Even the gentle waves crashed over him, till his eyes were wide with fear.

"Guess . . . my mother . . . was right," he said, spitting water. "She warned me. The Moreaus . . . don't belong . . . in the ocean."

I remembered Aidan's poor father, the sailor.

"Foolish of me to try this." Aidan kept pumping the water.

I closed the distance between us. "Hold on to me," I said. "I've got you."

He threw an arm over my shoulders and leaned on me. I laced my arm around his back and held his side. His weight pushed me under for a moment, but we resurfaced.

"That's right," I said. "Now just rest. Everything's all right."

Gradually Aidan ceased struggling. We bobbed up and down with the swell. My leviathan swam in lazy circles around us, splashing Aidan with the tip of his tail. Aidan began to experiment on his own and play in the water, always returning to my side if the water grew choppy. Or even if it didn't.

"So this is swimming," he said.

I nodded. There he was, looking at me, so close, his eyes so brown, his skin so tight and cold. For a moment I thought he was going to kiss me again. Then he turned away.

"Your teeth are chattering," I told him. "Let me take you to shore."

He came along, though reluctantly, it seemed, and I released him once his feet touched the bottom.

The sun was high over the university towers when we crawled back onto dry land and sat in the sand. I pulled my robe on immediately.

"I'd better get to work," Aidan said. "They'll be wondering about me by now."

"Tell them you were nearly eaten by a sea monster," I said. "It's mostly true."

He paused wiping his face with his shirt to laugh, then he pulled the shirt on.

"I've got to go too," I said. "Annalise will be wondering about me."

Aidan's face fell.

"What's the matter?" I said.

"It's just . . . How do you come, all of a sudden, to be the intimate friend of Princess Annalise?" he said. "Two days ago you were on your way to University, with nothing in the world, and now you live here?" He gestured toward the castle.

I didn't know how to approach his question. "You live here now, too, don't you?"

"In the workers' quarters," he said. "I don't go to parties with the king."

This annoyed me. "Do you think that's what I'm here for? Parties with the king?"

Aidan looked away. "Well, you never took your eyes off him when he was in Maundley."

"Oh, for pity's sake," I said. "He's the king. Everyone stares at a king."

"Well, what *are* you here for, Evie?" Aidan said, his voice lower now. "Why did you run off like that, from the Rumsens? I spent the whole day searching for you."

This was priceless. "You shouldn't need to ask me that."

How did we get to this awful place? Everything seemed so . . . neighborly, just a moment ago. Like old times. And now this.

"Have you written home yet?" Aidan asked.

"I plan to," I said, feeling guilty. "I don't really know what to tell Grandfather. Anything I say would make him worry. I thought, perhaps, after I reached University, I'd write from there." It was a hollow excuse, and I knew it.

Aidan was surprised. "You're still going to University?"

"Of course I am!" I said. "Why wouldn't I?"

"Well, classes have begun, haven't they?" he said. "And you're not there. You're here."

I hated how nothing seemed to slip by him. How dare he expose all my struggles? He couldn't understand about Annalise, and what she'd taught me, and all I owed her for it.

"I'll get there eventually," I said.

"What's happened to you, Evie?" Aidan said.

I looked at him sharply. "You mean the leviathan?"

"No," he said. "That's not what I mean."

I brooded over his question, and his nerve. Well might I ask him the same thing. From kissing me one moment to avoiding me like a leper the next—and he dared to ask what had happened to me?

"Are you going to marry Dolores Rumsen?"

Aidan's mouth fell open. I felt my face burn. Leave it to me to blurt out the worst possible thing. But Aidan only looked at the sand. He made no attempt to deny anything.

So, then.

My leviathan made his way up onto the sand, compacted now in size, sidewinding his way toward where we sat. He crawled over both of Aidan's boots, and Aidan didn't flinch a bit.

"He's a handsome creature," Aidan said, which disarmed me utterly. He stroked a finger over the leviathan's soft scales. Then he pulled on his boots and pushed himself up. "I'd better get back with that sand before they come looking for me. See you around, Evie."

I nodded and went to stand myself. Aidan offered me his hand. He pulled me up, then turned and walked away without a word or pause, leaving deep boot-shaped prints behind him.

Chapter 35

When I returned to the castle I found Annalise in her room, brushing her jet black hair.

"I wondered where you'd gone." She took in my wet appearance. "Enjoy your swim?"

I nodded and went straight for the drawer in the writing table where I'd put my University papers. It was empty.

"My documents!"

"What's the matter, dear?"

I pointed to the empty drawer. "My University documents that we put here the day I first arrived. They're gone."

"Are they?" She plied her brush through her hair. "Are you sure they were there?"

"This is where you told me to put them," I said. "Don't you remember?"

"Hmm . . ." She seemed to concentrate for a long moment. Then she gasped and bit her lip. "I'm sorry, Evelyn. Rhoda was tidying out that drawer, and she showed me those papers, and since I didn't recognize them, I told her they weren't important. She tossed them into the fire."

I collapsed onto the sofa and buried my face in my hands. Annalise flew to my side and threw an arm around me.

"What is it, child? What was so important about the papers?"

How could I have let this happen? If I'd gone straight on to the Royal University, as was my original plan, I'd be there, starting my studies. But now I'd lost my admittance twice. How could I get in now? The thought of going before Lord Appleton again made me shiver.

"Without the papers," I said slowly, "I can't go to University. I desperately want to go."

"Do you still? Are you sure?"

"Of course I'm sure!"

She rubbed my back. "Well then, in that case, when I return from my honeymoon as queen, I will decree that you shall have the funds and authorization to go."

"But you'll be gone a month or more," I said. "My opportunity to enroll may have to wait a full year. Couldn't you speak to King Leopold on my behalf so I won't have to wait?"

"Oh, my love, I would, but you know how busy he is today, with the wedding tomorrow. I don't think it would do any good, even if I tried."

I felt my eyes wanting to fill with tears, and I scowled

252

ferociously in an attempt to prevent them. "Then all my effort to get here, and leave my poor grandfather, has been in vain."

"Hush, hush," she said. "Surely you don't mean that. Why, we've found each other!"

I had no response to this.

"Will it really be so bad, staying here at the castle for another year?" she said. "You shall have everything your heart could wish for. Rhoda and Erma and Dorothy will tend to all your needs. You shall read, and swim, and take walks through the park, and visit the city and all the shops, with money to spend. And when I return, we shall be companions and friends, and my sole aim will be your comfort and happiness."

I blew out a long breath and tried to calm myself. "You make me feel like a brute for rejecting your offer," I said, "but I came to Chalcedon to learn to be a doctor. To help sick and injured people. And that's still what I want to do."

She gave me another squeeze. "Then you shall, Evelyn. I promise. Leave it all to me, and trust me. I know this . . . this temporary inconvenience is upsetting to you, but put your mind at ease. I will take care of everything." She gave me a friendly little shake. "All I ask in return is that you get me through these next two terrifying days."

I wiped my eyes with the handkerchief she offered me. What could two days matter now? It was Friday. The day would be spent in tedious wedding preparations.

Tomorrow would be the wedding itself. Like it or not, I was the maid of honor. My only job, for now, was to support and assist the bride. I could push University to the back of my mind for two more days. Even disappointed as I was, I could do that for Annalise's sake. It was the least I could do after all the kindness she'd shown me.

～

That afternoon I wrote to Mrs. Jeremy Thorndike in Hibbardville, enclosing money, more than we'd taken. I kept my promise to tell his wife and son he died thinking of them.

One duty discharged.

Then I tried to write a letter to Grandfather. I needed to tell him where I was. I should have done it sooner. He must be worrying about me awfully.

But the words that came from my pen were lies, and I knew it. There was no way I could overlook my leviathan and be truthful. What should I say? "Dear Grandfather, I regret to inform you that I am an affront to nature, a girl from a foreign land, attached for life to a huge and dreadful sea serpent. Did Father never tell you what kind of woman Mother was? Of course he didn't. If he had, I know you would have prepared me. In any case, I am now outcast from society, except for the royal palace itself, oddly enough. I will no longer be able to come visit you, but by all means do come and visit me, if you can bear up under the strain of the journey. Your loving granddaughter, Evelyn."

The shock would kill him. Maybe it would be better if he thought I'd died.

What a heartless thing to think!

I crumpled my paper and tossed it into the fire.

~

Later that afternoon, Annalise and I rode back from the cathedral to the castle in her graceful little carriage. We both kicked our slippers off our feet and groaned about the wedding planners. Annalise leaned back in her seat with her arm resting over her eyes, but I, who hadn't spent much time yet outside the castle walls, watched every sight that passed by. Such a press of people on every street, thronging the shops and the stalls and the vegetable markets! Elegant clothes and rough-spun brown trousers, carriages and milk carts.

"You'll be queen of much more than a castle and all its parties," I observed.

Annalise opened one eye. "Doesn't that make it all the more fitting that a serpentina should be queen?" she said. "Someone with extraordinary abilities ought to govern."

"Your confidence astounds me," I said. "I wouldn't want the job."

"And your lack of confidence is what worries me," she said. "You ought to know that you could rule this or any kingdom."

I saw something through the window that made me laugh out loud.

"It can't be them!" I cried. "La Commedia dell'Arte!"

"La what?" Annalise said.

Sure enough, there, performing on a street corner, their faces painted, still wearing the red suit and the black suit with matching trim, were Rudolpho and Alfonso. A small crowd of onlookers had gathered to watch. Our carriage passed them by, and they vanished from my sight.

"La Commedia dell'Arte," I repeated. "A comical pair of brothers, stage performers, whom I met on my journeys here. It appears they decided to come to Chalcedon."

"Comical?"

I laughed. "I should say so. And not always in intended ways. You should bring them on board your honeymoon ship if you really want to be amused."

Annalise smiled. "We already have the circus."

Then she sat up tall, suddenly more awake again. "But of course! Who wants to see a circus night after night? How many tricks can they do, after all?"

"Not a month's worth, I should think."

"But dramatic performers have dozens of plays in their repertoire, don't they?"

"I wouldn't know," I said. "It seems probable."

Annalise nodded to herself. "The more, the merrier. Of course!" She rapped at the window. "Driver, please turn about." The carriage turned a corner and began its way back.

"A favor, Annalise?" I said.

"Yes?"

"I . . . would rather that they not know it is I who pointed them out to you. Perhaps that could be a surprise for after the voyage. I'll just stay in the carriage."

Annalise waved her hand. "As you wish," she said. "Let the driver make the request."

The offer was soon extended. Even inside the carriage we could hear their effusive response. The driver told them to be ready at the docks where The Starlight, King Leopold's honeymoon ship, would depart by sunset tomorrow. Finally we drove on.

"Is it really tomorrow that you get married, Annalise?" I said. "Become a wife and a queen, all in one day?"

She closed her eyes. "I'll just be glad when it's all over."

"Aren't you looking forward to your wedding day?"

Her smile seemed tired. "Very much," she said. "After tomorrow, my love and I will have each other always. Even so, I'll be glad when the day is behind me."

Chapter 36

That night I lay on my couch talking silently to my leviathan, who was curled up once more in his favorite spot, next to my ear, half-hidden by my hair.

Annalise says you and Bijou aren't allowed to come to the wedding tomorrow, I told him. *She wants you to wait in the sea.*

He made a hiss of displeasure. *I won't make a single sound. I won't cause any trouble.*

That's what I told Annalise, I said. *I don't want to stand there in that huge cathedral of people without you there.*

What if something goes wrong, or someone tries to hurt you?

It's a wedding, not a war, I said. *People will be on their best behavior.*

People, as a whole, don't have any such thing as good behavior, he said, with a self-righteous sniff.

And you think they're food, I said. *You're a fine one to talk.*

You must come and fetch me as soon as the wedding is done, Mistress, he said. *I'll be miserable until you return.*

Do you need me that badly? I asked. *How did you manage all these years?*

He shuddered. *I don't want to talk about it.*

How could I not love something that devoted? I ran my finger down his soft back.

I made a promise to you this morning, leviathan.

I remember. I told you not to.

But I intend to keep my promise, and give you your name, I said.

Have you found a name?

I think so. Would you like to hear it?

He wriggled. *Please!*

It is the name of someone very dear to me. Someone I miss.

Oh?

Someone who taught me much, just as you have.

I had the sense he was working very hard to stay still and quiet.

It also means "clear," "pale," and "light," all of which seem to fit you, my handsome boy.

He held his jewel-cut head a bit higher.

My beloved teacher back home, the one who inspired me to become a scholar, was called Sister Claire.

He tilted his head to one side.

If we take the "e" off the end—not that you need to worry about spellings—it can be a name for a man.

He blinked at me.

May I call you Clair?

He climbed up onto my neck, which tickled me, and slid over and around my charms and onto my breastbone.

Clair, he said. *Clair.*

I found myself holding my breath, waiting for his verdict.

His whiskers twitched, and his wise eyes looked into mine.

Thank you, Mistress. I will be Clair to you.

I felt shy using the new name, but I made myself try.

You're welcome. Clair.

Chapter 37

~⁓~

"You look quite nice, Lady Bellinger."

We stood in an antechamber to the rear of Saint Bartholemew's Cathedral, a bridesmaid and I, milling around with the rest of the wedding party, waiting for the ceremony to begin. I was miserable, corseted and powdered and coiffed and swathed in more lace than the entire village of Maundley possessed, but all I could think of was Clair, in the bay, banned from the wedding. I couldn't hear his thoughts from this far away, and his absence was worse than a headache.

"Thank you," I told the bridesmaid, whose name I'd never learned. "You look nice also."

She nodded and drifted on, not in the mood for conversation. The feeling was mutual.

I peeked through an opening in the wall to see thousands of wedding guests, gorgeously dressed and peering through opera glasses at one another, no doubt comparing tailors. All the wealthy and noble of Pylander were gathered there, as well as guests from neighboring kingdoms. The aisle, which seemed long enough during yesterday's rehearsal, now stretched a hundred miles past those staring eyes to the nave with the altar, where priests prepared bread and wine for the bishop, who would perform the wedding mass. And I, Evie Pomeroy, who until recently was no more than a schoolgirl from Maundley, must walk that lonely aisle in minutes, as the closest attendant to the princess. Soon, queen.

The orchestra began to play the first processional song.

"My garters!" Annalise whispered to the other ladies. "I've forgotten to wear my wedding garters!"

The bridesmaids erupted into shocked whispers at this news.

"I *must* have my garters before the wedding reception," she said.

"I know where they are," I said. "I'll get them for you as soon as we're back."

A bridesmaid peered through a gap between the doors, saw the terrifying spectacle I'd just seen, and fainted, tumbling onto the floor and crushing her bouquet. The knights present all offered competing suggestions, while the ladies gasped beautifully.

How could people be so useless? I dropped my bouquet and rolled the girl over onto her back, straightening out her legs comfortably, and fanning the air in front of her face.

"Has anyone got smelling salts?" I asked the room at large. Of course no one did. I examined the pink mark on her forehead where she'd hit the floor, and determined that no serious swelling seemed to be taking place. She'd do no worse than bruise, it seemed.

"I knew I'd seen you before!"

I was too busy fanning the girl's face with my hand to pay much attention. It was a man's voice speaking, but whose, I didn't have time to find out.

"You'll have to tell the orchestra to play another song," Annalise told someone. "Quickly. We won't be ready to start."

"This girl hasn't revived yet," I said to anyone listening. "That should be our first concern."

"You're the healer girl. From . . . Maundley. Oh, what was her name?" The king was no longer addressing me, but consulting his own memory.

Oh, *no.*

I looked to Annalise for my cue, but her mouth was set in a line. "Darling, which knight could sit out and tend Joan? It won't do to have an imbalanced number of men and ladies."

"Evelyn," the undistracted king said. "You said your name was Evelyn. I see by your expression that I am right."

The fainted girl in my arms took a sudden, noisy breath, and at last I could do the same.

"What happened?" she said, noting the other brides-maids glaring at her.

"You fainted and hit your head," I said. "You would bene-fit from some rest. You'd probably better not walk down the aisle."

The girl nodded. She wouldn't need to be told twice.

"Darling," the king said to Annalise, who clutched his arm, "you told me she was your cousin Marie, from Merlia. Yet I saw her myself, in the Pylandrian provinces, perform-ing school recitations. One of my own subjects."

I dreaded to see Annalise's face. Her eyes flashed at me with annoyance for just a moment, then she reached up on tiptoe and kissed the king's cheek.

"The music has begun, my love," she said, her voice musical. "I can explain all of this, this harmless little mis-understanding. But pray, let us not keep our royal subjects waiting. In less than an hour, the king of my heart will also be king of my hand and body, and then there will be all the time in the world for explanations."

King Leopold looked back and forth between us. A priest appeared, beckoning him and his knights to follow him down the long aisle and take their places at the altar. The king hesitated, then kissed Annalise's hand and followed the holy father down the aisle. One by one, the bridesmaids began their parade to the altar.

Annalise blew out a breath, and I ran to her side. I was

still stinging from her look at me and eager to make amends, though confused at where my blame lay.

"I feared this," I began.

"Then that fear," she whispered in strident tones, "should have given you pause before putting on a show of heroics because some giddy bridesmaid has fainted. Think what you jeopardized!"

I was stung. "How could I not help her? No one else was! It was never my idea to—"

Annalise lay a finger over my lips. "Hush. There isn't time. Forgive me, child, I am in error here. It is not I that speaks to you so harshly. It's the terrors of a wedding morning. And such a wedding as this!" She nodded toward the open doors. "It's your turn, my love. Have no fear. I will repair everything. Now, go."

The last bridesmaid had left. It was time for me to walk into the abyss. I forgave her freely. Of course she was agitated by the wedding. The king's discovery had rattled me too.

Through the chapel doors I passed. One step. And step again. Right foot, pause. Then left, pause. I held my head high and straight, as the wedding coach had harangued, and painted on my lips the angelic, modest, maidenly smile we'd practiced. One step. And step again.

Ten thousand eyes were glued to me for that entire long walk, until I reached the priest, and then Annalise would enter and divert their attention from me.

The chapel itself was a daunting thing, with a painted ceiling soaring into the heavens and marble columns bearing it up. The walls were lush with splendid carvings and gilt detail. All of it was so vast, so opulent, as to remind mankind of its small and temporary state, contrasted with the infinite. It surely worked on me that morning.

Every twenty steps or so I passed a pair of stained glass windows, in which artists had created huge, vivid reconstructions of scripture scenes.

Jonah being swallowed by the great fish of the deep.

David slaying Goliath with a stone.

Moses, holding the tablets of the law, and the rod with the brass serpent, which would heal those bitten by fiery serpents, if they'd only look.

Abraham, and Isaac, and the altar, and the ram in the thicket.

Noah, and the ark of animals.

The creation of the world.

Adam, and Eve, and the fruit. And the serpent.

I dared not look at the windows anymore. Instead, I looked back at the faces watching me. Step, pause, and step again.

I stumbled. There, at the end of an aisle, and dressed in an elegant suit, with smoldering brown eyes with golden centers that bored holes through me, was he.

The highwayman.

Chapter 38

There was never a chance to warn Annalise. The wedding, with its ceremony and its pomp, its incense and songs, stretched on like a waking dream, like a spell being cast. The final incantation of the spell would make Annalise a queen.

I followed the steps of the ritual we'd practiced the day before, and suddenly it was over. Leopold and Annalise were man and wife, and I was carrying the train of Annalise's dress down the aisle, and avoiding looking at the highwayman.

The sun blinded me when we left the cathedral. Welcome fresh air filled my lungs. Mobbing the streets before us, as far as the eye could see, were throngs of waving, cheering people. King Leopold, holding Annalise's arm, paused to wave to his adoring subjects. He planted a long kiss on Annalise's mouth, and together they hurried into the golden carriage awaiting them. I climbed into another carriage with several of the bridesmaids and their companion knights, and endured the long, slow ride back.

When we reached the castle, we were directed to join Annalise and Leopold in the grand ballroom, but I broke away from the others and ran up to Annalise's chambers. I hadn't forgotten her garters. I viewed them as a sort of peace offering for the inconvenience I'd caused her.

The upstairs corridors echoed with my footfalls. I entered Annalise's chambers and took a longing look at her view of the sea. Nature had served up a perfect September day, and now the sea looked bluer than I'd ever seen it. How I wished I were swimming with Clair now.

The Starlight lay anchored some distance out into the harbor, and there along the shore near the boathouse lay the boats Leopold and Annalise would use to reach their honeymoon ship. Before the sun set today they would sail away for their bridal trip.

I went to the alcove where the armoire stood and opened the door.

Just then I heard Annalise's chamber door open, and a footfall on the flagstones. A heavy footfall, that of a man in boots.

Some instinct made me afraid. I climbed into the armoire and pulled the doors nearly shut behind me, then peered through the gap to watch.

The footsteps made their way slowly around the room,

but my view was too poor to see more than a dark blur when the figure passed by my hiding place. From the squeak of mattresses and wooden frames, I gathered he'd flung himself upon Annalise's bed. What kind of outrage was this?

I took a gamble and pushed the armoire door open another inch. No squealing hinges betrayed me. But now I could see who lay there.

The bandit.

He lay on the bed with confident ease, his ankles crossed, his hands resting behind his head, and elbows cocked. Even despising him as I did, I had to admit he was magnificent, dressed in leather trousers and a jacket of dark suede. Underneath was a snow white shirt, again with a lace ruffle under his chin, and a red sash belted around his waist.

What could he be doing here? Did he have some violence planned against the princess—or rather, now, the queen? Did he expect to catch her in an unguarded moment, here, returning to her room? And if so, what could I do?

Oh, for my leviathan! *Clair, Clair, can you hear me?*

But I knew he could not.

Neither Annalise nor I would be any match for this huge man, I knew. But perhaps together we could be. Perhaps, if we both fought him off and called for help, some help would come. I flexed my fingers and toes, bracing myself to be ready to fight when the moment came, and in the meantime, to hold steady my place.

And there we both remained, listening to the clock tick.

It chimed a quarter hour, and then a half. How long would my absence go unnoticed? Would someone come looking for me? Oh, please heaven, let them come. My legs screamed at the agony of crouching so long, but I didn't dare change position lest I give myself away.

The door opened, then closed. Footsteps crossed the room. Running footsteps—was it Annalise? A servant? Whoever it was, had she seen him?

The bed squealed again. I moved aside for a better angle. Was he rising from the bed to seize her? Was now the time I should burst forth from my hiding place?

What I saw made my heart stand still.

It was Annalise. She lay on her bed in her wedding dress, most willingly clasped in the bandit's arms.

Chapter 39

～⚮～

She lay upon his chest, gazing into his eyes. He reached up and wove his fingers into her hair, which loosed it from its careful configuration, spilling her dark curls over both their faces. She kissed him like I'd never seen her kiss King Leopold before. He closed his eyes.

"How much longer?" he whispered. "You can have no idea how I suffer."

"Nor can you imagine my pain," she replied. "Only a few more hours."

"The ship's captain will marry us," the bandit said, "or he'll feel a ball in his chest."

Marry us?

"You're too quick with weapons, Ronnie," she teased. "You need me to civilize you."

His deep laugh filled the room. "I'll enjoy watching

you try." He pulled her close for another kiss. "What about the girl?"

She traced her fingers around the buttons on his shirt. "Evelyn? What about her? She's not coming along."

I covered my mouth with my hand.

"She's dangerous," he said. "She recognizes me from the coach."

"Nonsense," Annalise said. "She never once spotted you at the soiree."

"When I was dressed as a *servant*," he scoffed. "I nearly dropped a fish fillet down her dress, and she still didn't notice. But two nights ago she saw me at the masquerade. Today at the wedding, she spotted me again."

Annalise frowned. "I told you it was reckless of you to come to the wedding. There were guests here from Danelind. You could have been seen! Shame on you."

"I had to watch," he growled. "I had to see that stupid, stuffed-up Leopold thinking he had made you his. It will help me, tonight, when I finish what we've started."

"But you could have been seen!"

"So what if I was?" he said. "Why shouldn't the prince of Danelind attend the wedding of the Pylandrian king and the Merlian princess? Father's always saying I don't tend well enough to my diplomatic duties."

Prince Ronald of Danelind? I cycled my mind back to my geography studies. Danelind. Ronald. He was ... second in line to the throne of our former enemy to the north. What was brewing here? More than an illicit liaison . . .

"Oh, Ronnie, stop," she said. "I nearly died when I saw you there in the church. Don't gamble like that with our future."

"If I weren't a gambler, we wouldn't be here," was his reply. "I was gambling when I won your heart in the first place."

"And I'm bringing two kingdoms with me for a dowry," Annalise said. "Merlia is mine, and tonight, Pylander will be too." She kissed him again, long and slow. Then she sighed. "If only you hadn't robbed that silly coach in the first place." Annalise tutted with her tongue. "Killing the driver? I ask you! What could be more foolish?"

"Leave my methods to me," Ronald said, with an edge in his voice. "I told you before. Father won't give me a drop of money past my allowance. Hiring those Rovarians and buying their silence wasn't cheap." His anger cooled. "A circus! Quite the cover, no? As it was, I didn't make much selling the coach and team. But I found money in other ways."

Annalise said nothing for a moment, but stroked his hair. "You need me to look after you, Ronnie." She raised her body a bit, with a new thought. "Did I tell you? I had a clever idea to bring a pair of actor brothers on board tonight. It was actually Evelyn who suggested it. But it's perfect. Throws less suspicion on us bringing the circus aboard in the first place."

"Brothers?" the prince said. "They could get in the way."

"Not them." Annalise laughed. "They're a pair of imbeciles."

"It's your little pet I'm worried about," Ronnie said.

"Who, Bijou? I've told you, he's not a pet."

"No. Not your killer cobra. Your little protégé. Elizabeth?"

"Oh, Ronnie, leave Evelyn to me," Annalise said. "She's one of my kind. I only need time to work on her. She'll be an ally. Be patient."

My stomach churned. I felt sick at her betrayal. Was this where all her friendship and kindness pointed?

"She could destroy all before we've even started." He sat up so that Annalise slipped off his chest and landed on the bed. "She's a risk. You tell me not to gamble with our future, and then you keep her around."

She ran her hand over his chest, his shoulders. "You're ten times the man Leopold could ever be," she whispered. "Rest easy, my love. I'll keep her in my sights today." She made a motion to get up. "I'd better get back before they send a search party to find me. Where will you wait?"

"I could wait here," he mused, and my heart sank into my stomach. Please, no.

"Better not," Annalise said, and it was the first good thing she'd said. "One of the girls might come here looking for something. Just wait with the circus performers." She laughed. "I can't wait to see you in your costume."

"I can't wait much longer for this to be done," Ronnie said.

"Tonight, my love." She lingered for another kiss. "You only need wait for tonight."

Chapter 40

Annalise slipped away, leaving me once again alone in the room with the brute. Ronald. Prince of Danelind and highway robber? How could it be? It was beyond sense, but there he lay, brawny and dangerous, still sprawled upon Annalise's bed, his chin thrust high in the air. He looked like a man savoring a sure victory close at hand.

Would he never leave?

At last he rolled himself off the bed and stretched, slowly, languidly, like a cat. And, oh, how he took his time about leaving! Wandering aimlessly about the room, wherever his curious eyes led him—to knickknacks on the mantel, to the drawer under the writing table, even to the contents of a trunk full of clothes. Not that he took anything. He simply touched it all, evaluating it, rejecting it, like one sampling a finger's worth of every dish on the supper table, but declining to sit and honestly eat a plateful.

When he rifled through the clothes I grew truly afraid. What would stop him from browsing through the armoire? What was *wrong* with this perverse man? If he had some devilry to do elsewhere, hadn't he ought to get on with it?

If he found me, I knew, he wouldn't hesitate. With his two bare hands he'd kill me on the spot.

And then my leviathan, Clair, not knowing why, would perish in the sea.

My eyes filled with tears. Most strangely, this thought made me sadder than my own impending doom. I squeezed the charms around my neck and prayed for deliverance.

Ronald, the bandit prince, laid eyes on the armoire and took a lazy step forward.

So much for deliverance.

The clock on the mantel chimed another quarter hour.

He stopped and looked at the clock, then changed his course and went to the chamber door, passing out of my view. For two or three endless minutes there was silence. He hadn't left. Nor had he come back.

But then there was a click, the faintest of sounds, like a door latching far away. I angled myself around for a better view.

I could not see him. Nor could I hear him.

For a dreadful stretch of time I waited.

At last I tumbled out the armoire door.

Sure enough, he was gone.

The clock on the mantel said three fifteen. The wedding celebration would be well underway. Afternoon sun gleamed off *The Starlight* like a warning beacon. Such a lovely ship, shaped as if carved from a single block of wood by a master's hand, and was it to be the site of a assassination? The Circus Phantasmagoria—what was their role?

And the architects of it all were a bandit prince and my own mentor and sister serpentina. Someone I'd shared my full confidence with. Someone I'd set aside my dreams for.

What could I do? How could I stop this? Who would believe me if I told them?

The king.

I should have warned him.

I could have, after the masquerade. Or even today, I could have tried to tell him my murdering bandit was a guest at his wedding. He would have doubted, but I could have made him believe. My reasons for not trying felt so petty now.

By this time my presence at the wedding reception would surely be missed. Should I make an appearance, I wondered? How could I slip into my seat near Annalise and pretend I knew nothing about her plans? I wasn't that good of an actress.

Actress!

Oh . . .

Could I possibly . . . ? Would it work?

It was suicide. Almost certainly. But after my cowardice, what else could I do?

It *might* save King Leopold, and the royal house of Pylander, if my gypsy luck could hold.

~~

I ran out the door and down the corridors, not toward the banquet, but toward the servants' hall. Through that large hall I could exit the castle unseen by the wedding guests.

Noise of the workers' wedding celebration reached my ears long before I found the door to the room. His Majesty's generosity had ordered ale, roast beef, and potatoes for the staff. In happier times, this was the party where I'd feel more at home. No one here bothered with a corset. I sprinted along one side of the room, as fast as I could go, and made my way for the door.

"Evie!" a familiar voice cried just as I'd reached the bottom step out into the vegetable gardens. "What brings you here?"

Aidan must have seen me racing through the room. He ran to where I was, misjudging the distance and nearly toppling into me.

"Sorry," he said, grinning. "I've been wondering where to find you."

"Well, you've found me," I said, "but I'm in a bit of a hurry." Except I needed to pause for a breath. Curse these corsets, they barely let a girl inhale.

"You look nice today," he said. He looked at his feet and said, slowly, like there wasn't a king about to be murdered, "I've been wanting to talk to you." Then he took a closer

~~

look at me. "What's the matter? Are you all right? Evie, what's wrong?"

I dragged him farther away from the building, beyond any listening ears. A friendly, familiar Maundley face was water in the desert to me now.

I took a deep breath to tell my tale and instead burst into tears. Confound it!

Aidan's face melted into concern. He reached out a hand, then hesitated.

"Oh, Aidan," I said, "I've been such a fool!"

His hesitation broke, and he pulled me close to him.

"There, there, Evie," he said softly, attempting to pat my head despite all the powder in my hair. "It's all right. It's long forgotten."

I wrenched myself out of his grip and wiped my eyes on my sleeve. "What? You . . . you think this is about *you*?"

"It isn't?"

"No!" I shook him off. "I haven't been a fool for *you*!" Perhaps that was a bit untrue. "This is someone else."

His face turned violet, but he thrust out his chin. "Someone else, eh? Already? Some castle dandy?"

"No! It's . . . oh, never mind. I don't need to explain myself to you. You're a fine one to talk. But I haven't got time! I've got to get to the ship." I took off once more for the beach.

He jogged effortlessly beside me. "Why, who's on the ship that's so important?"

"Nobody, yet," I panted. I could barely think straight.

My mouth just ran away with me. "It's who will be later on. Those actor brothers, remember? Rudolpho and Alfonso?"

"Oh, them, is it?" He chewed on this information. "That just figures. Them and their curly hair, and their speechifying. Tell me, which one do you fancy, or is one as good as the other?"

We reached the beach. It was harder to run through the sand. Far across the headlands, near the boathouse, I thought I could make out La Commedia dell'Arte's garishly painted wagon.

"Clair! Clair! I need you!" I called aloud, in case my voice carried farther than thought.

"Who's Clair?"

"My leviathan," I said.

"So now he has a name?"

"Yes," I said. "He does. Do you intend to keep following me around, asking me unwelcome questions?"

He folded his arms across his chest. I noticed for the first time the Sunday suit he wore in celebration of the wedding. In Maundley, he'd be the dapper young man about town indeed.

"Unwelcome, am I?"

"Clair! Clair!" I called till my throat hurt. "Where are you?" I took a deep breath. "Oh, come on, Aidan. It's just that I don't have time for this right now." I avoided his glare. "There's something much bigger than . . . Oh, never mind. I've got to get on that ship. *Clair!*"

"Why don't you ask your princess, then?" he said bitterly. "Or I should say, your queen."

"She's not my queen," I said. "Not anymore. *Clair!*"

Aidan's eyes narrowed. "What does that mean?"

A motion over the water caught my eye. Clair raised his shining, dripping head from the waves and bowed in greeting to both of us.

Here I am, Mistress.

Thank heaven, I thought.

I am ready.

For what? I asked.

You sounded like you were calling me to battle.

How did he know? *I am. Meet me down by the boathouse in a few minutes' time.*

Up at the castle, the music stopped and didn't resume. The celebrating voices faded. I didn't have much time left.

"Was it a nice wedding, Evie?"

The question was so unexpected, so bizarre, coming from Aidan, that all I could do was gape at him.

"Saint Bartholemew's," he said. "That's an impressive bit of stonework, that."

I nodded. "It was a nice wedding. Saint Bart's is magnificent."

I looked around me at the beach, the castle, the vast city of Chalcedon, and the university towers, painted rose by the setting sun. And Aidan's face.

He was wrong. His was a most welcome face to me,

whatever fool thing he might think or say. I wanted to tell him everything, about Ronnie and Annalise and the circus and what was brewing, but if I did, he'd only prevent me from doing what I must do now. Maybe I even wanted to tell him for that very reason. But I couldn't. I wanted to tell him to send a message of my love to Grandfather, when all was done. But we'd had that conversation once before, one that I remembered too often and too well.

If I made it onto the ship, whether I prevented a tragedy or not, I was sure I'd never see Aidan's face again. I did not expect to survive my encounter with the bandit, his murdering lady, and their hired killers. Perhaps I could warn and help the king. But one thing was clear. If I made it onto the ship, I would almost certainly never make it off.

"Yes. Well." Aidan looked out over the water, to where *The Starlight* was moored. "Good luck finding your actor brothers and getting on the ship, then," he said. "As for me, I've had my fill of ships. Mother's right. Don't expect I ever will sail again. Or swim."

I felt the sting in his words.

"Good-bye, Aidan," I said, feeling tears once again. It took all I had to force them back. "I think you'll become one of Chalcedon's great builders. You'll make your mother proud." He watched me without speaking. "I truly wish you well. But now I have to go."

Chapter 41

❦

Dressed as I was, I ran as fast as I could through the sand to the royal jetty and boathouse where the king's vessels were lovingly kept. The place seemed deserted. Was I too late?

Clair, I called to him silently. *Don't meet me in your full size. Can you make yourself small?*

I already have, Mistress. Come to the pebbly part of the beach.

I found Clair curled and concealed among the shiny gray stones and scooped him up. There was plenty of room for him inside my billowy sleeve, though he tickled awfully. I ran to La Commedia's wagon and rapped on the door. They didn't answer.

I ran to the edge of the dock and looked out over the water at the ship, but the setting sun blinded me. The ship was barely more than a dark spot, hundreds of yards out. This would be much harder to pull off if I ended up needing to swim.

"Looking for someone, miss?"

I whirled around to see a man sweeping the doorway of the boathouse. He was short and stocky and wore a fisherman's sweater. He had all the look of a retired sailor.

"The actors," I said, pointing to the wagon. "The ones going on the honeymoon voyage. Where are they?"

"Already on board," the boat keeper replied. "Them and the circus folks. There's a few crew members still gathering supplies. They're going to take the dinghy out and board when the king and queen do."

I couldn't very well sneak my way aboard that dinghy.

It was time to start practicing my acting skills.

"Oh, woe is me!" I cried. "I have missed my chance to join the ship, and I, I am the actress that the two gentlemen depend upon for all their shows."

The sailor squinted at me suspiciously.

"You? An actress?"

"Of course. How shall they perform tales of love without a young lady in the company?"

"Begging your pardon, miss, but you look a bit too respectable and, er, uppity for that sort of thing."

I held my nose high. "Uppity? How dare you? The stage is a noble art."

"That's not how I hear it. Especially about young ladies that act."

I sniffed. "I can't concern myself with what you hear. Kindly row me to the ship, sir, if you have any

285

compassion in you. Only let me first fetch my things from the wagon."

The sailor chewed on his lower lip, then shrugged. "Not sure as I've got much compassion in me, whatever that is, but I do have time to kill, so I don't care if I rows you out there to the ship or not. It's no skin off my pants."

I headed for the wagon, then turned and looked at him. "*Skin* off your *pants*?"

"Ain't you never heard the expression?"

"Oh, never mind."

I rattled the flimsy lock that held the wagon door shut, then shoved my entire weight against it, and the wood around the lock splintered easily. Inside the wagon were trunks lying open, with costumes and props strewn about helter-skelter. There wasn't much light to go by, but by feeling around I located wigs, trousers, wooden swords, and even sparkling gowns. Which of the brothers wore these, I wondered? I found a colorful skirt and a dark sweater, a black wig, and a pair of suede boots, stuffed them all into a sack, and presented myself to the boat keeper. He helped me into a small skiff and rowed me out toward *The Starlight*.

His strokes were straight and deep, and in no time he was calling to the captain to announce my arrival. The captain frowned down at us, but he accepted my explanation that I was one of the acting troupe, and lowered a rope ladder. Clenching my sack of costumes between my teeth and cursing the yards of silk and lace that made up my puffy skirt, I climbed on board.

"Odd thing," the captain said, frowning at my appearance. "None of those performing groups mentioned they were expecting anyone else to come along later."

Think fast, Evie! "We had an argument," I said, trying to borrow from the brothers' thick accents. "I swore to them both that I would never look at their donkey faces again. But then, today, I am thinking to myself, the poor king and queen, all alone on the ship, with plays that only my brothers . . ."

"Your brothers?"

"*Si*," I said, feeling my face grow red. "It's family. And I am thinking to myself, when my brothers perform without me, the audience, she will be yawning and wishing for death, rather than watch my tedious brothers. So I come. For the king. And his beautiful bride. To save the show. You see?"

The captain's eyes rolled back in his head. "Come along. I haven't got time to listen to this. You're one of them, all right. They do nothing but yap, yap, yap."

He led me to a cabin door. "They're in there," he said. "We pull anchor as soon as Their Majesties arrive, whenever that may be. You're to be ready to perform on short notice." He turned and strode off.

I took a deep breath and opened the door.

Rudolpho and Alfonso lay on bunks on opposite sides

of the room, their long legs dangling off the ends, their feet bare. One of them—Rudolpho, I was fairly certain—sat up so quickly he cracked his head on the empty bunk above him.

"*Signorina!*"

"The maiden in distress!" cried Alfonso. Then he frowned suspiciously. "If she *is* a maiden."

"Shut your mouth, idiot," Rudolpho cried. "*La bella donna* comes to us, and you, you say the stupid, offensive things."

"But why?" Alfonso said. "Why is she coming to us? Last time we see her, she is at that horrid place in Fallardston, that Badger Inn, where the hostess, she is pouring water in our beer and making us share the coldest room in the house. Now we perform for the king and queen! On a boat! From the castle in Chalcedon. And in walks la signorina? Where is the sense in all this?"

"Hush, both of you, please," I said, holding up my hands in front of me. "I . . . I came to take you up on your offer."

At this, Rudolpho jumped up from his bunk, seized my arm, and began kissing me all the way up from hand to shoulder.

"Not *that* offer," I said. "The offer to act with you. To join your company as an actress."

This didn't deter Rudolpho from kissing his way back down my arm, but Alfonso folded his arms across his chest. "See? When we are two poor traveling actors in Fallardston, she rejects our offer, but now, *phut!* We play for the king, and now she thinks to join us. I am wanting to know why. What is at the bottom of all this?"

I was spared from answering by the sound of voices coming from the water.

"Is that the king?" I said.

Rudolpho peered through the small porthole in their cabin. "No," he said. "It's just a boat carrying provisions and crew. They have been coming and going all day."

"Just as well," I said. "We need more time to practice our act."

"*Our* act?" Alfonso was going to be hard to win over.

"Out with both of you, if you please," I said, waving my costume at them. "I need to change my clothes."

"Don't mind us, signorina," Rudolpho said. "We won't watch."

"Out!"

They went grumbling and protesting, but they went. I wrestled myself out of my gown, popping several tiny buttons off the back in the process, and tried to make a plan.

I'm here on board the ship. That's enough of a miracle that it ought to give me hope.

But how can I protect the king?

And an actress? How can I pull that off?

I could never fool Annalise. Even if my head were shaved and my skin painted green, Annalise would know me for who I was. Bijou would know Clair was there, and he'd tell her.

I had walked into a death trap. But I knew that before I came.

I pulled Clair from out of my sleeve.

I'm going to have to keep you in the water, Clair.

He rubbed his chin along the palm of my hand. *I'll be ready. When do we fight?*

My skin felt cold and clammy at the thought. Fight?

Clair, I said. *Tell me. Does a serpentina ever go bad? What happens then?*

Clair seemed to puzzle over this question for some time. *A serpentina,* he finally said, *just is. I am not sure about good or bad.*

Have two serpentinas ever fought each other?

Oh, Mistress, he said sorrowfully. *That is a thing that must not be. You are sister and cousin and niece to all the other serpentina women, and I am family to the other leviathans. There should never be fighting.*

But if a serpentina wants to hurt other people . . .

Other people aren't worth feuding over, Mistress.

I disagree, Clair.

There was a knock at the door. "Signorina? You are dressed, yes?"

I scrambled to pull on my skirt and sweater. "Not yet! Hold a moment longer."

What is happening, Mistress, that you ask me such questions?

Oh, Clair, do I dare tell you?

I raised him up to my face. His tiny, wise emerald eyes

gazed at me for a long time. His flickering tongue brushed like a feather against my lips.

I *am with you to the death, Mistress, whoever your enemy may be.*

My heart melted. *Beautiful Clair. I know you are.*

Chapter 42

~∽∽~

"Attention!"

The captain's bellowing voice reached me in the cabin. I wrenched open the porthole window, tossed Clair out into the sea, then wrestled to tuck my straw-colored hair under the dark curly wig I'd swiped from La Commedia's wagon.

"Their Graces, King Leopold and Queen Annalise of Pylander, are now boarding ship! All crew report deckside!"

Rudolpho and Alfonso burst through the door, not bothering to inquire again if I was still indecently exposed. "You've taken long enough, signorina," Alfonso said. "We must dress for our performance." And they fell to pulling on stockings and shoes and dabbing their faces with sponges full of grease and powder.

I pulled my gypsy charms out from under my sweater

and displayed them around my neck. They were the perfect finishing touch to my gypsy costume.

"What will you perform tonight?" I asked, grabbing my own pot of makeup grease and applying it heavily. "Shall I try to memorize some lines?"

"Ah, no, signorina," Rudolpho said. "La Commedia dell'Arte does not use lines. Lines are for amateurs. We practice the high art of improvisation. The muses, they feed us our lines."

I turned to stare at him. "Do you mean that?" I said. "No lines at all? No prior plan for what you perform?"

"Oh, sometimes we have a plan," Rudolpho said. "We might say, tonight we play the revenge of the spurned lover, or the dairy maid's retribution upon the fat, greedy landlord. But other than that? No. No prior plan."

"I see," I said, wondering if I really did.

"It is not for the faint of heart, La Commedia," Alfonso said. "She requires her special genius. And years of practice. As for *you* . . ."

"I have an idea," I said. "For our performance tonight. Listen close."

～

A few minutes later I crept out of our cabin to see what was happening on the deck. Night was fully dark now, and the only light came from lanterns spaced at long intervals along the corridor. The cabin door next to ours was open. From the items strewn about on the floor, I surmised that it held the members of the Circus Phantasmagoria. A wooden box lined with velvet contained the dagger mistress's blades. A canvas wrapper lay open on the floor, covered with long rods with charred ends—the fire breather's batons.

Daggers. I'd seen the dagger woman's incredible precision. If she wanted to drive a blade between King Leopold's third and fourth ribs without shaving either bone, she could. Was this their plan?

Or was it fire? Or something else altogether?

I looked both ways along the deck to see if any of them were in sight. They weren't. Here was my chance to at least do something.

I ran into the room and gathered up the daggers and the sack of batons, lugged them out the cabin door, and tiptoed down the corridor. The sound of voices made me stop, draw up short, and pull back around a corner where I could see the deck without being seen. There amid bobbing shadows stood a solemn assembly of guards and sailors saluting the king and queen. Annalise laughed and complimented the men as she poured each of them a glass of wine.

"From the king's select cellars," she said. "We wish you to drink our health gladly. Only the best shall do for our escorts on our bridal voyage."

The sight of her playing her part, now that I knew what she really was, sickened me. How could I have been so stupid, so blind, so trusting?

I retreated back the other way, moving slowly toward the front of the ship. With the whole crew gathered to greet Leopold and Annalise, I encountered no one. Where were the circus members, I wondered?

I left the corridor of cabins and reached another section of the deck. Checking once more to make sure I was unseen, I went to the rail and heaved the weapons overboard. They fell with an ear-splitting splash that made me cringe, and disappeared in the black water.

My boldness made me giddy. That should make it harder for them to kill King Leopold.

From the corner of my eye I thought I saw a shadow. I turned, but no one was there. I tiptoed quietly back toward the corridor of cabins.

Then a hand seized my shoulder.

I whirled around. In the shifting light of a single lantern, I saw a hard, lean face leering into my own. The mouth was more scar than lip.

"You!" I said.

It was the fire breather, from the coach ride. I clutched my charms with a sweating hand.

His eyes narrowed. "Me, who?" he hissed. Then he shrugged. "I should send you overboard to fetch back what you sent to the ocean floor."

I willed my lips not to smile. A bath in the sea was the one thing I *wasn't* afraid of. But there were worse things he could do.

"Who are you? What do you know?" He shook me with each question.

"I don't know what you're talking about."

"Why'd you throw our things overboard?" His voice rose now.

I cast my mind about wildly. Luck, luck, help me! What could I say? "Queen Annalise told me to," I said. "I am her closest friend. She doesn't want you to carry out your plan."

My arrow hit its mark. His eyes widened with confusion and fear. His voice was still menacing, though. "Explain yourself."

If only I could. I, for one, would like to know where this story was headed.

"I don't have to explain myself to the likes of you," I said. "If you have sense, you won't get mixed up in this evil business. Take a dinghy and take your circus far from Pylander."

He laughed once. "You don't know what you're saying. The world's not big enough to hide from Prince Ronald."

"Prince Ronald won't survive this night," I whispered. "Flee, if you want to live."

Footsteps sounded down the corridor between the cabins. His eyes darted backward and forward. At last he shoved me down behind a bale of rope and hid himself behind it as well, his hand clamped over my mouth. We watched in silence as Leopold and Annalise passed by us, climbed a set of stairs, and entered a door on an upper deck.

"That's the salon, where we perform," the fire-eater hissed in my ear. "We're summoned to appear minutes from now. But first I want you to meet someone."

He dragged me down the hall to the circus's cabin and shoved me inside.

There they all stood in their colorful costumes—the tall clown and his chattering monkey, the skeletal dagger mistress, the lithe acrobat woman. And there was another.

He wore only a pair of canvas trousers that ended at the knees. His massive chest and body were bare and slathered with oil, which reflected the gold of lantern light on his skin, and the gold in the centers of his eyes.

"Meet our strong man," the fire-eater said.

It was Prince Ronald.

Gypsy charms or gypsy disguise, save me! Would he spot me through my wig and clothes and face paint?

"What's this?" the bandit prince said. "What have you brought me, Gerry?"

"I'm only an actress, sir," I said, bowing, the better to hide my face. "I must get back to the other actors."

"I caught her throwing our things overboard," Gerry the fire-eater said in a whiny voice, like a tattling child. "My rods! Genevieve's knives. She sunk 'em."

The strong man took a step toward me. "And why would you do this?" His voice was a lethal whisper.

My runaway mouth failed to rescue me this time.

"She said Annalise told her to," Gerry said. "She said you'd be dead before the night was over, and that we should escape if we could."

Prince Ronald's lips compressed against each other. He plucked off my wig and my corn-silk hair came spilling out.

He raised his arm, and I closed my eyes.

"Circus!" The door opened with a bang. "Circus Phantas ... whatever you're called, come immediately. Queen's special request."

I opened my eyes, but the captain had already moved on. I could hear him repeat his summons to Alfonso and Rudolpho. They followed the captain into the hallway and spied me through the open door.

"Signorina!" Rudolpho cried. "Why are you wasting the time with these circus people? Come, come, our time is now. The show, she does not wait!"

He seized my hand and dragged me from the lion's den, completely ignorant of how he'd saved me. In a flash impulse, I snatched my dangling wig from Prince Ronald's hand as Rudolpho pushed me out the door.

"Put your wig back on," Alfonso barked. "Pronto! Pronto!"

I stuffed my hair back under as best I could and pressed the wig onto my scalp, hoping it wasn't too far askew.

And then all of us, La Commedia and the Circus Phantasmagoria, went up the stairs and entered the glittering salon, lining up in a row and bowing for King Leopold and Annalise, his snake-in-the-grass bride and queen.

Chapter 43

The king clapped his hands loudly. "Welcome! Welcome! You've come to entertain us, have you? We await you with great pleasure. Even though"—he kissed Annalise's hand— "I have all the entertainment I need in my radiant queen."

Annalise's eyes were riveted to me. Whatever shred of confidence I still had drained away. She knew me immediately.

She'd never looked more beautiful than she did this night. Her cheeks were flushed red, her eyes, dark and broody, her hair now flowing down her back, with only the sides pulled off her face and tied in a true love's knot at the nape of her neck. She was no mere queen of Pylander. She was an immortal fairy queen.

She looked at Ronald, and back at me. Her nostrils flared. Her eyes were full of suspicion.

She would hate me, I realized. And in that moment, in

spite of all I knew, in spite of what I'd come to do, this hurt me most. Withdrawing her affection would leave a gaping hole in my heart. What terrible wounds she could inflict with only her scorn.

Why, Annalise, did you do this?

"My darling," King Leopold said, "have we any more of that wine you poured for the crew? Sixty-seven was a splendid vintage. Wouldn't it bolster our performers also?"

"Alas, my king," Annalise said, never breaking her gaze upon me. "The thirsty crew has finished even the dregs from the bottles."

"A pity," said the king. "We shall ask the captain what he has in the ship's supply."

I broke away with effort from Annalise's spell and looked at the king. There he sat, so handsome, so alive, dressed in his wedding clothes, sampling a platter of delicacies and sharing morsels with the woman he idolized, never dreaming she had murder in mind.

Pity overwhelmed me.

In the same moment, my own life stretched before me, all my dreams jumbled together. University. Medicine. Healing the sick, delivering babies, riding the undersea waves with my leviathan to discover what the ocean could teach me. A lifetime with Clair. Tending Grandfather in his declining years. And somewhere in all those dreams, the possibility of someone else beside me. By boarding *The Starlight* tonight, I had forfeited my future for the king's.

Precious though he may be to Pylander, I wished I didn't need to die for him. Not if there was any other way.

The only way I could see, however faintly, was putting my plan in motion.

"What shall we do first?" the king said, reaching for another appetizer. "The circus, or the theater?"

"As my lord wishes," Annalise cooed.

"Then . . . the theater," King Leopold announced. "Here! Get off with you!" The monkey had loped across the floor and climbed up into a chair at the king's table, where he tried to reach for the savories on the platter.

The circus clown clacked his tongue, and the monkey bounded to his shoulder.

"Cheeky devil," the king said. "No respect for God or the crown. He was aiming for my onion tart."

The circus performers removed themselves to a table at one side of the room while the brothers and I took possession of the open area of the salon, making it our stage. Rudolpho stowed a box of props behind a chair.

"My lord the king," Alfonso cried, stepping forward with both arms outstretched. "We come before you tonight to grace the celebration of your most beautiful marriage to your most beautiful queen, with our humble little performance. We are La Commedia dell'Arte, the, er, three of us. We've performed in Florence and Milan, Barcelona and Rome, and tonight we play for you and your fair bride. Our show tonight? She is called, 'The Jealous Love of the Bandit Prince'!"

Annalise's knuckles whitened around the stem of her glass.

"Ho ho!" Leopold cried, leaning back in his chair. "Is that me, darling? Your bandit prince? I love you jealously, to that I'll swear."

Annalise forced a smile for him, then blasted me with her full scorn. I ignored her fiery look and my heart thumping in my chest. We had a show to put on.

"Once upon a time," I said, trying to sound theatrical, "the prince of a foreign land came to Pylander, disguised himself, and became a bandit on the highway, robbing and plundering the people that passed by."

Rudolpho marched along as a jaunty traveler, until Alfonso leaped out at him and began pummeling him with the flat of a wooden sword. I winced to see the blows. They *were* acting, weren't they?

"No one knew he was a prince. They only knew he was a ruthless killer."

"Have mercy!" Rudolpho the victim cried. "Spare me, I pray you . . . *aaaaghh!*"

A battered and, I could almost imagine, bloodied Rudolpho lay splayed out across the floor. Prince Ronald the strong man folded his arms across his chest and glowered at Annalise.

"But the prince was wealthy in his own right. Why did he need to plunder and steal? Was he mad?"

Alfonso rubbed his greedy hands together.

"It was his lady," I said, entering the scene as the guilty woman herself. "His princess lover, from another far-off kingdom, with her insatiable appetite for gold and jewels, for carriages and pleasure boats, for palaces and kingdoms." I sauntered across the stage area, wearing a painted tin crown nestled atop my wig. Alfonso presented me with a sparkly tin necklace and I smiled at it, then beckoned for more, more, more.

"So on the bandit prince went, robbing and terrorizing the countryside, with no one to check his wicked ways."

Poor Rudolpho took another beating from Alfonso. Annalise rested her chin in her hand and watched the show, mildly amused.

"The princess was betrothed to the king of Pylander," I said, "but her heart belonged to the bandit prince. The two of them conceived a wicked plan. They would make off with the entire kingdom of Pylander!"

Alfonso and I pretended to whisper together, but all the while I watched King Leopold, desperate to see some glimmer of understanding in his eyes, but he just went on sampling his food, chewing, and watching the show.

"On the day of the marriage, the bandit prince followed the king and queen onto their honeymoon boat," I said.

Rudolpho, now the king, escorted me onto an imaginary boat, while Alfonso crept along after us, crouching and tiptoeing like a villain. Oh please, King, open your eyes and see!

Prince Ronald saw. He kept his fist wrapped tightly around the hilt of his sword. The other members of the Circus Phantasmagoria exchanged uneasy glances. The monkey scampered back and forth along the chair rail behind the tables.

"Before they could even finish their bridal supper, the bandit prince struck, slaying the Pylandrian king where he sat, striking him down in cold blood on the night of his marriage."

"You think you have wedded my lady love?" Alfonso cried. "We shall see!" He plunged his wooden sword into Rudolpho's armpit, and the mortally wounded actor-king sank to the ground in a fine display of groaning and burbling out his bitter end.

King Leopold paused in his chewing.

Did he begin to see?

If not, then . . .

Clair? Are you close by?

I am here, Mistress, in the water beside the ship.

Is Bijou with you?

No, Mistress.

"Why do you suffer such a tedious performance to drag

out?" Queen Annalise said. "I regret that I invited these second-rate performers onto our ship, my lord. Let's send them back from whence they came."

"Tedious? I think they're droll." King Leopold waved a tiny drumstick at us. "Go on."

I swallowed hard. I'd lost. If he didn't see yet, he never would until it was too late.

"The bandit prince and the treacherous queen ran off together, and returned from the bridal trip months later, telling Pylander that the king had died of illness, and that the child the queen carried in her womb was the king's own son. In time they were married, and they ruled Pylander as though it were their own. And the royal bloodline of the house of Pylander was cut off, and the land itself sold through treachery to the foreign prince and his sons. And all because the Pylandrian king loved hastily, and trusted blindly. The end."

King Leopold wiped his mouth with his napkin. "But what kind of a tale is this for our wedding day?" He nudged Annalise playfully. "Next trip, I'm choosing the entertainers. Tell me, you actors, what happened to the bandit prince and the treacherous queen? When and how were they brought to justice?"

"Only you can tell, my lord king," I said. "If they succeed in carrying out their wicked plan, there will be no one to swear that the king's death was not an accident."

"*Chick-chick-chick-eeeet!*"

The monkey jumped up onto the table once more and grabbed for King Leopold's wine cup, but the king ignored him.

"What do you mean, *if* they succeed?"

"Pay her no attention, my lord," Annalise said. "Let's move on with the circus, and send these actors back where they came from."

"My lord king!" Rudolpho cried. "Look!"

We all followed his pointing finger.

It was the monkey, pouring a packet of powder into King Leopold's cup.

The king snatched the packet from the creature and sniffed at the powder. Then he rose from his chair, toppling over the wineglass as he did so. Dark wine spread like blood on the snow white tablecloth.

The Circus Phantasmagoria rose to their feet, too, with swords and daggers drawn.

Chapter 44

"Guards!" Leopold shouted. "*Guards!*"

"They won't come, my lord," I said, suddenly seeing all. "They're asleep, if they aren't dead. Queen Annalise has drugged them with her wine."

King Leopold looked dazed. He shook his head. "Annalise?"

Prince Ronald pointed his sword straight at Leopold's heart.

King Leopold whirled upon the queen, breathing hard from his nostrils.

"Tell me the truth of this, Annalise," he said. "Tell me this is not your doing."

The Circus Phantasmagoria pressed in closer, forming a ring around the king's table. Ronald dragged me with him by my collar and threw me against the table.

The monkey was back on his master's shoulder, chattering, baring his gruesome teeth, twitching his long tail.

Clair, I called to my leviathan. *I'm in danger.*

I'm coming to you, Mistress!

No, I said. *Instead can you upset the ship?*

"My lord the king," Annalise cried in a fluttery voice, "I know nothing! These performers must be hired by some foreign power plotting against us!"

The fire breather exchanged an uneasy glance with the dagger mistress.

"You see?" I said. "What did I tell you? She'll betray you, too, in the end."

Annalise opened her mouth, then closed it again. The ship groaned and creaked as if it were being compressed by a giant nutcracker. Then it lurched sharply to one side, causing dishes and silver to topple off the table and slide to one wall. The clown fell backward, and so did the fire breather, while Prince Ronald fell forward, nearly crushing me.

Good, Clair. Good! Do more!

Queen Annalise, who only tipped over slightly on her cushioned couch, pulled out her small velvet purse and slipped out Bijou. She gave him a kiss and then set him on the floor. He flashed away like a golden bolt of lightning, wriggling his way over the wreckage and out the door of the salon.

King Leopold saw him go and looked at Annalise with new terror.

"What in heaven's name," he panted. He backed away from Annalise. "What are you?"

She smiled at her husband. Her charade was over. "Princess of Merlia, by my birth," she said. "Now queen of Pylander, through your grace."

"Soon to be queen of Danelind as well," the strong man said, lifting Annalise by her waist and kissing her. She drew her arms up around his neck and kissed him back, long and full. The circus members drew in closer.

The king scrambled sideways to get away from them both. "Treason!" he cried. "Treason and murder! Is there no one to hear?"

The ship lurched to the other side. Churning waves began hitting the windows of the salon. Up till now the sea had been perfectly calm. The circus members stumbled and fell once again. Out the windows of the salon I could dimly see the thrashing forms of our battling leviathans, gleaming against the dark.

The fire breather pinioned King Leopold's arms to his back.

Annalise turned to me with a face full of malice. "So this is how it ends, little sister," she said. "I would have made you a queen. See how my love is repaid."

There was a loud crack. The fire breather relinquished his grip on the king, who broke away from him with a cry.

The fire breather toppled to the ground. There behind him stood Alfonso, looking astonished, holding his wooden sword high.

"Stop the actor fools!" Ronald cried, but too late. Rudolpho had smashed a heavy chair over the clown's head, and taken a nasty bite from the monkey as payment.

The ship rocked once more, snuffing out several lamps in the salon. In the shadowy light I saw the dagger mistress raise her arm to take aim at the king. Where she'd found more knives, I didn't know. I whipped off my tin crown and flung it in her face as hard as I could. Her knife missed the king, but hit Rudolpho in the arm. Alfonso pounced on her.

The king recovered his wits enough to draw his own sword just as the acrobat girl came within reach of him, lashing and kicking at him with powerful, precise movements. But the king managed to reach his sword to her throat.

"Never before have I injured a woman," he said, panting, "but I will, if you move another inch."

And still the ship rocked and reeled in the unseen battle of the leviathans.

Clair, are you all right?

I *am here, Mistress,* was his terse reply.

It wasn't just their battle now. Angry winds had roared up, bringing clouds that hid the waning moon, churning up waves that rocked the ship and smashed salon windows. I remembered Clair's words when I asked him if he'd caused that other storm. *It isn't natural. The ocean abhors it.* I wondered, how did the ocean feel when two leviathans waged war?

La Commedia and the Circus Phantasmagoria lay bruised and beaten amid the shattered glass on the salon floor.

"Enough!" Prince Ronald roared. He snagged me in one brawny arm and disarmed the king with one fierce stroke of his other, sword-bearing arm. Annalise raised the hem of her skirt and picked her way daintily over bodies and wreckage, following as Ronald dragged us out onto the deck.

Even Ronald stopped a moment to take in the dreadful sight. Silver blue Clair, thirty feet long, with green eyes flashing, darted his long neck in and out to avoid and counterstrike lethal blows from amber Bijou. His horns dripped with seafoam and blood, his whiskers were plastered against his scales. And still Bijou struck, and struck again, almost faster than the eye could see, knocking my beautiful beast back, and farther back, in the water.

"Heaven help us," the king breathed, and crossed himself.

Winds buffeted and rain lashed against *The Starlight.*

"You shall not prevail, Evelyn," Annalise said. "Relinquish now and I will spare you. Otherwise, you and the king die together."

Rain pelted us all, soaking gowns and wedding clothes.

Only bare-chested Ronald seemed unaffected by the storm. If anything, it animated him. He herded the king and me into a pathetic pair, poking his long sword at us both until we cowered against the outer wall of the salon, while behind Ronald, the battle in the sea still raged.

King Leopold placed himself between me and Ronald's blade.

"Choose!" Annalise cried to me. "Or the beast dies, and you with him."

How could I kill Clair? What did I dare do? I reached once more for the charms around my neck. Love had abandoned me. Luck couldn't reach me here. And snakebite? I never needed that one in the first place. Silly schoolgirl, to think gypsy trinkets could ever do anything, much less help me now!

I was beaten. I opened my mouth to give Annalise my answer.

Then Ronald's sword clattered to the slippery deck and slid under the rails and out to sea.

Something had dealt a crushing blow to his shoulder.

That something was Aidan Moreau.

Chapter 45

Aidan?

Ronald bared his teeth and turned to face his new opponent.

"You?" he snarled. He remembered the Fallardston coach.

Aidan laced his fingers together and swung his double fist against Prince Ronald's face, sending him staggering across the deck to the ship's rail, his nose streaming blood. Aidan followed quickly, bringing both elbows smashing down onto the bandit prince's chest.

Our moment of hope was short-lived. Ronald roused himself and met Aidan's next attack by sliding his legs out from under him. With a roar he dropped onto his knees on Aidan's belly and set his massive fists pounding Aidan's chest and face. Aidan kicked to fight him off, and the king lunged forward to help, but Annalise met his move with a bright little dagger pressed into his belly.

"You witch," the king spat at her. "To think I ever gave you my heart."

"Silence," Annalise said.

I sprang to Ronald and flung myself at his back, gripping around his neck with one hand and clawing at his eyes and face with my other. He reached his arms back and plucked me off easily, but that moment's pause gave Aidan a chance to get back onto his feet. I ran back into the salon to find a weapon, picking my way over groaning bodies. When I returned the tide had turned. Aidan had Ronald backed up against the rail once more, smashing blow after blow on his face and chest.

I handed Aidan the blade I'd found, and he held it to Ronald's throat.

"Stop!" Annalise cried. "You shall not harm him!"

And then, in a dreadful moment, I realized. The sea had gone calm. We all looked around, stupefied, wondering what it meant.

Bijou reared up in the water and pushed his great body onto the deck of the ship, his nether parts coiling up slowly, wearily, after the head and neck. His face was damaged, haggard, and, I almost thought, grieving.

I searched the water frantically.

Clair! Clair! Where are you?

There was no answer.

Clair! Can you come to me?

And then, most horrible sight, a flash of white, as Clair's

long belly bobbed to the surface, then dipped below again, a white corpse half-submerged, half-floating.

I sank to my knees. Waves of nausea and pain swept over me.

"Evie!" Aidan cried. "What's happened?"

"Take the young man, Bijou," Annalise said, not bothering to communicate silently. She was busy tying the king's hands behind his back with her ripped-off sash. "Hold him at bay while I say good-bye to my sister."

Bijou snaked golden coils around Aidan and pinned his arms to his sides. Aidan writhed against him, trying to reach me, but his knife clattered to the deck as Bijou's horned head hovered over him, his fangs wet with venom.

Ronald, flopping over onto the rails, retched into the water.

I collapsed onto the deck, my pulse ringing in my ears.

Clair was gone, and I would soon follow.

"Evie!" Aidan cried. "Evie, wake up!"

All I could see were Annalise's slippers standing before my eyes.

"Perhaps I am to blame for this, Evelyn," her voice said, far above me, far away. "I didn't teach you enough. If I had, you never would have crossed me like this. You are still my sister serpentina, and I will forgive your memory."

With all my strength I raised my head for a bleary glimpse of her face.

"I will even spare your loyal stonemason," she said, "for

bravely coming to your rescue." She smirked a little. "That is, if I can persuade Ronnie."

She knelt and stroked my hair. "Oh, Evelyn, Evelyn," she said. "I loved you dearly. But I have to love Ronnie more. Someday, you would have understood."

I lay my cheek back down on the wet deck. Blackness stole around the edges of my vision.

They'll throw my body into the sea, I thought. At least I'll be with Clair.

Annalise went to Ronald and exclaimed over his bruises, rubbing and soothing him. He groaned and let himself be ministered to.

Then a voice I thought I'd never hear again sounded in my ears.

"Release the lad and the king, and help the girl," it said, "or I'll drive this through the leviathan's neck. I've killed one before, and I'll do it again."

I tried and failed to raise my head. "Grandfather?"

Chapter 46

❧❧

"You said you'd wait in the boat!" It was Aidan's voice protesting.

"So did your mother, but she climbed the ladder the moment you were gone," Grandfather's voice replied. "I had to chase after her to make sure she didn't get into trouble."

Aidan groaned. "Where is she now?"

"Tying up the last of those entertainer folks."

Perhaps I'd already died, and this was some delusion or dream, combining the horrid present on *The Starlight* with my gentler past in Maundley.

"What is the meaning of this mockery?" Annalise cried. "Who are you, old man? And why do you pretend to bravery where my beast is concerned? It could rip you to pieces."

"Ah, but he isn't now, is he?" Grandfather said.

Fighting back death, I rolled myself over, the better to

see. There stood Bijou, towering over Grandfather yet quailing with pain at Grandfather's fierce grip on his whiskers—which weren't, of course, made from hair. Grandfather held a knife pointed straight into the soft scaly tissue directly behind the joint of Bijou's jaw. His hand holding the blade wobbled, but the tip stayed wedged in place.

Bijou's tail thrashed in terror. Annalise tried to rise, but Grandfather pressed his knife in farther, and the leviathan hissed in fright.

"What's going on here?" It was Widow Moreau, brandishing the iron skillet she bought from the gypsy caravan. "Lem Pomeroy! You make that snake let go of my boy!"

"Patience, Eulilly," Grandfather barked. "Let a man do his own work for once, without you bossing him around three-quarters of the time."

"Let the beast go free, old man," Annalise said, "and I promise no harm will come to you or any of yours."

"Look at the child," Grandfather said. "It's a bit too late for that."

I closed my eyes.

"Evie! No!" It was Aidan, calling from another time and place. I was falling, falling now.

"Bijou," I heard Annalise's voice command. "Let the boy go."

"Surrender," Grandfather ordered.

There was a long pause, then Annalise spoke. "We do."

"Now save my daughter," Grandfather said. "I watched

her mother die this death, and I won't stand by to see it again."

My daughter?

"It's too late," Annalise said.

The leviathan hissed once more.

Darkness closed all around me. From across eternity, I heard a voice.

"Are you sure?"

Chapter 47

It was cold in the water. I lay upon the waves, rocking gently, sandwiched between dark water below and dark sky above. It was cold, but that was all right with me.

As it had on my first swim in the water, the darkness under the sea began to grow lighter, and I could make out, dimly, shapes and currents, plants and creatures, moving, swaying, far below me.

She was full of life, the ocean. So much more alive than dry ground and harsh air.

She was full of life, but here on the surface we floated, Clair and I. Dead, and cold, and tranquil.

I saw my leviathan now, stretching like a cord across the surface of the sea. Even in death he was beautiful. The water caressed him, carried him, let him still sway to the ocean's dance in death.

I reached toward him but found I couldn't really move,

couldn't really swim. I could only will myself toward him, and hope the waves would nudge me closer.

There was a flash of gold before me, so bright it burned my cold eyes. Like a comet racing across the sky, this streak of gold raced to where my beautiful Clair lay and kissed him.

Or did it bite him?

No. Oh, no, don't do that to my sweet Clair. Leave his sad body be.

My peaceful cold was broken then by sharp bursts of heat, and pain, and light. I coughed and choked on seawater. My limbs stabbed with needles of pain. My stillness became spasms and jerks that I couldn't control. The soft sea beneath me became hard, rude, scraping boards.

I opened my eyes to three sets of flaring nostrils and anxious eyes—loving faces peering over me.

"She's coming round!" Widow Moreau cried.

"Not so fast, Eulilly, those are just tremors," Grandfather said.

"No, they ain't," Widow Moreau said. "Unless that's a tremor kicking me in the shins."

"You there, Evie?" Aidan said. "Are you with us?"

My body rose off the deck in a racking cough, but none of them even flinched.

"Raise her up," Grandfather ordered, and Aidan's hands slid under me and lifted me off the floor. I let my head fall against his chest, and felt him tuck me under his neck and cradle me close to him.

We heard a loud splash. Aidan turned to see what it was.

The space where the injured Prince Ronald had been splayed was empty. Before I could even cry out, Annalise flashed me a venomous look I would never forget, then vaulted over the ship's rail easily to join Ronald in the water.

"She just lifted him up herself, like he was a bag of oats, and dumped him overboard," Widow Moreau murmured, incredulous. "Is she trying to kill him?"

"Look," Aidan said.

Down in the dark water, lit by the sheen of Bijou's gold scales, we saw Annalise maneuver Ronald onto the leviathan's back. She straddled Bijou behind him and wrapped her arms around him. Bijou rounded the ship and took off swimming.

West. Toward Merlia.

Good-bye, Annalise. Take your lover and your anger back to where you belong. Pray heaven that we do not meet again, for I fear your vengeance.

And still, my eyes filled with tears.

That doesn't mean I will not miss you.

Chapter 48

⤜∾⤛

"Excuse me," came a voice from across the deck. "I don't suppose someone could release me?"

"Laws a mercy!" Widow Moreau cried. "Sorry we forgot all about you there, King." She hurried over and unraveled the knots in the queen's sash.

Mistress?

Clair!

Help me?

"Grandfather," I said, "my leviathan needs help to board the ship."

Grandfather hesitated, then leaned over the rail. He lowered a rope, and moments later pulled it up with a small, silver blue Clair wrapped neatly around the knot at the end. He held the rope high, grimacing, unwilling to touch my bright leviathan. Aidan reached for Clair and placed him on my shoulder, where he curled like a necklace around my throat.

"Let's get inside," Widow Moreau said. "C'mon, into this room that used to be so fancy."

They climbed over debris and glass and entered the salon. Aidan still carried me.

"Here, lay her down on these couches," Grandfather said, but Aidan sat on the couch himself and held me in his lap. I looked around me at the wreckage, and saw gagged and writhing bodies, tied with stout cords, piled up in a heap against one wall. There was the fire breather, the clown, the acrobat and dagger mistress—and Alfonso and Rudolpho!

"Grandfather!" Even speaking hurt my head. "Grandfather. Those two men with the curly hair. Release them, please. They aren't our enemies."

I felt a rumbly, growly sound rise from Aidan's chest. "Are you so sure?"

"Let them go," I said. "They were heroically helpful."

"Heroic," Aidan muttered. "Hmph."

In no time the actor brothers were spitting the lint from their gags out of their mouths and staggering about on jellied legs, massaging their wounds.

"Signorina the brave," Rudolpho said, throwing kisses in my direction.

"Signorina the dangerous," Alfonso added. "No more do we let a female decide what show we perform. I go to bed."

The king went off in search of drugged crew members to see if he could rouse any, and Widow Moreau began setting the chairs and tables back in order and tossing cushions back onto the couches. She found a broom and began tidying up the broken glass, while Grandfather sat next to me.

I still felt weak and dizzy. Aidan wrapped his arms closer around me.

"Grandfather," I said, "why are you here?"

He thumped his walking stick on the floor. "Well, you didn't think we were going to sit still and do nothing when we'd gotten word about the coach robbery, did you?"

"We set out straight for Fallardston, along with the Hornbys, to make sure you were both all right," Widow Moreau said. I noticed she was sweeping awfully near to the circus performers' faces.

"And when we got there, the lady at the inn said you'd gone on her nephew's ship, which had been wrecked," Grandfather said. "We feared the worst, naturally. So we had to keep on going to find any word of you."

"But that tale you told!" Widow Moreau scolded. "Telling that innkeeper you and Aidan was married. You ought to be walloped, Evie Pomeroy. You *ain't* married, are you?"

I felt very small. "No, ma'am."

"Well, we'll set things right soon enough," she said. "Anyway, when we got to Chalcedon we looked up the Rumsens. What a relief to know you both were all right.

But they were saying strange things about you, Evie, and all they knew about Aidan was that he was working on a building project at the palace."

"It took no end of trouble to locate him there," Grandfather said. "How were we to know we'd be arriving on the day of the wedding?"

"We found Aidan ranting about you having gone on some ship, so we just borrowed us a boat from that dock there, and Aidan rowed us out."

"*Borrowed* a boat?" I said.

"We'll bring it back." Widow Moreau tipped a serving table upright.

I leaned against Aidan's shoulder and closed my eyes. All was well now. Wasn't it?

"Grandfather."

He raised his tired, sad eyes toward mine, slowly, as if it gave him pain.

No one spoke.

Even Widow Moreau's broom stood still.

My question hung in the air between us. It didn't need to be spoken.

I waited.

"I was an old man, Evie," Grandfather said. There was pleading in his voice. "Not as old as now, but old enough to have known better. I met your mother, and I . . . She . . ."

His eyes clouded over with wet. Widow Moreau fished around in her bosom for a handkerchief.

"She was like a fire, child. A beautiful flame. And I was an old bachelor who wasn't prepared for how I felt about her. Nor for how she felt about me."

I tried hard to follow the words as he spoke them, but they darted and dove around in my head like barnyard swallows. I couldn't pin them down.

"You mean my mother?"

Grandfather nodded. "That's right. Your mother was one of my students. Then she became my wife." He winced. "Not my daughter-in-law."

My mind seized hold of the image of Grandfather holding Bijou at knifepoint, and suddenly I felt cold, colder than the ocean could ever chill me.

I didn't know how to speak. Grandfather seemed to read my face. He took my hand.

"She was different from anyone I'd ever known, but even till the end I never knew just how different. The day you were born, child, was so joyful for me, for your mother. But her creature—her leviathan . . ." He swallowed hard. "I was jealous of it. Always, from the beginning. Jealous of how she adored it. I thought she loved it more than me."

I stroked Clair, lying next to my throat, and felt the thrum of Aidan's heartbeat.

"When the creature first saw you, it slithered toward you and opened its mouth, and"—he was working hard to keep his face composed—"I thought it was going to bite you, child. I thought it was as jealous of you as I was of it.

And I had my knife handy for just such a time." He wiped his eyes with his sleeve. "I wouldn't believe Rachel when she told me to trust the beast."

Clair uncurled himself from my neck and crawled toward Grandfather. His bright eyes studied his creased and grief-stricken face. Grandfather couldn't return the leviathan's gaze.

I clung to Aidan, grateful for his solid mass while everything else I thought I knew floated away around me. "And that is how my mother died?"

Grandfather's hand holding mine trembled. "That is how, child. I swear I never meant to harm her. I just didn't know.

"I buried your mother here, in Chalcedon, along with the body of her beast," Grandfather said, "then I took you and fled as far away from my old life as I could. I found a nurse in Maundley"—here Widow Moreau looked away—"and there I stayed. Townspeople assumed without asking that I was your grandfather, and I saw no reason to correct them. I thought it would be simplest for you to know me as your grandfather. Then you wouldn't press me for more information about your mother." He let go of my hand so as to cover his face with both of his own. His voice was choked with sobs when he spoke again. "And I could pretend not to be the man who had unknowingly killed his dear young wife."

It hurt me so to see tears trickling out from between

Grandfather's fingers—for I still must call him Grandfather, at least until I'd had time to work out another name. I reached out my arms to him, and he came to me, and Widow Moreau, too, and there we all sat, hugging and crying.

Poor Grandfather.

Poor Mother.

Poor leviathan.

We pulled ourselves together finally, and just sat there, tired and weak and spent, and glad that nothing more was expected of us just then.

The salon door opened, and in came King Leopold, followed by a groggy-looking ship's captain. He surveyed the damage with a look of mingled horror and headache. I felt suddenly self-conscious sitting there in Aidan's lap, so I sat up and rose to curtsy for the king.

"Arrest these four," the king said, pointing to the fettered Circus Phantasmagoria, "and secure them in the hold until we can take them to prison." The captain called to some crew members loitering in the doorway, and they dragged the assassins away.

The king crossed the room to me and bowed deeply.

"My dear young lady," he said, seizing my hands and kissing them, "whether you be"—he wrinkled his nose in distaste, as if he couldn't bring himself to say Annalise's name—"*her* cousin or no, you have been my salvation this night."

"Not me alone, Your Highness," I said.

"Call me Leopold," he said. "Please."

Aidan cleared his throat.

"I won't soon forget what you've done," the king went on. "I will spend a long time considering what I might do to repay your loyalty and devotion. But for now, ask what you will of me. I insist."

I was too stunned by all that had happened to think clearly. All I could think of at that moment was a wish for a soft, warm bed.

"I have a wish to make of *you*," the king said with a bow, "and that is, that I might have the chance to know you better."

I saw in that moment just how young the king was. Priscilla was right. He was far from thirty, and handsomer than any king had a need to be.

I glanced around me. Widow Moreau was sweeping holes into the parquet floor. Grandfather watched me out of the corner of his eye, and Aidan, whose face was now a fine mix of purple and black bruises, only looked at his calloused, swollen hands lying in his lap.

"Then you must meet my family," I said. "Over there, Mrs. Moreau has been my friend and neighbor my whole life. She's practically kin to me."

"Howdee doo, Majesty," Widow Moreau said, with a wrinkly smile and a squatting sort of curtsy.

"This is her son, Aidan Moreau," I said. "He works as

a stonemason at the palace. The youngest and most talented master stonemason in all of Chalcedon."

"Excellent," the kind said, shaking Aidan's hand heartily. "We need more young men like you to build the kingdom!"

Aidan grunted in reply.

"And this," I said, pointing to Grandfather, "is my . . ."

And I stumbled in my speech. It all hit me then. The realization that he was my father before I died. Bijou saving Clair, thereby saving me. Annalise must have told him to.

Oh, Annalise! Why did you have to turn wrong?

My eyes filled with tears.

"My dear young lady!" the king remonstrated.

"It's all right, child. I will introduce myself. My name is Josiah Lemuel Pomeroy. I am Evelyn's father," the man I'd always called "Grandfather" said. "I'm a retired professor of medicine at the Royal University."

"Josiah?" Widow Moreau wrinkled her nose. "*Josiah?*"

I stared at him. The grandfather who wasn't my grandfather was the professor of medicine whose books I'd grown up reading?

Well, who else could have written them?

King Leopold bowed. "I am honored to meet you, Dr. Pomeroy," he said. "If I recall rightly, you treated my mother in her illness before she died, these eighteen years ago."

Grandfather nodded. "That is true. I remember."

He came to my side and squeezed my hand.

"I have a favor to ask of Your Majesty," Grandfather said.

"Anything you wish," King Leopold replied.

"We need the ship's captain to perform a marriage."

Aidan and I looked at each other, then looked away. What on earth? Did they intend to make an honest liar out of me?

"What do you say, Eulilly?"

I gaped at Widow Moreau. Her hands still pushed the broom, but her eyes were soft.

"All I can say, Lem Pomeroy," she said, "is that it's taken you long enough to come around. I never have known a more stubborn man, and that's a fact."

Chapter 49

I left my new room in the castle and ran down the corridor to the stairs.

"Excuse me," I said to a serving girl—the first one I'd met when I arrived at the castle. "Which way is it to the chapel?"

She hoisted her tray up higher and wedged it into her waist to balance on her hip.

"Down the stairs, turn right, and on till you hear the organ playing. They were setting up for something in there earlier this morning."

"I know." I smiled and hurried on.

Mistress is happy today.

Clair was tucked in my pocket. I was happy to hear from him. Since his ordeal in the sea he'd done little but sleep. I hoped it would speed his healing.

The little chapel was full of flowers. Sweet organ music

filled the room. I ran to the dear friends seated in the pews.

"Prissy!" I cried. "Mr. and Mrs. Hornby. And Miss Jessop. So glad to see you all here!"

Prissy threw her arms around my neck. "Wouldn't miss it for the world," she said. "I'm so glad the king persuaded your, er, . . . father to wait."

Rudolpho and Alfonso appeared, dressed in their pressed red and black suits, and slipped into a pew toward the rear. Rudolpho winked at me, and I waved in reply.

I reached under my collar and pulled out my charms. Love, luck, and snakebite. I owed much to each of them. I wished I could meet the gypsy woman again and tell her so. But I'd fastened the love charm on Widow Moreau early this morning. It was her turn to use it now.

"Something borrowed on a wedding day is good luck," she'd said cheerily. "I don't mind a little secondhand love."

Aidan appeared in the chapel doorway, dressed in a new suit, with his hair combed back. The bruises on his face were purple and green today. I needed to find time to work on those and get them on their way to healing faster. I'd hardly seen him since that night on *The Starlight*.

"Good morning, Aidan," I said.

"Morning, Evie."

"I suppose I must congratulate you."

"And I you."

I sat down in a pew, and he sat next to me.

"You look very fine today," I said.

"I look like a street brawler," he muttered.

I leaned over and placed my hands over his blackened eye. "No, you don't," I said. "Why can't you just accept a compliment?"

He placed his own hand over mine, closed his other eye, and said nothing.

"How goes your work, Aidan?" I asked, grasping for a way to start the conversation.

"The menagerie project's been dropped," he said. "The workers have been let go."

Oh, no. "I'm sorry to hear it."

Aidan lowered my hand and looked at me.

"No matter," he said. "King Leopold introduced me to the chief architect at the university. I start next week as the head mason for their new library."

I squeezed his hand. "What wonderful news!"

He tried not to look too pleased.

"You *will* be the greatest stonemason in all Pylander someday, laddie. I'm sure of it."

We sat and listened to the music.

"I've been thinking, Aidan," I said.

"Hmm?"

"With your mother marrying my father, does that make us brother and sister?"

He scowled. "It had better not."

The king appeared in the rear of the chapel, thronged

by a quartet of guards. He was never without them these days.

"The king's been awfully attentive to you lately," Aidan observed. "I suppose you and he have had time to decide upon all the wishes and favors he's going to grant you."

"Leopold has been tremendously kind," I said. "It was his insistence that we hold the wedding here."

"A wedding's a wedding, wherever you hold it," Aidan said.

"Must you be so ill-tempered, Aidan Moreau?" I said. "On today of all days!"

The music changed, and I turned to see the bride and groom, standing in the rear of the chapel. The tribe of royal tailors had done themselves proud in Widow Moreau's rose-colored dress. I could only imagine her sharp tongue at their fitting sessions.

And Grandfather. I had decided that was what I would always call him. He supported Widow Moreau's arm with one of his, and stuck out his chest proudly.

Priscilla and Mrs. Hornby made no pretense of hiding their handkerchiefs as they dabbed their eyes. Nor did I.

We stood to greet the lovebirds as they walked down the aisle and stood before the priest. He welcomed us, and the cantor sang, and the ceremony began.

No royal wedding could compete with this one for sweetness, however beautiful the princess bride might be, however handsome her kingly groom. I thought I'd swell to bursting with love for Grandfather. And Widow Moreau. Though I really couldn't call her that anymore after today. What would I call her? Mother? It didn't matter. After all we'd been through, our family was together. And I realized, there in the chapel pew, that we had already been a family for a long, long time.

"You may kiss the bride," the priest said.

Grandfather and Widow Moreau, or Mrs. Pomeroy, as I should say, turned around slowly and beamed at us. Grandfather, looking nervous, leaned toward his bride.

Mrs. Pomeroy dropped her bouquet and threw her arms around him.

The bride kissed the groom. He didn't seem to mind.

We all rose up, clapping and cheering and laughing. A pair of young girls from the castle scattered rose petals down the aisle, and the newlyweds made their way out of the chapel to jubilant organ music.

"May I?" Aidan held out his arm, and I let him lead me down the aisle. We embraced the bride and groom, and everyone else there, and stood there watching and laughing and smiling until my cheeks were sore.

We were a small wedding party, but King Leopold had spared no expense for us. Servers in starched uniforms led us to a private room decked with flowers and tables of food. French doors opened onto a terraced garden with benches. A string quartet, stationed in one corner, played elegant, stately music, until Widow Moreau told them to liven it up a bit, which they obligingly did.

I danced in a circle around Grandfather, ate dainties and cake, and even kissed the priest on his cheek. I felt in love with the entire world. Even King Leopold danced with me to a little roundelay. It was kind of him to stay for the entire wedding, I thought. He'd taken quite a shine to Grandfather.

I left the king dancing with a blushing Priscilla, and looked for Aidan. He wasn't there.

I went outside and roved around the gardens. He sat on a bench, shielded by sculptured shrubs, facing down across the park and out to sea.

I tiptoed as quietly as I could toward him and placed my hands over his eyes. He didn't flinch, but took my hands in his and pulled me around the bench until I fell into the seat beside him. I looked for some merriment in his expression, and was surprised to find none.

We sat together in silence. It began to grow awkward. Who could read this boy? Not I!

Aidan broke the silence. "You'll be staying on at the castle, I take it?"

I fixed my eyes upon the sea. "I'll be living with my father and stepmother in their new home. Grandfather's old chambers at the university."

"What?"

"Prissy's coming too," I said. "We shall study with Grandfather this year, and enroll in classes next year."

Aidan seemed to be breathing rapidly, a flush spreading under his purple bruises.

"But . . . you'll be spending a lot of time at the castle, all the same," he said.

"I don't see why I would."

Aidan's lower jaw was working. I wondered what idea he was chewing on, but I figured the best way to find out was to wait.

"What *did* you tell the king you wished for most, Evie?" Aidan said.

"I asked for Grandfather's quarters back for him, and his place of honor restored at the university."

Aidan watched me sideways. "And?"

"And what?" I said. "That was the extent of it."

He wouldn't look at me. "And did he ask you anything?"

King Leopold *did* ask me something, and only one person in a thousand would say I wasn't a fool for how I answered.

I hoped I was sitting next to that person.

"He did," I said, "and that conversation will remain private."

Aidan's face flushed as red as the rose petal he was grinding to a mash underneath the heel of his boot. Oh, but he was ruddy perfect, bruises and all.

"I suppose there'll be many more of those *private conversations*."

"I suppose you invited the Rumsens to the wedding," was my retort. "I wonder why they didn't come? I was so hoping to see Dolores again."

"I did no such ... oh, you!"

"What is it you want, Aidan Moreau?" I said. "Why don't you ask me now, instead of pestering me all day?"

He turned toward me and gazed full at me. Suddenly I had no more quick jabs to offer. I looked back at him and felt I was seeing him for the first time. Familiar, yes. Handsome. But there was so much more to my childhood fishing partner now.

"I never thanked you for coming after me, Aidan." My voice felt small. "You risked yourself to rescue me."

His eyes never left mine. "I would do it again."

I knew he would. I squeezed his hand. "I hope you'll never need to."

He caught my hand in his, and then in one swift movement pulled me close, and kissed me.

But once he'd started, he took his time.

The bench, the ground, the castle gardens fell away from under me as his warm lips drew mine in and held me. Nothing, not even riding the ocean waves, felt this thrilling, or this free.

Clair awoke in my purse. *Fish?* he said. *Nice fish?*

Go swim, Clair, I said. *I'll meet you later.* He didn't need to be told twice.

Aidan paused to watch my leviathan crawl across the flagstones and down toward the beach. Then he wrapped his arms around me, cradled me close, and rested his cheek against mine.

"Evie?"

I felt shy of him, and so safe with him, both together. "Hmm?"

"What I want is another swimming lesson."

I smiled. "It'll be awfully cold. For you."

"I need to learn, though, if I'm going to keep up with you."

At last he released me, rose, and held out his hand. I took it, and together we headed back into the party. Before we entered, though, he paused to finger the charms around my neck. "Your love charm is gone," he said. "You never needed it, you know."

I thought of King Leopold, and Alfonso and Rudolpho, and the lads back in Maundley. "You can't deny that it worked."

"Not on me." He traced his finger over my face, down my nose, and tapped my lips. "Evie, there's something else I want from you."

Even as warm and comfortable as I was with him, I felt a moment's nerves. What could he want? Maybe we'd better hurry inside.

"I want your snakebite charm," he said. "Just in case."

Acknowledgments

This book wouldn't exist without two friends who opened their homes and offered me a quiet sanctuary. Margaret Lazenby and Julie Keenan, I cannot thank you enough.

I'm grateful to my posse of devoted advisors, Diane Sampson, Whitney Johnson, Julia Blake, Jamie Larsen, Cindy Jermasek, Ron Scott, and again, Julie Keenan.

Ginger Johnson read draft after draft. Michelle Nagler's patience, insight, and encouragement sustained me. Alyssa Eisner Henkin was always in my corner. And a special basket of love goes to Vermont College of Fine Arts, the faculty, the alumni writers' community, and, in particular, the unstoppable Cliffhangers.

I put my husband, Phil, through the heavy-duty cycle this year, and still he comes out, wash after wash, sparkly fresh and wrinkle-free. Thank you, Joseph, Daniel, Adam, and David, for fixing meals and loading the dishwasher. (Someday you'll thank me.) To the Vosler family, thank you for adopting me. To my litter of siblings, and my adorable mother, I love you a bushel and a peck.